STIR IN A MURDER

A WITCHY, COZY MYSTERY

LE DOUX MYSTERIES
BOOK SEVEN

ABIGAIL LYNN THORNTON

STIR IN A MURDER

"Stir in a Murder"

Le Doux Mysteries #7

To my family.
I'm only here because of your support.
You're amazing and you help
me be brave enough to reach for the stars.
Thank you!

ACKNOWLEDGMENTS

No author works alone. Thank you, Cathy.
Your cover work is beautiful!
And to Laura, for your timely and thorough editing!

CHAPTER 1

"But I don't want a glass wall," Wynona argued, rubbing her forehead. She was positive she would need some tea when she got home. This morning had been nothing but one argument after another. Was nothing in life ever easy?

"It'll give the room character," Celia argued, jabbing her finger at the computer screen which held a digital rendering of the large dining area for the tea shop. "It'll also allow your customers to see you working in the kitchen. It'll bring them in with you and allow them to feel part of the action."

"Celia," Wynona said in exasperation. "I'm not looking to bring them into the kitchen. It's a private space and I aim to leave it that way. While I'm grateful for your suggestions, the wall simply isn't going to work."

Celia's bright red, plump lips pinched into a thin white line and her black brows pulled together. "You don't like any of my ideas."

Oh brother, Violet grumbled. *Here we go again.*

"That's not true," Wynona said gently. She had hired her sister to help redesign the tea shop, trying to give Celia's new career a boost, but the tension between the siblings was proving to be anything but subtle. Celia liked bold and bright, while Wynona liked clean and simple.

Only a couple of months ago they had argued over Wynona's cottage when Celia had tried to redecorate without permission. Now they were doing it over design and decor. A double whammy.

"Your designs are wonderful," Wynona assured her sister. "But they aren't what I'm looking for in the shop. I want warm and homey. I want people to feel cozy and welcome. Sharp angles and contemporary lighting will pull away from that." She folded her arms across her chest, determined to stand her ground. "It's a tea house, not a museum."

Celia muttered under her breath. "Fine," she snapped. "But don't blame me when people hate it."

They didn't complain before, Violet argued. *And this'll be nicer than it was.*

Thank you, Wynona sent back to her familiar. *I'm glad someone understands.*

Violet huffed and began to clean her whiskers.

The whole morning had been like this. One fight after another. It was enough to make Wynona want to pull her hair out. Did Celia treat all her clients like this? Did she try to push them to her way of thinking or let them pick out their own tastes? Wynona was convinced that her sister's career would be short-lived if that was the case.

Celia snapped her laptop shut and stuffed it in her oversized purse. "We can discuss this more later. I have a client meeting coming up."

"Good luck," Wynona said through a tight smile. She watched her sister strut to her motorcycle and get situated before roaring down the road. Wynona closed her eyes and let out a breath once her sibling was gone. When she opened her eyes, she realized half of the construction crew was still watching the street.

Wynona rolled her eyes and walked back to her Vespa. Apparently, her sister's cat walk wasn't meant for Wynona's benefit. Just as she reached her vehicle, a large truck pulled up on the curb. Wynona paused and smiled wide as she watched her fiance step out of the cab. She sighed internally. *I still can't get used to it.*

If you swoon any more, you'll be a puddle on the ground, Violet muttered.

Rascal's grin grew, letting Wynona know he had heard their little mental conversation. "Hey, babe," he said in a husky tone as he stepped up and wrapped an arm around her waist.

His kiss left her breathless and pulled a couple of hollers from the construction crew, who had managed to pull their gazes from Celia's departure.

"Hey," Wynona said breathlessly as she pulled back. She smiled. "What brings you here? I thought you were working the long shift today."

"I am," Rascal said with a nod. He turned to look at the partially constructed tea shop. "But I took an early lunch break so I could see my two favorite girls." His golden eyes were glowing when he turned back to look at her.

Wynona patted his chest. "You need food, don't you?"

Rascal chuckled and kissed the tip of her nose. "You know me so well."

Wynona sighed deeply, pretending to be put out. "Now I see why you're marrying me. It's only about my skills in the kitchen."

Growling, Rascal brought his mouth to her neck. "Don't get cheeky with me, woman."

Wynona laughed and pushed him away. "You're ridiculous."

"And you're beautiful."

And I'm going to be sick.

Rascal looked at Violet and gave her a look. "Stop messing with my mojo. I'm trying to woo a witch."

A witch which you've already won. Violet stood up in her basket and put her front paws on her hips. *I'm starving here. Quit with the smooching and let's get back to the house before I faint.*

"If she faints, it won't be from lack of food," Rascal muttered under his breath.

"Play nice," Wynona warned the two of them.

Violet chittered, but backed down and Rascal grinned.

Wynona pointed at him. "Don't think I was favoring you," she scolded. "I've had enough arguments this morning. I don't need you two going at it all day."

Rascal's smile fell. "What arguments? I thought you were meeting with Celia about the plans."

Wynona rubbed her forehead. "I was."

He folded his arms over his broad chest. "What did she do?"

Wynona shook her head. "She just has a different vision than I do." Wynona blew out a breath and forced a smile. "Let's just go eat. I'm sure your time is limited and I don't want to spend it talking about my sister."

"Good point." Rascal turned and waved toward his truck. "Come on. I'll drive."

Wynona raised an eyebrow. "I need to bring my scooter home. I'm not coming back this afternoon."

Rascal's lower lip poked out and he widened his eyes.

"Don't you dare give me puppy dog eyes," Wynona said with a laugh. "I'm not leaving my scooter here. You'll just have to ride to the house without me."

Rascal huffed and turned off the look. Those gold eyes with his dark lashes and the fact that he truly was part canine meant he was far too good at getting his way, but Wynona was determined to be better about standing her ground. She couldn't let him win *all* the time when they were married. He'd have to learn to share the victories.

Still grinning to herself, and with Violet's squeal of excitement, Wynona straddled her mint green Vespa, pulled on her helmet and headed home. The twenty minute ride was peaceful, except for the loud, massive truck riding right behind her. She wasn't sure how he ever snuck up on a scene in that crazy thing.

Pulling into the garage, Wynona stepped out to the driveway to walk with Rascal. They walked inside, hand in hand, only to come to a screeching halt. "Lusgu?" Wynona asked, her eyes wide as she looked at the house.

A grunt met her call.

"What the he—" Rascal choked off when Wynona gave him a look and the tips of his ears turned pink. He rubbed the back of his neck. "What's going on here?" he asked weakly.

Wynona walked further in, careful not to slip on the ultra shiny floor. Lusgu had been living with her since the fire and had been wonderful about keeping the house clean, just as he kept the shop clean, but this…was too far.

Lusgu stood in the kitchen, his head tilted back as he watched a rag scrub a cabinet above his head.

"What are you doing?" Wynona asked.

"Varnish." Lusgu grunted. "Wood needed it."

"Okay…" Wynona's eyes couldn't stop roaming. Everything…*everything*…was shining. Her little cottage had been owned by a wood nymph and was on the border of the Grove of Secrets. The magic there was heavy and deadly, which meant Wynona was left alone, a state she truly appreciated after escaping her horrible family.

But living in a cottage also meant everything in the house was made from wood. Wood floors, wood walls, wood cabinets…and apparently, Lusgu had decided to not only clean them, but add a thick layer of varnish, leaving the cottage gleaming like the top of a troll's head.

Lusgu rolled his beady eyes and went back to watching the rag.

He was bored, Violet explained.

"What?" Wynona responded out loud. She stiffened when Lusgu gave her a questioning glance. *I mean...how do you know?*

Violet shrugged from her place on the floor. *I just know. He needs something to do. A purpose. Or you might find the whole Grove of Secrets just as shiny.*

"Oh dear…" Wynona rubbed her forehead. That headache was only getting worse. She sighed in relief when Rascal began to massage the back of her neck.

"Use your magic," he reminded her.

She huffed. Why did she never remember that herself? Focusing on a slight trickle of power, she sent it to her aching head and the pain immediately dissipated. "So much better," she whispered, smiling at Rascal. "Thanks for the reminder."

He smirked and pumped his eyebrows.

Wynona laughed softly. "Come on. Let's get you fed."

"Music to my ears."

Now that her magic was warmed up, Wynona used it to whip up a quick lunch and everyone, including Lusgu, sat down for a meal. It had taken quite a few invitations before Lusgu had been willing to join Wynona and her ever evolving group of friends to break bread, but Wynona had been persistent enough that it was now simply part of the process and Lusgu no longer grumbled about it.

"How was your morning?" she asked Rascal, taking a bit of the chicken salad. "Busy keeping criminals off the street?"

Lusgu snorted, but his eyes never left his plate.

Rascal grinned. For reasons Wynona could never figure out, the wolf shifter enjoyed riling the brownie. It had been that way since they'd met and the tension between them didn't look like it was going away any time soon.

"We book 'em as fast as we can," Rascal bragged, his eyes on Lusgu, obviously knowing the words would set the brownie off.

"Can't leave better enough alone," Lusgu grumbled.

"What would you have us do, Lu?" Rascal asked. "Let people break the law willy-nilly?" Rascal tsked his tongue. "The whole city would be chaos."

Lusgu was far from impressed. "Leave people to their lives," he said in his gravelly tone. "If they're not hurting anybody, they shouldn't be kept track of."

"That's the problem," Rascal argued. "They *are* hurting people. That's what committing a crime is all about."

Lusgu paused before stuffing a bite of chicken in his mouth. "Not everyone who breaks the law is a criminal."

"Okay!" Wynona said loudly, putting her hands in the air. "I think that discussion is over, you two."

Rascal and Lusgu continued to glare at each other, completely ignoring her. "Are you saying you broke the law, Lusgu?" Rascal leaned in, his eyes flaring. "Because it sounds like you have personal experience with this."

Lusgu leaned in as well, though it didn't have nearly the same effect. Only being waist high, with long floppy ears and a thin, pointed nose made for a much less intimidating picture than Rascal's broad shoulders, glowing eyes and wild hair.

"Boys," Wynona said sharply. Neither of them moved. Wynona pinched her lips together and sparks began to play on her fingertips. She could feel the magic building, but her frustration was also mounting and they were egging each other on.

Squeezing her eyes tight, she forced herself to remember the time she zapped Rascal. It had terrified her and she never wanted to go through the pain of hurting a loved one again. Though the shock had been small, she still didn't want to do it. It wasn't in Wynona's nature to strike out at other creatures unless it was in defense of a life.

She barely registered a scrambling sound before two men grunted…loudly.

"Vi," Rascal said in shock. "That hurt."

Wynona opened her eyes, her magic dropping off at the sight of the small mouse standing between the two men, her tail whipping back and forth.

Then maybe you'll stop being such a nincompoop and stop fighting. Are you three or thirty?"

Rascal frowned. "What about him? He's older than I am."

Violet began chittering too fast for Wynona to follow, but she was clearly giving both men what-for.

Lusgu's lip twitched.

Wynona stared. That was an action she'd only seen once…maybe twice…before. Though, Lusgu and Violet had always had an odd sort of a connection. Not that Wynona understood it and neither party was willing to share what brought them together. In fact, Lusgu, as a whole, was simply…a mystery.

Every time his hard, grouchy veneer cracked, Wynona caught the tiniest glimpse into something simmering below the surface. But the look was never long enough to truly understand what she was seeing.

One of these days, she was going to start digging. And she would refuse to take no for an answer.

Standing, she began to gather the plates. "Now that the temper tantrum is over..." She gave the men a significant look. Neither looked the least bit repentant. "How about we clean up? I have an appointment with Prim later today."

Lusgu snapped his fingers and the dishes all left the table, floating nicely to the sink where the water turned on and a cleaning line commenced.

Wynona sat back down, shaking her head. "Lusgu, you're amazing."

"Hey!" Rascal cried.

Wynona smiled and turned to her fiance. She leaned over and kissed his scruffy cheek. "And you're handsome."

"Handsome *and* amazing, right?"

Lusgu groaned. "Wolves," he grumbled, getting down from the table. "Messy, messy, messy."

Rascal chuckled darkly and stood up, grabbing Wynona's hand. "Come on. Walk me to my truck so I can give you a proper goodbye without Old Lu watching."

Wynona happily tripped after him even as she shook her head. "You need to stop. Lusgu's a good guy."

Rascal winked at her as he guided her out to the driveway. "Probably." He hesitated. "But something in my gut tells me he hasn't always been on the good side."

Wynona let that thought simmer. She had to admit he might be right. "But he's good now," she admonished. "And that's all that matters."

She hoped.

CHAPTER 2

The greenhouse was heavy with moisture as Wynona stepped inside and she immediately felt her hair begin to wilt.

Magic... Violet reminded her.

Wynona shook her head. After thirty years without the use of her powers, she was really going to have to change her lifestyle in order to remember she had full use of it all now. Closing her eyes, she concentrated for a moment and felt her hair spring back into shape. "Much better," she murmured.

"That you, Nona?" Prim called from deeper inside.

"Yep," Wynona answered back.

Prim stepped through an opening between two fronds, wiping her hands down the front of her apron. She was grinning wildly and her pink hair stood out a little more than usual. "Are you so excited? I'm so excited! I've never done flowers for my best friend's wedding before! We're going to make it so perfect!"

Wynona laughed as the small fairy rushed over and grasped her in a hug. "I've never been to a wedding at all," Wynona admitted. "So I guess we're both newbies."

Prim pulled back, her face despondent. "Ah, man, Nona. I'm sorry. I didn't mean to bring up bad memories."

Wynona shook her head. "It's fine. The weddings my parents attended would have been pretentious and stuffy. And the food was probably all made with magic."

Prim made a face. "I don't see the appeal. Magic food doesn't fill you up."

"Ah..." Wynona grinned. "But it also doesn't hurt your waistline."

Prim put her manicured hands on her hips. "I'll keep my curves, thank you very much. No one's taking my favorite walnut, spinach salad from me."

As a fairy, Prim was a vegetarian, which was in direct contrast to Rascal's wolf side, which craved all meat. It was a delicate balance having everyone eat dinner together, but Wynona loved the time shared.

She clasped her hands. "Okay. You said you would have ideas for me to look at?"

"Oh, yes." Prim *poofed* into her human form, which provided her with much longer legs, then rushed back to a side table, grabbing a binder. "I've been working on it all week and I think I've got some great ideas for you." She shoved aside trowels and dirt on her main work table before plopping the binder down.

Wynona paused just long enough for Violet to climb to the floor and disappear in the foliage, before following her friend. She grabbed a stool and sat down, waiting for Prim to show her ideas.

"What do you think of this?" Prim asked, the excited undertone in her voice clearly audible. She turned a page and proudly displayed the pictures.

Wynona's eyebrows shot up. "Wow...that's...a lot." Massive sprays of flowers decorated the page in every color of the rainbow. The flower colors almost didn't look real and Wynona had to assume they were enchanted in some way.

"We've got roses, of course," Prim gushed. "You know...because... hello! Love and passion!" She pointed to a bright orange flower. "These are carnations. We can dye them whatever color we want, but I personally love this tone. They stand for motherly love." Prim scrunched her nose. "And let's face it. You won't get that from your actual mother, so why not get it from a flower instead?"

"Uh…"

"Oooh! And this one! Sunflowers are for longevity and loyalty!" Prim nudged Wynona's shoulder. "With a dog at your side, loyalty is perfect, right?"

"Prim, I don't think…"

"And the protea!" Prim explained, her excitement growing to the point where she was bouncing on her toes. If she had been born with wings, Wynona was sure her friend would be fluttering above the ground, but instead, Prim rose up like a ballerina whenever her emotions got the best of her. "This one is really rare," Prim said, dropping her voice to a tension-filled whisper. "This one stands for courage and hope. Both are attributes you have in spades, but a little more never hurt…right?"

Wynona stared at the nearly bald flower and swallowed hard. It was…sort of pretty…in an odd sort of way, but it definitely wasn't what Wynona had in mind.

"And what about—"

"Prim." Wynona put her hand over the images.

Prim's mouth snapped shut and she turned large, pink eyes to Wynona. "Is there a problem?"

Wynona chewed the inside of her lip for a moment, trying to think of a nice way to tell Prim that she hated it.

Just say it, Violet grumbled.

I can't. She's my friend.

Your friend who picked flowers that are nothing like you at all. Doesn't sound like much of a friend to me.

Before Wynona could respond, the sound of snickering caught her attention. Blinking out of her mental conversation with Violet, she looked at Prim who was so red, she nearly matched the roses on the page.

"You should see your face," Prim said, still trying to swallow her laughter.

When Wynona frowned, Prim lost it.

Doubling over, the fairy burst out laughing, barely able to catch her breath.

Wynona's shoulders fell and she gave her friend a look. "I've been had."

Thank goodness, Violet snapped. *There's no way that last one smells good.*

Wynona pursed her lips and studied the picture again. "It's sort of pretty…in an odd way."

Violet's snort was covered by the continued gaity of Prim's laughter.

Wynona rolled her eyes and sat back down, waiting for Prim to get control of herself. She tapped her fingernails on the table. "Prim…"

Prim nodded and wiped at her eyes. "I know… Sorry…I couldn't resist." Her pink eyes were bright with humor, her lily white skin flushed dark enough to nearly match said eyes. "Turn the page," she instructed when she could finally talk. "The real ideas are there."

Wynona turned to the book and followed Prim's instruction. Sighing in relief when she saw bouquets much more to her liking, she began to study the images. *Turns out she does know me after all.*

Violet huffed. *Never did like fairy humor. They never think of anyone but themselves.*

Wynona shrugged. *It was fine. I'm just glad I don't have to come up with a way to tell her no.*

"So…what do you think?" Prim scooted closer and studied the pages. "I thought the peonies were particularly lovely." She turned to Wynona. "Do you know what colors you want? With your dark hair, I'd be a little careful."

Wynona nodded. She had her mother's coloring. Black hair, black eyes and bright red lips, which contrasted with her porcelain skin. There was no question that Wynona's heritage was anything but a witch. She fit the mold perfectly.

"Of course my dress will be white," she murmured, still studying the flowers. "I love the softer colors, but you're right, I'm a little afraid that my hair will stand out like a sore thumb if I surround myself with pastels."

Prim pursed her lips and tapped the bottom one. "We could make it work, but it would have to be more neutral. What if you used soft shades of gray and white as your colors, but gave small accents with something else? It would be easy to go for a garden party type look. Lots of greenery to break it up, but all the colors could be soft."

Wynona tilted her head back and forth. "I like the idea of gray or even a soft silver, but do you think it would be too much to use a bold accent? Like a red rose?"

Prim's eyes narrowed and grew unfocused as she contemplated the question. "That's slightly trickier, but I think we could do it. The red would need to be very strategic." She grabbed the binder and began pulling out the pictures. "Hold on…" she muttered, engrossed in her work.

Wynona watched and waited. Prim was the premiere florist in Hex Haven. This was definitely a time to sit back and let the expert work. Wynona's knowledge of flowers included phrases like, "t's pretty," rather than how a plant actually worked or what it meant.

"What about something like this?"

Wynona's eyes widened. "Prim…that's lovely." The fairy had pulled a picture of all red roses for the bridal bouquet, solid white arrangements for the wedding, gray tulle and ribbon, with a splash of reds thrown in random places in the arrangements. "I think this is where I'd like to start. I love the idea of a garden party, but having something slightly bold is also appealing. This allows me a little of both."

"I know." Prim preened.

Alright…let me see. Violet came scrambling across the floor and climbed up Wynona's leg.

Once in her lap, Wynona lifted Violet to the table and let her study the mix of pictures and fabrics.

Violet's pink nose twitched for several seconds as she studied the ideas, then she finally sighed. *She did good. For once.*

"She likes it, doesn't she?" Prim said with a smirk. "Otherwise, she'd be screaming at me."

Wynona winced. She definitely wasn't telling Prim everything Violet said. The purple mouse was sometimes a little on the crabby side and she liked very few people. It was easy to get on her bad side and early on in their relationship, Violet had taken a dislike to Prim's excitable nature. Nothing had been able to mend the gap ever since. "Of course she likes it," Wynona assured Prim. "It's beautiful." She smiled and leaned back slightly. "Now that we have a good idea of colors and flower ideas, I can move forward with other things as well." She glanced at her watch. "Speaking of, I actually do need to go shopping today."

"Oooh, shopping! What do you need?"

"I need to replace all my tea sets," Wynona said sadly. "My whole antique collection, including the ones from Granny's personal stash, are gone."

Prim's face fell. "Oh, Nona. I'm so sorry. I didn't even think about that. I was only worried about the building itself."

Wynona nodded. "I know. I don't think most people knew that the teacups were anything but a simple tool of my trade, rather than part of my inheritance."

Prim rubbed Wynona's shoulder comfortingly. "Where are you going to look for them?"

Wynona stood and shrugged. "Antique shops, mostly. I always found the best ones there." She smiled softly. "Daemon said I had a knack for picking out ones with residual magic and that it enhanced my teas."

Prim had stiffened at the mention of Daemon and Wynona immediately felt bad. The two had had a falling out and had yet to reconcile. Daemon said Prim needed to mature enough to realize her actions were capable of hurting others and Prim thought Daemon was being a controlling stick in the mud.

Though Wynona loved the idea of her two good friends together, she struggled to see how their differing personalities could overcome such a large gap. "Anyway," she said, pressing on, "I wanted to hit a couple before they closed today. Celia was finalizing the plans for the decorations, and I want the tea sets to be part of that, so I need them sooner rather than later."

"Can I join you?" Prim asked, hopping up from her stool. "I don't have any other appointments today and I'm so sick of dead-heading that I'm going to take someone's real head instead if I don't get a break."

Wynona laughed softly, grateful the change in subject had worked. "Absolutely. I'm going to Aster's first. We'll meet there."

"Perfect. See you in a few." Prim flounced off, disappearing through a door behind some plants.

Wynona picked up Violet and walked toward the outside entrance.

Did she have to come?

"Hush," Wynona scolded. "One of these days, you're going to have to accept the fact that Prim is my friend and quit trying to bite her head off."

It's not her head I'm worried about. Her ego is too big. I can probably only manage her nose...but if it'll do the trick...

Wynona gave the mouse a look. "Enough. Can't you just choose to get along? Prim just built me the most wonderful bouquet of flowers. She's going to make my wedding an absolute delight. Why not look at the good things she does rather than worry about the mistakes she makes?"

Violet sniffed. *Because her mistakes always seem to hurt the people I love.*

Wynona stopped right before getting on her Vespa. She looked down. "Aw, Violet. You do have a heart."

Violet rubbed her face vigorously. *Don't let it get around. I wouldn't want to ruin my carefully built reputation.*

Wynona kissed the purple head, then set the mouse in her basket. Pulling her keys from her pocket, she sat down and started the engine. "Ready to do some shopping therapy?"

If you're asking if I'm ready to spend all your money, the answer is ALWAYS yes.

Wynona laughed. "Well, get ready, because we'll do some damage to the bank account today for sure."

CHAPTER 3

Wynona stopped her scooter along the side of the street, tucking neatly between two vehicles, and pulled off her helmet. One of these days she was going to start practicing porting again. She adored riding the Vespa, but once in a while it would be nice to save time by simply poofing herself where she wanted to go.

Maybe Celia will help teach me.

And maybe Celia will leave you in the in-between to rot.

Wynona huffed. "Do you not have a good word to say about anyone?"

Violet wrapped her tail more securely around Wynona's neck. *Not ones that don't deserve it.*

Choosing not to respond to that, Wynona pulled open the glass doors and headed into the musty shop. *I think they do this on purpose,* she thought with a grin. The antique shop was exactly what someone would expect of a paranormal place of business. Dust and cobwebs seemed to be everywhere. Suits of armor sat in one corner, while creepy, wide-eyed dolls sat in another.

Glass cases filled with stones, gems and knives were on full display right next to herbs and essential oils that would help someone looking to cast a specific spell.

Of course it's on purpose. Why bother to clean if you don't have to? Violet scrubbed her whiskers.

"Maybe because cleanliness is nice to look at?" Wynona offered, though she smiled as she said it. She absolutely adored stores like this. They were full of all kinds of exotic finds that could do anything from blast a hole in a wall to giving a creature perfect hair for the rest of their life. She never knew what she was going to find, and Wynona lived for the hunt.

"Can I help you?" an elderly man asked in a dark tone.

Wynona looked around until she saw a gnome glaring at her with black eyes from the front of the store. "I'm looking for tea pots and cups," she said, giving a friendly smile.

The only real trouble with shopping in an antique store was that they were usually run by creatures who loved to hoard treasure. The items might technically be for sale, but that didn't mean the owners enjoyed giving them up. Sometimes it took a great deal of work to get a purchase to go through.

The gnome never took his eyes off of her, though his arm raised and a short, stubby finger pointed to the side.

"Thank you," Wynona responded. She walked toward him until she reached the aisle he was directing her to. As she got closer, she realized that the gnome was glaring not at her, but at Violet. *Do you know him?* she asked on their mental connection.

No. But don't you dare set me down. Violet's tiny body shivered. *I'm pretty sure I'd become part of his collection, given half a chance.*

Wynona nodded. She agreed. The gnome was a little too interested. Pretending all was well, Wynona walked to a china hutch full of exactly what she was looking for. "Hmm…" she said in her throat, excited to see what drew her eye.

Try sensing the magic, Violet suggested. *Now that you know it exists, maybe you can seek it out.*

"Good idea," Wynona murmured. She closed her eyes, trying to remember exactly how it felt when she caught visual glimpses of magic. It had only happened a couple times and Wynona was still figuring out exactly what her powers could do, so she wasn't truly proficient at anything yet...except warming up a cup of tea.

Purple sparkles began to burst behind her eyelids and Wynona blew out a long breath.

Focus... Violet urged. *Remember, you're in charge. We don't need a torch if we're only lighting a candle.*

Wynona's lips twitched. It was true that she sometimes lost control of her magic. It was stronger than anyone else's in Hex Haven and with no true teacher, Wynona was stuck learning how to control it herself. *I should get back to reading those grimoires. They probably have some help in them.*

True, but not right now. Focus.

Wynona nodded, her eyes still closed. The electric feeling she associated with her magic began to trickle down her arm and she strained to keep it thin and small, until it reached her fingertips and they buzzed with energy. Opening her eyes, Wynona barely noticed the small ribbons of purple that were floating around her head. Her eyes scanned the shelves of teapots and cups and she allowed her hand to rise, gently moving it through the air as if to touch the objects, though never quite coming into contact.

A neon orange teapot with silver trim rattled as she passed over it and Wynona paused, tilting her head. She ran some of her magic up her chest and into her eyes. The lightest haze of red floated around the object, but there was something...off about it.

Wynona narrowed her gaze and looked closer. The red smoke had, what appeared to be, bubbles in it. There were holes in the smoke, as if it wasn't quite attached to itself properly.

The bell over the front door rang and Wynona was jolted from her musings.

"Hey, hey!" Prim hollered, delicately dancing her way through the overcrowded aisles. She sidled up to Wynona. "Find anything good?"

Wynona shook her head to rid herself of the residual magic. "Uh, I don't know." Carefully, she took hold of the orange teapot. She wasn't normally drawn to neon colors, but she was intrigued by whatever leftover power she'd detected. More particularly, why was the power so odd looking?

The teapot felt warm in her hands and she frowned. "Here. Touch this." She handed it to Prim. "Do you feel anything?"

Prim pursed her lips and shrugged. "It feels like it recently came off the stove. That's it." She scrunched her nose. "You don't really want to get that one, do you? The color is hideous."

"Dragon fire."

Both women spun around and stared at the small man. Wynona raised her eyebrows. "Excuse me?" she asked, not sure she had heard him correctly.

He grumbled under his breath inaudibly and waddled over, pointing at the teapot. "Dragon fire," he snapped. "It's enchanted with dragon fire to stay hot at all times."

"Ooooh," Prim said with a slow nod. "Gotcha." She grinned at Wynona. "That's cool. It almost makes up for the horrible color."

Wynona took back the pot and examined it. "But I don't think it works properly," she murmured.

The gnome's eyes narrowed.

"What makes you say that?" Prim asked. She tilted her head. "I don't see anything wrong with it."

Wynona turned it over a few times in her hand. "I don't know…but it doesn't…feel right." She wasn't about to tell them about the magic haze with holes in it. Most of Hex Haven was already terrified of Wynona's powers, she had no desire to advertise them unless necessary.

"You have the sight."

It wasn't a question, but a declaration. "The sight?" Wynona asked.

The shopkeeper folded his arms over his chest. "You're the Le Doux witch."

Wynona hesitated. There was something about the way he made that statement that irked her. Technically, there were three Le Doux witches. Why was he singling her out? "I'm one of them," Wynona said carefully.

The gnome shook his head. "No. You're the one." He waved a hand at the pot. "Take it. Lusgu will want it."

"Lusgu..." The man began to walk away and Wynona chased after him. "How do you know Lusgu?" she asked.

The gnome shook his head and snapped his mouth shut.

"At least tell me how you knew *I* knew him," Wynona pressed.

The shopkeeper went behind the counter, forcing Wynona to stop, then climbed up a short ladder behind the register. He waved a hand for the teapot.

Wynona looked back at Prim, who shrugged, then slowly handed the object in question to its owner.

He scanned it with a rock, punched a few numbers into the register and handed it back. "I needed to mark it for inventory purposes." He grunted. "Now out with you."

Wynona didn't move. "Please," she whispered. "Why won't you tell me anything?"

Black eyes bore into hers. The silence was heavy and long and Wynona felt suffocated by it. She was the eldest daughter of the current president of Hex Haven, though her father ruled more like a king. Her family were viewed as celebrities and hate it as she did, Wynona was often treated with fear and deference simply for being related.

And yet, it seemed that almost the entirety of Hex Haven knew more about Wynona and her powers than she did herself.

"Did you know my grandmother?" Wynona asked.

His eyes flared. "Not my place," he said, his voice low and hoarse. He tilted his chin toward the pot. "Lusgu can help you fix it. That's the best I can do."

Wynona hesitated only a moment longer before nodding in acceptance. There had been many more pots and cups on the wall to look at, but she was done. Clutching the warm pot to her chest, she turned and walked out, hearing Prim following behind her.

"I don't like it," Prim said harshly. "What's wrong with the old coot?"

"I don't think anything's wrong with him," Wynona corrected. She turned to stare at the shop. "But he knows something he's not telling me." She studied the pot again. "Why is this important?" She turned it around, trying to figure out what the shopkeeper saw.

"Do you find it weird that he never offered his name?" Prim asked, putting her hands on her hips.

Violet chittered angrily and Wynona had to hold up a hand.

"I can't understand you when you speak so fast."

She doesn't get it! Violet cried. *This is why she drives me crazy. Something is wrong and Primrose is worried about stupid details that mean nothing.*

Wynona gave her familiar a look. *How do you know it means nothing? Maybe his name would have been part of the key.*

Violet growled slightly and turned in a circle until she was settled on Wynona's shoulder. *Let me know when we're home.*

Prim was still glaring at the front window of the shop, not the least bit perturbed that Violet was complaining about her. "So what are you going to do?"

"Do?" Wynona asked blankly.

"Yeah. Do?" Prim waved her hand at the pot. "He told you to take it to Lusgu. Are you going to obey? Or did you have something else in mind?"

Wynona pursed her lips as she considered her options. She finally shrugged. "I suppose I will take it to Lusgu," she said. "I'd like to try and understand what's going on and maybe Lusgu will have answers."

"Fat lotta good that'll do you," Prim grumbled. "He's closed up tighter than an ogre's purse."

Wynona ran a finger over the silver detailing. The metal was cool, which was in direct contrast to the warm porcelain. "He said it had dragon fire in it," she murmured.

"It's definitely not hot enough to have dragon fire in the enchantment," Prim argued.

"Maybe part of the enchantment is that it won't burn the pot holder."

Prim tilted her head back and forth. "That could be it. But it seems weird. Isn't dragon's fire like…super powerful? How could it be enchanted into a pot?"

Wynona walked over and put the pot inside the front basket. "I guess there's only one way to find out," she declared. She set Violet down in the basket as well and grabbed her helmet. "I'll let you know what I find out."

Prim rolled her eyes. "I hate how you always get to have all the fun."

"I suppose we can bind your powers, put you with an evil family, have you escape after thirty years, break the curse and then have to learn how to adjust your whole life back to normal," Wynona said with a wide smile. "Then you can have all the fun too."

Prim shook her head. "You're amazing. In case I haven't said that lately."

"Aaaannd, that's why we're friends," Wynona teased. She stepped forward and gave Prim a hug before hopping back to her scooter. "Thanks again for the flower ideas. We'll do some more planning soon!"

"We better!" Prim hollered over the sound of the scooter engine. "I have to live vicariously through you!"

Wynona waved and pulled out into traffic. The ride home only lasted about fifteen minutes, but Wynona's heart was pounding like crazy the entire way. There was something odd about this pot. But what? And why was Lusgu involved? There were very few dragons in Hex Haven, so where did it come from?

Her magic hadn't reacted badly. In fact, Wynona had been pulled to the teapot, rather than repelled like she'd been toward the dark grimoires.

Her garage door moved half as fast as usual, she was positive, as she waited on the driveway for the chance to pull inside. She edged inside as quickly as she could in a safe manner, determined not to let her curiosity get too out of control.

"Lusgu!" she shouted, walking through the house door. "Lusgu!" Wynona paused, waiting for him to hear her. When no sound came from the house, Wynona set Violet down. "Can you go get him please?"

Violet frowned but nodded, scurrying toward the broom closet where the entrance to his portal was.

Wynona paced the kitchen. She didn't have the patience to sit down. This was just another piece of the Lusgu puzzle and she was desperate to know what it was.

Finally, she heard shuffling behind her and turned to see him step through the wall.

"Well?"

Wynona held out the pot. "I was told you would want to see this."

Lusgu's permanent frown deepened and he walked toward her, stopping with his nose just shy of the pot. He sniffed and his eyes flared before he snatched it out of her hand. "Where did you get it?" he demanded.

"At an antique shop," she explained, watching him carefully. "The shop owner was a gnome, though he never offered his name and he didn't take any money for the pot. Said you would want it."

Lusgu's eyes were glued on the piece of crockery and he took another sniff. "It's barely there," he muttered.

"What's barely there?" He didn't respond. "Are you talking about the dragon fire?"

Lusgu's head snapped up. "What do you know about dragon fire?"

Wynona shrugged. "Only that the shopkeeper said it was enchanted with it. Was supposed to keep anything inside hot." She touched it lightly. "But I think it's broken."

Lusgu studied it again. "How can you tell?"

She pinched her lips together, unsure what to tell him. Lusgu was a closed book and Wynona wasn't always sure he was completely trustworthy, but…she wanted him to be.

Tell him, Violet encouraged. *It'll be alright.*

Wynona took in a slow, long breath. "I used my powers to change my vision and I could see a light red haze around the pot, but…"

"But?"

"But it had…holes in it, like something was missing."

Lusgu's face fell and he nodded. "That sounds about right."

"Can it be fixed?" Wynona asked. "Who made it? Why did the shopkeeper think you should have it?" She tightened her jaw. Too many questions, too fast. Lusgu would never respond to them all.

He sighed and handed her back the pot. "It doesn't matter now. It was ages ago."

"Lusgu," she began.

He shook his head. "The only way to get it fixed is to find the inventor."

"And you know who that is?"

He hesitated, then nodded. "Yes."

"Will you tell me?"

Another long pause ensued. "Zullorayn Brownhide," he whispered almost reverently. "But everyone calls her Dr. Rayn."

CHAPTER 4

*D*r. Rayn...Dr. Rayn... Wynona couldn't seem to get the woman's name out of her head, but neither could she place it. Once again, she seemed to be out of the loop somehow and she wanted to break the cycle...but how? She ground a little harder at the dried herbs in her mortar and pestle.

After her chat with Lusgu, he'd clammed up and refused to say anything more, disappearing back into his portal and not coming back out. It had left Wynona to her own thoughts and they were swirling with curiosity and worry. Lusgu had appeared...sad. That was a very unusual emotion for him. Grumpy, grouchy, rude, stubborn...those were all words that Wynona would use to describe the brownie. But sad simply didn't fit.

"Why did the mention of the doctor's name upset him?" she murmured.

Maybe it's time for another library visit.

Wynona smiled and looked across her work table to where Violet was munching on a strawberry. "That...is an excellent idea." She had visited the library for the first time ever on her last case and it had been a dream...at least it would have been, if her attention hadn't been spent on trying to catch a criminal. "If Dr. Rayn is some kind of inventor, surely there's a record of her and her inventions, right?"

Violet nodded and began cleaning her face.

"Let me just finish this," Wynona said as she began pouring the newly made tea tincture into a jar. Ten minutes later, the tea was labeled, shelves and the work table wiped down. "Great." She rubbed her hands against the side of her pants. "Let's go."

The day was overcast and Wynona kept watching the skies, afraid it would rain as she drove through town. There was nothing worse than driving through a downpour on her Vespa. It simply wasn't made to handle that kind of weather.

"Something's on the horizon," she said softly to Violet as they parked on the side of the street.

Dark clouds loomed behind the buildings, looking heavy with moisture, but it was more than that. They appeared menacing, as if they were villains looking to destroy everything in their path.

As she stared, a rumble in the distance began to build, until the sound sounded as if it were directly overhead. Wynona could have sworn she felt the reverberations in the ground, right before there was a crack loud enough to wake the dead.

Clapping her hands over her ears, she rushed up the library steps and tucked herself safely under the roofline. But the storm kept her from going inside quite yet. Instead, she continued watching, worried but curious about what would happen.

Something's wrong, Violet grumbled, burrowing into Wynona's hair.

Wynona frowned. "What do you mean? It's just a fall storm."

Violet began to shake. *My fur's standing on end. It's more than that.*

"Are you sure?"

Check for yourself, Violet huffed indignantly.

Wynona let her magic out, filling her limbs with the electric sensation. It reacted immediately to the electricity in the air, causing Wynona's skin to tingle almost painfully. She shut off her own powers quickly and rubbed her arms. "That's worrisome. I wonder who's causing this."

Or why.

Wynona nodded. "That as well." She pursed her lips. "It could be a spell gone wrong. Or maybe one of the witches is brewing something for a client?"

How many creatures do you know that can cause a storm this size? Violet argued.

"Not many, for sure." Wynona jumped when another crack of thunder boomed through town. She wasn't the only creature diving for shelter. The streets were almost bare at this point, only the occasional person darting into the buildings.

Wynona shrugged. "There's not really any way for us to figure any of that out. Maybe we'll see something on the news later." She turned and reached for the library door, only to pause when she heard a scream and saw the remnants of a flash.

Take cover! Violet screamed.

Wynona winced from her familiar's volume, but turned and looked for whoever was in trouble. Smoke was filtering down the street and Wynona squinted.

Are you insane? The lightning! Violet cried. *Get down!*

"Someone needs help," Wynona murmured, her attention glued to the street. A sense of anticipation began to grow and she was sure something was coming. She could feel it.

The screaming came again, followed by another blinding flash of light.

"Where are they?" Wynona cried, running down the steps.

Your sense of preservation is broken, Violet snapped, scrambling down Wynona's side. She darted back up the steps and tucked herself behind a plant.

Wynona ignored the anxious rodent. She couldn't back down now. Raindrops began to pelt the top of her head and Wynona called her magic to her fingertips, creating a shield to keep herself dry.

Another scream, this one truly in distress, echoed down the road.

What's going on? Rascal demanded. *I can feel your stress.*

The storm, Wynona yelled back mentally. She could have sworn she saw movement and began to move forward. *I'm in front of the library. Someone's screaming, lightning is flashing...this isn't normal.*

Stay where you are, he ordered.

I need to help them, Wynona shot back.

Wy!

Wynona tuned him out, knowing Rascal would be there in a matter of moments, and began to jog. Her ballet flats were far from exercise-worthy, but the pain in her feet was small compared to what someone else was going through. The smoke grew thicker and another flash of lightning brought Wynona to a halt, covering her eyes from how close it was. This time the scream came *after* the lightning and the sound was filled with pain instead of fear.

"Where are you?" Wynona cried, peering through the smoke. Another dark body moved and she turned in that direction. A knocking on her shield had her pausing for a second. She looked down to see Violet standing with her hands on her hips.

Do I really need to ask permission?

Wynona concentrated just long enough for the mouse to get inside and up her leg before securing the shield. Pain began to pelt the purple bubble in earnest, making it even harder to see where she was going.

"I thought you weren't coming," Wynona muttered as she tried to track the person moving.

Another flash, and this time a manly yell.

"Oh my word, there are two of them," Wynona moved faster.

I didn't want you to die alone, Violet explained.

"Gee, thanks."

Anytime.

"There!" Wynona pointed to a black shape that wasn't moving and hurried over. Right before reaching the creature, she fell back when a bolt of lightning hit the ground right in front of her feet, just outside the shield, shaking the ground and releasing a burst of smoke from the heat. Wynona screamed and ducked back.

Can it penetrate the shield? Violet asked.

"I don't know," Wynona admitted. "I've never tested it against lightning." She glanced at the sky and edged toward the prone creature again. Her heart fell the closer she got. The shape wasn't moving.

Wynona knelt down, noting the pale skin and unmoving chest of the creature.

Any chance it's alive? Violet asked.

"I doubt it," Wynona responded. "Even vampires breathe." She moved the shield over the body, stopping the rain from continuing to drench them, and reached shaking fingers down to feel for a pulse. The skin was clammy and wet, but there were no signs of life.

Squatting back on her heels, Wynona shook her head. "How sad. It looks like they got hit by the lightning," she said, noting the blackened slash of skin on the woman's chest.

Didn't a man call as well?

As if her words were a premonition, there was a slam against the shield and Wynona yelped before turning to see a man with glowing green eyes pressed against the purple bubble.

"Let me in!" he bellowed, pounding on the wall. His eyes were wide and terrified as he glanced up. "No, no, no!" he screamed. Bending over and covering his head, he screamed in pain as a flash of lightning struck him in the back of his leg, blasting his body away from Wynona and her shield. He rolled several feet before coming to a stop and laying still.

"Oh my word," Wynona whispered hoarsely. She scrambled to her feet, her knees knocking together, and rushed to the man's side. She could see a black spot on his pants, but there didn't appear to be any blood. As she drew closer, she realized his chest was rising and falling, though erratically, and Wynona let out a breath of relief. She immediately knelt at his side and covered him with the shield. "Hurry, Rascal," she whispered.

Sirens rang through the air and the smoke began to clear in great bursts of wind.

A police car raced up and screeched to a halt only a few feet from Wynona, startling her, but her eyes kept straying back to what was causing the wind. Just like before, she could feel something was coming and she wasn't sure if it was friendly or not.

The man on the ground was still out, so Wynona stood and watched the distance, hoping her instincts were right.

"Wy?"

Wynona glanced over. "Rascal. Someone's coming!" she shouted, pointing to the billowing smoke.

Of a sudden, the smoke swirled, creating a whirlwind and shooting upward. In the middle of the street stood Celia, her hands stretched to the sky and her hair whipping around her face. The storm clouds were being pushed across the horizon, taking the rain and lightning with it.

Wynona's eyes widened. Celia had mentioned that wind was her specialty, but Wynona had only seen it in action once.

Dang, Violet complained. *She's more powerful than I thought.*

"I don't know how people can say I have more power," Wynona whispered.

You do. You just don't have as much control over it.

"Wy, let me in," Rascal said in a growl.

Wynona could see his eyes blazing gold, letting her know his wolf was close to the surface. Her safety had always been a difficult trigger for him and Wynona immediately dropped the shield. "Oof." He grabbed her in a hug so tight she could barely breathe.

"What did you think you were doing?" he demanded, once he'd pulled back.

"I was trying to save them," Wynona responded, cupping his cheek. She sighed and looked over her shoulder at the female body. "But I was too late."

"Paramedics!" Rascal hollered, stepping back to walk to the woman. He stood at the victim's feet and blew out a breath before looking at Wynona. "She was dead when you found her?"

Wynona nodded, wrapping her arms around her middle. She was feeling unusually cold and goosebumps broke out over her exposed skin. "She was screaming and I'm pretty sure she was hit by lightning." She pointed to the man. "I saw him get hit."

Rascal walked over, calling for another crew, who all followed his orders immediately. "This one's alive!" he shouted, bringing a bigger array of officers and first responders.

Rascal stepped back to let them work and Wynona came up to his shoulder. "He had just run to my shield when he was hit," she whispered.

Rascal wrapped his arm around her shoulders, tucking her into his side. "It's not your fault," he murmured. "The injuries were completely random and could have happened to anyone. I'm glad you were protected by your magic."

"Actually…"

"Actually, what?" another voice demanded.

Wynona waited until Chief Ligurio had finished walking up, though she knew his paranormal hearing would have allowed him to understand her response.

"Actually, the lightning seemed to be targeting the man," Wynona said, knowing she sounded crazy, even for a witch. "The hit was too precise to be anything but planned."

Chief Ligurio scoffed. "You're telling me that you think someone was throwing lightning bolts, Ms. Le Doux?"

Wynona shrugged. "I'm telling you what I saw," she responded.

"No one's that powerful," Celia offered as she walked up. Her skin was flushed and her eyes bright and alive. Using her magic suited her.

Apparently, Chief Ligurio also noticed because he cleared his throat and shifted his weight from side to side as if uncomfortable, though his red eyes couldn't seem to leave Celia. "You know every paranormal in the city?" he challenged.

Celia smirked. "Close enough." She turned to Wynona. "Now you…I could see being capable of this…someday."

Rascal's arm tightened around Wynona. "She didn't do this."

Celia rolled her eyes. "No, she didn't. But she possibly could with the right training."

"Let's focus on what happened this time, not what is capable of happening in the future," Wynona suggested.

"Why don't you tell us what you saw," Chief Ligurio snapped.

Wynona opened her mouth to do just that, but another officer came rushing up. "Sir….sir!"

Chief Ligurio turned.

"This was found just down the back alley," the vampire said, handing a large box to Chief Ligurio.

Wynona frowned. The design was sort of similar to her teapot. Only instead of being made of porcelain, it had metallic sides, but the silver trim was the same.

"What is it?" Chief Ligurio asked. He turned to each of them and everyone shook their heads.

"Where's Daemon?" Wynona asked.

"Skymaw!" Chief Ligurio bellowed.

A tall man came loping through the crowd. "Yeah, Chief?"

Chief Ligurio handed over the box.

Daemon frowned, nodded a greeting to Wynona, then looked back at the box. His eyes went black, then flared. "It's covered in red magic," he said. He leaned back away slightly. "And it doesn't look very stable."

"What could that have had to do with the storm?" Rascal demanded.

"Can anyone read the writing on the sides?" Daemon asked.

Wynona leaned closer. "No…it's not a language I recognize."

We need to talk to Lusgu, Violet said softly.

Both Wynona and Rascal turned to look at her. "Why do you say that?" Rascal whispered back.

Because I think it's dragonese, Violet continued. She looked at Wynona meaningfully.

Wynona closed her eyes. "Dr. Rayn."

"Who's Dr. Rayn?" Chief Ligurio growled.

Wynona shook her head. "I'm not sure and it's kind of a long story. Why don't you finish up the crime scene and we can all meet up at the precinct. I'll go talk to Lusgu and see if I can talk him into helping."

Rascal snorted.

"Be nice," Wynona reminded him.

He kissed her temple. "I'm always nice. But sometimes I'm also realistic."

She shook her head. "I didn't promise I'd succeed, just said I would try."

"Not good enough," Chief Ligurio argued. "If you think Lusgu has information we'll need, then we'll come to him. Your house. One hour."

Wynona watched everyone else begin to leave. She blew out a breath. "Guess that settles that."

"I'm going to study the scene. Want to help?" Rascal asked.

Wynona pinched her lips. "Sure. But I don't know if I want to get involved in this one. That kind of power really frightened me."

Rascal shrugged. "We'll take all the help we can get. As always." He kissed her cheek and walked back to where the man had fallen, Wynona following on his heels.

.

CHAPTER 5

"Thank you," Wynona said, grasping Rascal's shoulders as he helped her down from the truck. She hadn't won this battle and he had driven her home, promising they would get the scooter later.

She hated leaving her Vespa around town, but Rascal was so insistent, she'd given up arguing.

"I better get some tea going," she murmured. "Everyone's bound to be starved."

Rascal put his hand on her lower back as they walked inside.

Violet climbed down Wynona's side and disappeared as soon as they were in the door.

Wynona knew the mouse was going to speak to Lusgu. She'd let Violet talk to the brownie first. Their relationship might be helpful if the police were going to get any information out of the grumpy janitor.

The door opened by the time they reached the kitchen and footsteps piled in behind them.

Wynona headed straight to the cabinet, letting Rascal handle the guests. She pulled out her jar of ashwagandha. They would need all the calm and clarity they could get.

Using her magic, she heated up water and got the tea brewing. Once done, her eyes landed on the orange teapot. She probably ought to show that to the chief. It might help add credence to what she had to say.

"What is it this time?" Lusgu snapped as he stepped out of his portal.

Wynona turned around, resting her weight against the counter. "I'm sorry, Lusgu," she began. "But…something happened in town today and I think you might be able to offer some help."

Lusgu's frown deepened. "What do you mean?"

"She means that we found something that might belong to your friend Dr. Rayn," Rascal interrupted, stepping into the room

Wynona held her breath. She wasn't quite sure how Lusgu was going to react. He was still a mystery to her in a lot of ways.

"Rayn?" Lusgu asked hoarsely. He spun, glaring at Rascal. "Why are you talking about her?"

Rascal folded his arms over his chest, emphasizing his size, which was massive compared to the small brownie. "Because a person was killed today and another seriously injured by a contraption that Wynona said has markings similar to a teapot she bought." He leaned down a little. "A teapot that you knew the maker of."

Lusgu blanched and stumbled back a couple steps before catching himself. "Let me see it," he said softly. "Please."

Wynona's eyes widened. She'd never heard Lusgu be polite. Ever. "Did Chief Ligurio bring it with him?" she asked Rascal.

Rascal was still staring at Lusgu, but he nodded. "Yes. Everyone's in the other room." His golden eyes flashed to Wynona. "Celia came as well. Better brace yourself."

Wynona nodded. Fireworks were never far away when Celia and Chief Ligurio were in the same room. She wiggled her fingers and finished putting together the tea tray, including a cup for each person, then straightened her shoulders and marched to where her guests were waiting. After setting the tray down, she passed out the cups.

"Thank you," Celia said with a nose scrunch. She sniffed. "What is it?"

"Ashwagandha."

"Bless you," Celia said with a smirk.

Lusgu growled and Celia leaned away from him.

"It was a joke, sheesh."

Lusgu shook his head and went straight for Chief Ligurio. "Where is it?"

Nice to see his manners lasted all of two seconds, Wynona thought wryly.

This isn't easy on him, Violet argued. *Be patient.*

Wynona nodded subtly. Violet was sitting on Lusgu's shoulder and seemed to be trying to comfort the brownie, but Wynona was still confused as to why.

Chief Ligurio raised one black eyebrow, then nodded to the box on the coffee table.

Lusgu's hands were visibly shaking as he pulled out the device. It was nearly half the size of the brownie, but he carried it with ease. He studied it for what seemed like forever, his eyes reading through the markings as if he could understand each and every one. The entire room stayed quiet, as if collectively holding their breaths while they waited for Lusgu's analysis.

Finally, he set it down gently. "Rayn had a design similar to this," he admitted in a low tone. "But this isn't hers."

Chief Ligurio leaned forward. "How do you know?"

Lusgu's head snapped and his lip curled. "Because I know."

Wynona moved to intervene, but Rascal held her back.

Let them talk, he urged. *You can't keep saving him from hard things.*

Wynona took a long breath and leaned back, trying to stay calm. She hated seeing the brownie so upset even if she didn't understand what was going on. She hated seeing anyone in distress. She'd spent too much of her life under that exact emotion and she wanted to help others any way she could.

He's a big boy, Rascal assured her. *Let him work it out.*

Wynona nodded. Rascal was right…but it was hard.

Chief Ligurio tilted his head and instead of snapping back like he normally would have, he stayed calm. "That's not good enough," he explained. "This is a murder investigation, Mr. Lusgu. I'd appreciate your cooperation, but I'll use the command of the law if I must."

Lusgu's nostrils flared and a moment later his shoulders slumped. "Zullorayn Brownhide is a dragon shifter," he said. "She's an inventor. Lives inside the Grove of Secrets."

"No one lives in the Grove of Secrets," Daemon argued.

Wynona had nearly forgotten the black hole was there. His large size should have made him hard to overlook, but his serious and silent stance helped him blend into the background.

Lusgu shrugged. "Believe what you will."

"Why is she such a big secret?" Wynona asked.

Lusgu's head hung forward. "She was disgraced…many years ago…"

"Disgraced? What do you mean?" Chief Ligurio pressed.

"She used to work for Paratech," Lusgu responded. He slumped down onto the hardwood floor.

Wynona's jaw dropped. Paratech was the biggest tech company in the paranormal world.

"How long ago?" Rascal asked hesitantly.

"Maybe three hundred years?" Lusgu responded.

"But…" Wynona held off again. If her memory was correct…

Lusgu looked up, his eyes mournful. "Yes. She was one of The Five."

Several gasps went through the room. The original five members of that tech company were some of the wealthiest paranormals in the world. Each of them had strong magic, but their money and technology spoke louder than their powers.

Chief Ligurio tapped his knee. "Dr. Rayn…" he muttered. "Dr. Rayn…" He pinched his lips together. "Why does her name not sound familiar? I thought I knew the board well."

"She was the silent partner," Lusgu explained. "She wanted to be in the lab rather than the spotlight."

"Oh, yes!" Celia cried, sitting up straighter. "I remember that there was always one partner whose name was kept blocked. The media loved the mystery of it." She smirked and sipped her tea. "It was a brilliant advertising move."

"It wasn't about advertising," Lusgu growled, glaring over his shoulder. "It was about privacy. She *was* brilliant. All their best inventions were hers."

Wynona leaned in. "What happened to her, Lusgu? You said they had a falling out."

He sighed. "The details don't matter, but there was a…fight. She was ready to move in a different direction, one based more on philanthropy and helping the less fortunate. But the board wanted her to continue building what was selling. They weren't interested in helping others. They only wanted to line their pockets." His lip curled. "So she left."

"Just…left?" Chief Ligurio asked.

Lusgu took a moment to respond, but ultimately shook his head. "You can find it in the ghost reporter archives if you want more," he grumbled. Standing up, he began to walk away.

"Mr. Lusgu," Chief Ligurio said with a warning in the tone.

Lusgu stopped but didn't turn around.

"I'd like to know more about the device," the vampire said.

Lusgu shook his head. "It's not hers," he insisted. "But if you need more proof, you can find her yourself." With that parting shot, he disappeared.

Wynona jumped. She had gotten used to seeing Lusgu leave through his portal and walk into a wall, but she'd never seen someone simply vanish in thin air. Even those who ported required a little more preparation than that.

"Well, well, well," Celia cooed, looking smug in her seat. "The brownie has more secrets than we thought."

Wynona blinked rapidly. "How did he do that?" she asked softly. No one had an answer for her.

After a few moments, Chief Ligurio slapped his hands on his knees and rose to his feet. "I'm thinking we have some work to do. Strongclaw. Head to the hospital and see if you can talk to the victim. Find out who he is and what he was doing with the box."

Rascal nodded and raised his eyebrows at Wynona.

She knew what he was asking, and though she was intrigued, she shook her head. "I don't think I'll go this time."

"Quitting before we get started?" Chief LIgurio asked coolly as he walked toward the door.

Wynona stood, sliding her hands down the front of her pants. "I don't think Lusgu would ever forgive me."

Chief Ligurio hesitated before nodding. "Understood." He paused before walking through the front door. "If you change your mind, you're always welcome."

"Am I?" Celia asked, her chin held high in challenge. "Are you going to welcome yet another Le Doux into your inner circle?" She stood and sashayed toward the chief. "Or are you still too…put out about our little tiff a few years ago?" Celia walked two fingers up the chief's chest.

Wynona couldn't tell if Celia was serious or toying with the vampire, but she couldn't look away either.

Chief Ligurio grabbed Celia's hand so quickly, Wynona had trouble following the movement. "If you call betraying me and breaking my trust 'little,' then I think you have your answer," the chief said tightly. He dropped Celia's hand, then looked at the rest of the room and nodded. "Move it, gentlemen."

Wynona watched Celia stare at the door after the vampire closed it behind him. She wasn't sure how often her sister had been told no, but it wasn't much in her life. That kind of public rejection had to be difficult for someone with Celia's ego to handle.

Spinning on her heel, Celia smiled, though her cheeks were red. "Looks like I'm done here." Holding up a hand, silver began to shimmer around her fingers, until she snapped, porting herself from the room in a small puff of sparkles.

Rascal pinched the bridge of his nose. "I'm not touching that with a ten foot pole."

"Hear, hear," Daemon echoed.

"Looks like you're with me, Skymaw," Rascal ordered.

Daemon nodded. "Thank you for the tea, Wynona." His face softened just a touch. "Have you seen Primrose lately?" he asked softly.

Wynona nodded.

"How is she?"

Wynona shrugged, not wanting to lie. "She's…Prim," she said, thinking of the fairy's joke about the flowers. The odds of Prim ever calming down were slim to none.

Daemon nodded and turned to his superior. "I'm ready when you are, Deputy Chief."

"Let's go." Rascal wrapped an arm around Wynona's waist. "You're sure you don't want to come?"

Wynona shook her head. "No. I don't want him hurt any more than he needs to be." Inside, however, she was dying to know what all had happened.

Rascal nodded and kissed her forehead. "I'll talk to you later."

"Come by for dinner," Wynona replied and rose up on tiptoe for another kiss.

"I might be late."

"I'll keep it hot."

Rascal grinned. "Thanks." Letting go, he walked away, Daemon following.

Once her house was empty again, Wynona slumped onto the sofa. She was exhausted. Using her magic didn't drain her as badly as it used to, but her emotions felt like they had been pulled through the wringer. All she wanted right now was a blanket and a nap.

I'm staying here for a while, Violet sent her way. *Go ahead and rest.*

Thank you, Wynona sent back. Knowing Lusgu wasn't alone helped Wynona feel better about the situation. Grabbing an afghan off the back of the couch, she leaned over and rested her head on a pillow. A nap would help her have a clearer head when Rascal got back. She might not be working directly on the case, but her curiosity was through the roof. The only thing holding her back, however, was her loyalty to her friend. She'd never been put first growing up and

Wynona had determined long ago to be the exact opposite of her family.

Letting out a long breath, she promised herself that even Lusgu's grumpy behavior wouldn't keep her from backing him up. He needed someone in his corner, and she was just the witch to do it.

CHAPTER 6

"Learn anything interesting?" Wynona asked Rascal as she passed him the bowl of salad.

He grimaced, but dutifully put a few leaves on his plate.

Wynona held back a grin. It made her laugh how much the predator hated vegetables, but she also wanted her fiance to be healthy, so she insisted he have at least a few. Sometimes it was like dealing with a toddler, however.

"The guy in the hospital is still in a coma," Rascal complained. He cut a chunk of steak and stuffed it in his mouth. "The lightning strike cut open his leg, but also shocked him with the electricity, so his mind kind of shut down."

Wynona's eyes opened wide. "Is he going to be okay? He's not brain dead or anything?"

Rascal shook his head. "No. The tests show his brain is fully functioning, just had a shock."

"And they can't bring him back?" Wynona wiped her mouth, then set the napkin back on her plate.

He shrugged. "Doctor said it would be better for him to let it happen naturally. Something about how brains are more sensitive to trauma, so if in a few days the guy doesn't come out of it, they'll use magic for something more." Rascal raised an eyebrow. "We could always have you come try. I doubt you would hurt anything by coming to cure him."

Wynona scoffed. "I'm no doctor," she argued. "They know what they're doing and are just as capable at healing as I am."

Rascal leaned back slightly in his chair. "Maybe. Your healing doesn't leave any kind of trace. I wonder if it has to do with the immense amount of power you have."

Wynona felt her neck grow hot. She didn't love talking about her powers. She'd spent thirty years without them and suddenly being the most powerful being in all of Hex Haven was a transition she wasn't sure she wanted.

"Have you done any more research into those grimoires?"

She shook her head. "No. I've been a little scared to, but I do think it would be helpful."

Rascal nodded. "We can pull them out after dinner if you want. I've got nothing going on tonight. And until the guy in the hospital wakes up, I've got nothing to work with on the case."

"Is someone analyzing the box?" Wynona asked.

Rascal nodded. "Yeah. Our tech team is on it, but nobody has any idea how it works. And so far no one can read the writing either."

"Does the department have access to a dragon?" Wynona pressed. "Violet said something about it being in dragonese. I'm assuming that's a language."

Rascal pursed his lips. "Maybe. I never was very good at history, but dragons are about as old as paranormal beings get, so it's possible." He grinned. "Maybe we need to take that visit to the library together."

Wynona smiled back. "I'd love that. But I'm still not joining the investigation."

Rascal chuckled. "We'll see."

"You don't believe me?"

His smirk stayed firmly in place. "I think you're too curious and I also think you're dying to know more about Lusgu." Leaning over the table, Rascal's eyes twinkled. "I give you three days before you can't stand it anymore and have to be involved."

Wynona sniffed and looked imperiously at him. "I don't know what you're talking about." His laughter was soothing and deep and it warmed Wynona all over. How she loved this shifter. Their soulmate connection was such a gift and she wondered, not for the first time, just how she'd gotten so lucky.

The only downside to having a soulmate was how well he knew her. She *was* horribly curious. She wanted to be part of the investigation, but she also wanted to maintain her relationship with Lusgu. He was obviously deeply connected, or had been at one point, with this mysterious Dr. Rayn. It seemed to pain the brownie to even speak of her, and Wynona didn't want to cause her friend any more heartache than was necessary. So, she would curtail her busy brain and put it to good use elsewhere.

"Prim and I think we figured out flower colors," Wynona said. "Want to see them?"

Rascal's smile was less than enthused. "Can't I just trust you to do it the way you want?" He put an elbow on the table and rested his head on it. "The only thing I'm interested in with the wedding is the part where I'm told you're mine for the rest of eternity."

Wynona laughed. "You're such a guy."

He spread his hands to the side. "Did you want something else?"

Wynona shook her head and stood up, gathering plates. "No, but still, I'm excited for flowers and colors and dresses. The least you could do is at least pretend."

He came up behind her at the sink, crowding into her personal space. "Oh, I'm excited. Because once it's all together, it means exactly what I said a minute ago." He kissed the side of her neck and Wynona sighed. "That you'll be mine…" He kissed the edge of her ear. "And only mine."

Wynona spun and wrapped her arms around his neck before planting her lips on his. Their wedding couldn't come fast enough.

"Uh, hm." A voice intruded on their moment and Wynona squealed, jumping back from Rascal, only to hit the edge of the counter.

"Ouch."

Rascal turned. "Lu…was that necessary?"

Lusgu glared at them. "I wanted to know what you found out," he said gruffly.

Wynona rubbed her lower back.

Magic, Violet reminded her. She was perched on Lusgu's shoulder. She'd been with the brownie all day and Wynona was glad to see the snarky mouse was alive and well.

Rascal sighed and pushed a hand through his hair. "Nothing," he admitted. "The guy is still in a coma."

"Rayn had nothing to do with any of this," Lusgu said fiercely.

Rascal held up his hands. "No one's accusing her of anything," Rascal said. "But if the technology is similar to hers, then speaking to her would be a good thing. She could give us an alibi and that would be that."

Wynona waited, wondering if Lusgu would give in and share Dr. Rayn's location. Surely the brownie had to see that it would be helpful to the police as well as Dr. Rayn. Wouldn't she want her name off the suspect list?

The problem with inventions was that *anyone* could have gotten ahold of it to use it. Which meant Dr. Rayn wasn't necessarily the only suspect. But until the creature in the hospital woke up or the police were able to speak with Dr. Rayn, no one could be set aside as no longer of interest.

Lusgu didn't move, but the stubborn set to his jaw said it all.

Rascal's shoulders relaxed. "I'm sorry I don't have more news for you."

I'm starving, Violet said, scampering down Lusgu, then back up the table. *What's for dinner?*

Wynona was grateful for Violet's interruption of the tension in the room. "I haven't put anything away yet. We had steak and salad. Lusgu? Can I interest you in something?"

The brownie waved her off and shuffled back toward the portal door. "I want to hear when you find something," he said to Rascal right before disappearing.

Wynona gave Rascal a commiserating smile. "See why I can't join in? It'll make him feel like we're all against him."

Rascal shook his head. "We are against him, if he continues to not cooperate."

Wynona wrapped a hand around her hair and brought it to the side of her neck, running her fingers through it. "He said all this happened a few hundred years ago. I wonder just how old Lusgu is."

Violet snorted, but continued munching on a crouton.

Rascal rolled his eyes. "I don't even want to know. Dragons live forever, practically, and it looks like brownies aren't too far behind." He sighed. "Let's talk about something else though, huh? Sourpuss janitors aren't high on my priority list at the moment."

Wynona laughed softly. "Okay. What would you like to talk about?"

Rascal stepped into her space again. "I think you know," he said in a husky tone. "But we've got kids present."

Violet muttered under her breath. *Exactly. Please don't scar us for life.*

Wynona smiled and patted Rascal's chest. "Soon," she whispered.

"Better be," he grumbled.

"You said you'd look through the grimoires with me," she said, changing the subject. "Should we do that now?"

Rascal glanced at his watch. "Shoot. Yeah. I don't have as much time as usual though. I really should be at the office early, so I can check on our coma patient."

Wynona nodded. "That's fine. Why don't I feed you dessert instead and we can read another night."

Rascal kissed her cheek. "Now you're speaking my language."

Wynona squished her lips to the side. "I'd like to try making something with my magic. You up for that?"

Rascal's grin widened. "If it results in a delectable treat, I'm always up for it." He stepped back and sat down at the table. "Go ahead, chef."

Wynona stood a little taller under his praise. She actually enjoyed baking, but she'd seen it done so much faster with magic and she wanted to try her own hand at it. She'd learned how to make tea and cook meat. How hard could a cake be?

Apparently, it was harder than she thought. It took Wynona four batches to get it right. The first cake deflated, the second was overbaked and the third was too dense. But the fourth was pretty tasty, if not quite as delectable, as Rascal had been hoping for.

The wolf wiped his mouth with his napkin. "You do good work, beautiful." He stood. "But I gotta run."

Wynona pouted. "So soon?"

Rascal put one hand on the table and the other on her chair, caging her in. "So soon? It took almost two hours to make that cake. It's late evening now."

Wynona slumped a little. "I know. Sorry." She played with the button at the top of his uniform shirt. "I just wanted to make you a treat."

"You're a treat." He gave her a short, fierce kiss. "But now I have to go. Next time, I'll help with dishes."

"No need." Wynona sighed. "Every time I try, Lusgu appears and takes them out of my hands."

Rascal chuckled and shook his head. "I just can't seem to get a handle on that guy."

Wynona shrugged. "Me either. But I'm determined to be his friend anyway."

Rascal gave her one last lingering kiss, then slipped out of the kitchen. The front door opened and closed and Wynona sighed.

She looked at Violet. "How is he?" she asked softly. She had no idea how much Lusgu could hear from the house, but he always seemed to have a finger on the pulse of the comings and goings.

Violet stopped munching and looked away as if in thought. *He'll make it. But it's hard.*

"Is there any way we can get him to share more?" Wynona pressed.

Violet shook her head. *Not until he's ready.*

Wynona folded her arms on the table and stared at her familiar. "You know all about him, don't you?"

The mouse shrugged.

"Is he…" Wynona looked for the right word. She didn't want to offend, but she also wanted to be sure.

Safe? Violet asked with a smirk.

Wynona tilted her head back and forth. "That's one way of putting it, I suppose. I just…sometimes I feel like he's one of the family. But at other times I get the sense that he's a complete stranger."

Violet's nose twitched. *It's his story to tell. But you're safe.*

"Me?" Wynona's eyebrows went up. "But not the others?"

Unless he or you are threatened, there's no need to worry.

Wynona frowned and rested her chin on her fist. "I wonder what Granny had on him. It seems odd that he's so dedicated to me."

Violet laughed, the sound high and squeaky.

"What's so funny?"

The mouse shook her head. *Nothing. Everything.*

Wynona pushed back her chair and stood up, yawning and stretching. "You're as vague as he is."

With a snort, Violet went back to eating.

"I'm going to get some rest," Wynona said. "I'm tired and I'm meeting with Celia again tomorrow. If the construction magic goes well, we should be decorating in only a few days."

Violet nodded and waved. *See you in the morning. I'm going to spend the night with Lusgu.*

Wynona sighed. "Alright. Thank you for keeping him company. I'm worried about him."

And you wonder why he's loyal.

Smiling tiredly, Wynona headed through the family room and down the hall. She didn't bother with the dishes. Lusgu would only scold her in the morning for putting them away in the wrong places. She, unfortunately, knew this from personal experience.

Her bedtime routine was done in a haze with her mind stuck on the odd storm and Lusgu's possible role. The intrigue was eating at her something fierce, but she'd promised herself to put Lusgu's interests first.

Looking in the mirror, she pointed a finger at herself. "No more," she scolded. "He's your friend and more important than your curiosity. Let it go." Nodding firmly, she headed to her room. Slumber sounded heavenly right now and hopefully in the morning, she'd have better control over her thoughts. Then she could move ahead with her business and her wedding and forget that anything else ever even existed.

CHAPTER 7

"I don't think I've been in a library since I was in high school." Rascal rubbed the back of his neck.

"Then it's a good thing we're going now," Wynona said, tugging on his arm. "A little reading never hurt anybody."

"I don't know. I'm pretty sure paper cuts are a thing. And what if someone threw a book at your head? Have you seen the size of those medical volumes?"

Wynona rolled her eyes and pulled on the door handle. "Quit being such a baby and come on."

Rascal paused by her ear. "I'm not a baby." He grinned. "I was a pup."

"Oh my word, you're ridiculous." She pushed him and walked inside, leaving the wolf to catch up. The musty smell of dust and paper hit her nose immediately and Wynona paused to take in the pleasurable scent. She'd spent a lot of time in her library at the castle while growing up. It was her only communication with the outside world and the best way she could keep herself informed about life.

But even her parents' library couldn't compare to this one. The one at her parents' was bright, shiny and untouched. This one was homey, peaceful and full of dark, warm colors… It was perfect.

"Where to?" Rascal asked under his breath.

"Why are you whispering?" she asked.

"Because librarians are scary and I don't want one of them to yell at me."

"I'm guessing you have experience with that," Wynona quipped as she headed toward the left.

"You don't want to know."

She glanced over her shoulder, giving him a coy look. "Of course I do. But we can wait until later." He sent a playful growl her way and Wynona smiled.

Can we focus? Violet asked. *I'm getting nauseous.*

"Sorry." Wynona reached up and scratched behind Violet's ears. "I'll get back to task." She began running her fingers along the spines of different science journals. There had to be something here that could tell her about Dr. Rayn. Being one of the original five of Paratech would definitely make her a topic of conversation in print and word.

"Ah-ha!" Wynona pulled a magazine off the shelf. It was older than Wynona. A lot older. But the front cover had a picture of four creatures on it. Three men and one woman, all looking classy, wealthy and serious as the cover announced that their company had reached the grand old age of one-hundred.

"You think they'll mention her?" Rascal said, scratching behind his ear. "Lusgu said she was kicked out about that time."

Wynona wiped dust from the sleeve and nodded. "I'm assuming they'll at least mention her. And maybe that will give us something to check out further."

"So you're simply hoping for a stepping stone?"

Wynona nodded. "Come on." She headed to a table and sat down, carefully turning the pages. She didn't want to tear anything, even if the pages were preserved by magic.

After finding the article on the tech company, Wynona began to skim.

Rascal bounced his foot and was quiet for a couple of minutes before asking, "Find anything?"

Wynona shook her head with a frown. "No. So far it's only about these four." She paused and bent a little closer. "Wait a minute...Rascal?"

"Hm?"

"Does this man look familiar to you?"

Rascal glanced at the magazine, tilting his head. "Uh...yeah..." His eyes flared. "Isn't that the creature in the coma?"

"That's exactly what I was thinking," Wynona murmured. She quickly read the words under the picture. "His name is Meldaeon Thathion and he's a gorgon."

"That would explain the greenish tint to his skin," Rascal said wryly.

Wynona tapped her finger against the picture. "I didn't notice it when he was lying unconscious on the street."

"It was so foggy, it's a wonder you saw the body at all," Rascal said. He sucked in a long breath. "Now I'm even more eager for him to wake up. How is it that one of the CEO's of the paranormal world's biggest tech companies, who hasn't been seen in public in years, was running around the streets of Hex Haven? And who was the woman with him?"

Wynona nodded. "It is odd, I agree. I mean, I've heard the names, but none of the other original five have been in the spotlight since well before I was born."

"Are they even still working with the company?"

"I have no idea," Wynona admitted. "Everyone calls them the 'Original Five,' but that doesn't really mean they aren't still around." Her brows scrunched together. "But Gorgons don't usually live hundreds of years. And the man didn't look ancient by any means. How is he still here?"

"What kind of creatures are the rest of them?" Rascal asked.

Wynona studied the page again. "This man, Ceraon Solarspike, is a griffin. Eve Guanaco, is an eagle shifter. And Ebus Toleus, " she tapped her finger against his face "is half troll."

"Huh." Rascal leaned back. "Half troll? What's the other half?"

"Judging from his face, I'm guessing human," Wynona said with a gasp. Trolls were notorious for being unattractive to everyone but other trolls, but this man actually looked good. The lines of his face were slightly sharper than average, but they simply made him look masculine and strong. But human combinations with paranormals were rare. Like...really rare. Humans, other than a select political few, didn't know the paranormals existed and the magical world preferred to keep it that way.

"Or a witch," Rascal pointed out. "Witches and warlocks look like humans. Does it say he has magic?"

Wynona shook her head. "Doesn't say. But I suppose it's possible." She shut the magazine. "We need more. This doesn't say anything about Dr. Rayn and it really only talks about the company itself. We need bios on the board."

"Better check digitally then," Rascal said. "There might not be actual books on the topic, but there'll be articles and such."

"Good idea." She stood, put the magazine in a rack to be re-shelved and headed toward the computer area. Grabbing one of the empty seats, she sat down. "So...I've never done this before."

Rascal's eyebrows went up. "You've never used a search engine before?"

Wynona gave him a look. "I didn't exactly get out much." She looked at the screen. "I can guess how it goes, but it would probably be more efficient if you told me what to do or simply switched places with me."

"No need," came a soft voice.

Wynona looked around, but couldn't find anyone.

"Down here."

"Oh. I'm sorry." A tiny wood nymph, no higher than Wynona's knee, was at the side of her chair. "I, um..."

The nymph pushed her glasses up her bark nose. "You said you don't know how to use the computer?"

Wynona felt her cheeks flushed as a couple others turned when the librarian spoke. "I've never been here before."

"Do you have a library card?"

Wynona shook her head and the nymph tsked, causing the leaves on her head to shake. "To use a computer, you must first have a library card and then sign the agreement that you won't look up illegal spells or any other underhanded dealings."

"Can you help me get a card?" Wynona asked. "I don't even know where to start."

The nymph's silver eyes widened and her leaves trembled. "Well, yes…come." She turned and began hurrying away, quickly weaving between furniture and legs as she headed toward the front desk.

"Guess this is what we're doing now," Rascal teased.

Wynona shot him a glare. "How was I supposed to know? I didn't need a card at my parents' house."

Rascal chuckled and put his hand on her lower back. "It's fine. We all have to learn sometime. I'll even admit I didn't know you had to sign an agreement to use the computers."

"Yeah, but you also said you haven't been here since you were a teenager." Wynona snapped her mouth shut as they arrived at the desk. She waited for the nymph to climb some steps so she was tall enough to work at the desk.

The librarian pushed her glasses up again and shook the mouse to wake up her computer. "Now…a card." She tilted her head back, looking through the bottom of her lenses. "Name?"

"Wynona Le Doux."

The nymph gasped and her head snapped toward Wynona. "How did I…" She swallowed hard. "You look just like your mother," the librarian said in a tiny squeak.

Wynona gave a wan smile. "I've heard that before."

Looking wary, the nymph went back to the computer. Her eyes kept darting back and forth from the screen to Wynona. "Are you… are you the *oldest* daughter?" she whispered.

Wynona held back the desire to close her eyes and sigh. Between her family and the massive breaking of her curse, the entire community knew who she was and it led to a reputation Wynona didn't want or deserve.

Rascal growled low in warning, but Wynona put a hand on his arm.

"Yes," Wynona replied calmly. "I am." She raised her eyebrows. "Am I still eligible for a card?"

"Oh, of course!" the librarian said too quickly. Her bark-like skin, however, paled and her typing grew a little too fast. "Let me just get…" She grabbed several things under the counter and ended up scattering pens and cards everywhere. "I'm so clumsy," the nymph cried, disappearing down her ladder.

Wynona shook her head and walked around the desk, getting down on her knees to help the nymph. "Here. Let me help."

"No, no," the librarian said quickly.

Wynona rested her fingertips on the librarian's shoulder, careful not to press the small creature hard. "I insist," she said softly.

The nymph frowned slightly, but nodded. "Okay."

Wynona helped gather the papers, scooping the pens into a basket before putting them on top of the desk. "There." She walked around to her side again.

"T-thank you," the librarian stuttered.

Wynona smiled kindly. Someday, people would know it wasn't her they needed to be afraid of.

Bozo, Violet muttered from her place in Rascal's pocket.

Wynona ignored her familiar. "I sign here?"

The librarian nodded. "Yes, please," she squeaked.

When all was said and done, Wynona had a new library card in her back pocket and permission to use the computer.

"Would you like me to teach you how to search?"

Wynona's smile grew more genuine. "I'd love that. Thank you."

The front door slammed and all heads turned to the loud sound. "Oh my goodness," a fairy said, her hand on her heart. "What are we going to do?"

Wynona's eyebrows pulled together and she looked at Rascal, who shrugged. He stepped forward. "Is there a problem?" he asked, holding out his badge.

"Oh, thank goodness," the elderly fairy gasped. "An officer." Her wings fluttered and she floated their way, wringing her hands. "The media…the ghost reporters…they're all outside and I don't know how much longer I can keep them there."

"What do they want?" Wynona blurted out before she could think better of it.

The fairy looked at her, then gasped, a trembling hand going over her mouth. "You're she. The president's daughter."

Easy, Wynona warned Rascal when he growled again, causing the fairy to duck behind the desk. "Yes. I'm Wynona Le Doux. Can you please tell me why the ghost reporters are outside?"

"They want to talk to you," the fairy said in a whisper.

"What? Why?" Wynona asked. She could feel the presence of dozens of eyes from the other patrons in the library, but at this point she didn't care. Something weird was going on and she needed to know what she was facing. Chief Ligurio usually tried really hard to keep the media out of her business. But she hadn't been doing anything, so why were they here now?

"They're saying you helped save Meldaeon Thathion in that freak storm yesterday," the fairy stammered. "He's in the hospital and no one can get close enough to speak to him, so they want to talk to you instead." The librarian shook her head. "They said you were in here, but I didn't believe it." She pointed to the door. "You need to go speak to them."

Wynona shook her head. "No way."

"But you must!" the fairy shouted, rushing toward Wynona. Rascal's growl had her floating backward again. "They're talking about you, and Eve Guanaco and the griffin, and even that old dragon, Dr. Rayn."

Wynona stilled. "They're asking about Dr. Rayn?"

The fairy nodded. "Someone said it was her storm device."

Wynona and Rascal looked at each other. *Where are they getting all this information?*

Rascal shook his head and straightened, becoming the officer he was. "Where's your back door?"

The fairy shook her head, whimpering.

"I'll show you."

Wynona gave the wood nymph a grateful smile. "Thank you," she said softly. "I appreciate it."

Nodding, the nymph climbed down and guided them to the back of the building, which was much larger than Wynona would have guessed, before opening an emergency exit. "Good luck," the nymph said softly.

Wynona stopped just outside the door. "Thank you for the library card. I'll look forward to the computer lesson another time."

The librarian smiled. "You're not what I expected."

Wynona's smile widened. "I also get that a lot." Turning away, she took Rascal's hand and they ducked down the alley. It was time to get home.

CHAPTER 8

"It looks like you're going to be involved whether you want to be or not," Rascal grumbled as they drove toward her house. His brows were pulled into a deep "V" and Wynona had the urge to press the skin with her fingers, to straighten it out.

Maybe pushing away the wrinkles would push away the media as well.

One can only hope.

Wynona rubbed her forehead. "I hate how everything always comes back to my name. If I was born to some poor creature on the far side of town, no one would ever care that I ran into Mr. Thathion yesterday."

Rascal's hand landed on her knee and he gave it a squeeze. "I like you for being Wynona," he said with a sad smile. "I don't even care about your last name. We're about to change it anyway."

She laughed softly. "I guess that's something."

He blew out a breath. "But we do need to figure out what the ghost reporters are saying. Can we use your computer when we get back to the house?"

"Of course." Wynona grew quiet and the rest of the ride home was comfortable, but the air had a slight wave of tension to it. Both of them were worried about what the news was reporting and who they were chasing.

They chased Wynona, a lot. Between her help with the police and being the oldest daughter of the reigning president, she struggled to stay out of the limelight, despite her best efforts.

Pulling into her driveway, Wynona waited for Rascal to walk around and get her down. She loved feeling his large hands on her waist and how he always left a short peck on the tip of her nose when he pulled her close.

"Thank you," she whispered, smiling up at him.

Rascal smiled back. "Someday, all this hubbub will be a distant memory."

Wynona shook her head and patted his chest. "Someday…will never happen," she told him flatly. "I've been thinking that since I escaped my parents."

Rasca shrugged and turned toward the house. "It was worth a shot."

Once inside, Wynona set Violet carefully on the edge of the couch. The mouse was sleeping deeply. She apparently wasn't nearly as worried about the media as the other two.

"Be right back," Wynona said, dashing down the hall to her room. At the last minute, she stopped herself and concentrated. This was exactly what her magic should be helpful for. Making life just a little easier.

Wiggling her fingers, she used her powers to bring her tablet out of the bedroom and into the sitting room. Grabbing it out of the air, she headed to the couch and waited for Rascal to join her.

After trying a couple different catch phrases, Wynona finally got a series of hits.

"Oh my word…" Wynona breathed. "Disgraced Tech Giant goes from Isolation to Prison."

"You've got to be kidding me," Rascal muttered. He read the next headline. "Is Eternal Life Worth It? How One Creature Went Crazy from Isolation and Killed Her Partners."

"What are you reading?" Lusgu shouted from behind them.

Wynona nearly jumped out of her seat and Rascal jumped to his feet, growling low in warning. "Lusgu," she scolded, only to cut off when she noticed how intensely he was focused on the tablet. Her heart fell. She hadn't even thought about how the news would affect the brownie.

She looked to Rascal for help, but he shrugged.

Give it to him, Violet said with a yawn. She stood on her hind legs and stretched. *He needs to know.*

Hesitantly, Wynona walked forward and handed the tablet to Lusgu.

He nearly took her fingers off as he hastily grabbed the object and began scanning the page.

Several heartbeats went by and Wynona felt each one clear to her bones. She wanted…*needed*…to know what he was thinking, but she was terrified at the same time.

Lusgu's fingers tightened around the tablet until she could hear the plastic and metal begin to break.

Wynona screamed and ducked when the whole electronic exploded, shooting shards toward her and Rascal. A warm body covered hers and she glanced over her shoulder to see Rascal tucking himself over her. Her eyes widened when she noticed a small drip of blood begin to run down his temple.

This has gone too far.

Without any more thought and her usual sense of hesitancy, Wynona threw up her magical shield and locked Lusgu inside. She ignored the raging brownie, though she could feel him pounding the barrier with his own magic. He was strong. *Really* strong. But right now Wynona's righteous anger was stronger and it lent her strength.

Turning her back to him, she faced Rascal. "What were you doing getting in harm's way like that?" she scolded, trying to keep the mood light, though the situation called for something much more explicit. She reached up and touched his face, quickly pulling out the plastic piece and healing his skin.

Rascal growled. "Like I would leave you to get hurt?" he asked in his low, angry tone. His eyes were flashing and claws were extending on his fingers.

This was about to go downhill fast. Nothing brought out the wolf faster than Wynona being in danger.

She cupped his face and brought his attention back to her, closing her eyes for just a moment to reinforce the shield again. She wouldn't be able to hold off Lusgu for much longer. "Thank you," she whispered, giving him a pixie soft kiss. "But I need you to calm down."

"I will when he does," Rascal ground out, his teeth growing as fast as his nails.

"No. Now," Wynona ordered. "I can hold him with my magic, but I can't handle two of you." When Rascal didn't back down right away, Wynona raised her eyebrows. "Please," she whispered.

Listen to her, wolf man, Violet said in an uncharacteristically meek voice. *Lusgu needs help, not a beating right now.*

Rascal sighed and closed his eyes.

Wynona took the opportunity to do the same, once again sending a wave of power to keep the shield in place. How in the world did that small creature contain such strength? It was unprecedented!

Slowly, Rascal's features went back to normal, until he opened his eyes to the usual caramel gold, rather than bright metallic.

Wynona gave him a hesitant smile. "Thank you."

"Don't thank me yet," Rascal said, stepping around her and facing Lusgu. "If he puts a finger on you, I'm ripping him to shreds."

"I don't think he's trying to hurt me," Wynona said, though she couldn't help but wince even as she said the words.

Rascal's growl immediately deepened.

"I'm fine," Wynona assured him, resting her hand on his arm. "He just caught me off guard."

"We need Skymaw," Rascal stated bluntly.

Again, Wynona shook her head. "I won't make it that long. Lusgu's too strong."

"I don't like it," Rascal said.

"Me either, but here we are." Stepping forward, Wynona put out her hands. "Lusgu," she said in as authoritative a tone as she could. "If you will calm down, I'll lower the barrier."

Lusgu stopped flinging magic, but his eyes were wild and he appeared unstable.

Wynona stepped a little closer, ignoring Rascal's warning growl. "Lusgu," she said more softly. "I know you're hurting, but we're here to help. We're friends. Please…calm down enough for us to talk this out."

Lusgu's small body was trembling and heaving from his tantrum, but he jerkily nodded his head.

Wynona looked at Violet.

Let him out, Violet said.

Trusting her familiar, Wynona lowered the shield. No sooner had the bubble begun to pop, than Lusgu threw up his hands, causing it to explode the rest of the way and sending Wynona flying across the room, her head slamming into the wall.

The room spun and Wynona couldn't get her lungs to suck in a breath, they were frozen along with the rest of her body. She registered maniacal growling, but couldn't turn her head to see what was going on.

The growling diminished and a dark head appeared above hers. "Never restrain me again," Lusgu said in an icy tone, his black eyes pinning her in place.

Electricity built in Wynona's fingertips. If Lusgu was above her, then Rascal was being held.

Stay calm! Violet shouted. *Everyone needs to calm down!*

For the first time in a while, Wynona completely ignored her familiar. Her soulmate bond was screaming in panic and it was the only thing she could feel. Her fingers twitched and Lusgu's eyes darted to the movement.

Acting on complete instinct, Wynona threw out her hand and twisted it, clenching her fist at the end as if holding a rope tight. Lusgu gasped and was sucked to the floor, lying flat on his back. His hands clawed at his neck, but nothing was visible.

Wynona climbed to her feet, feeling weightless, as if she still wasn't quite part of her body yet. She registered the brownie gasping for breath, but felt nothing. The edges of her vision were sparkling with a purple so dark it was nearly black, and she focused in on her wolf.

Rascal had shifted at some point and was muzzled and bound with shining black magical cords.

Wynona ran her nail through the air, slicing them in half and freeing her predator. She rested her hand on his shaggy head when he trotted to her side, before turning back to the creature still thumping on the floor.

She pursed her lips. Her brain seemed a little fuzzy. Why was he there? Wynona tilted her head, studying the small one struggling for breath. Her wolf whimpered and she scratched behind his ears, but the sound intensified.

The wolf stepped forward, nudging the creature, then looked up at Wynona with soulful eyes. Wynona blinked. What did it want? Why was she even attached to the wolf? What did it mean to her?

WYNONA! a voice screamed in her head.

Wynona blinked. Was that her? Was that voice calling to her? She looked around and noticed a bright purple streak run across the room, aiming for her leg. Reacting before thinking, Wynona sent a zap of magic at the movement, but the tiny creature didn't even hesitate. It finished running to her and clamped down on her calf.

"Ouch!" Wynona cried, leaping back. As soon as the word broke through her mouth, she felt her lungs begin to move and she paused long enough to take in several deep breaths, her chest hurting with each expansion.

"Rascal," she breathed, noting he was in his wolf form. "Rascal, are you okay?"

He whimpered and looked down.

Wynona followed his gaze. "Lusgu!" she screamed. Scrambling over on her hands and knees, she put a hand on his chest, sagging in relief when she felt it rise, though his eyes remained closed.

A sting on her leg brought her mind back around to what had caused the troublesome reaction in the first place. "Violet?" Wynona called out, spinning on her knees. "Violet?"

I'm here. Violet came crawling up Lusgu's side, sitting primly on his chest. *Are you back?*

Wynona pulled back her hand, which had been reaching for her familiar. "What?"

Are you back?

She looked at Rascal, who had separated himself from her by a few feet, and a dull ache began to build in her chest.

"I don't understand."

Violet nodded at Rascal and went down on all fours, tapping Lusgu's chest a few times. *Heal him and we'll talk.*

"What happened?" Wynona asked, immediately going into nurturing mode.

Heal first.

Wynona bit her bottom lip to keep it from trembling; they weren't telling her something. And she had a terrible feeling that it was bad. Really bad. Gingerly, she rested a couple of fingers on Lusgu's sternum and sent the slightest jolt of healing his way.

His eyes immediately shot up and he sucked in a deep breath.

Before she could pull back, however, Lusgu grabbed her hand, his long fingers crushing hers.

"I wasn't sure I believed it," he rasped.

"You're hurting me," Wynona whispered, trying to extricate her limb.

Lusgu blinked and tightened his hold, causing Wynona to wince in pain. "You're the only one who can help."

Wynona shook her head. "I don't understand what you're talking about. Help what?"

"Help…" Lusgu swallowed and his eyes darted to Violet, then back to Wynona. "I need you to help Rayn," he whispered hoarsely.

"The dragon?" Wynona asked. "The inventor?"

Lusgu nodded. "You're the only one who can do it."

"I didn't want to get involved," Wynona explained. "You seemed so upset."

"You're the only one." He finally released her hand and closed his eyes. "You're the only one."

CHAPTER 9

Wynona rocked back on her heels and looked around at Rascal and Violet. Both of them appeared uncomfortable. "I don't understand what's going on," Wynona said. "You're hiding something from me."

Rascal and Violet exchanged a look. *We have to tell her*, Rascal said through their combined mental link.

Violet hesitated, then nodded. *We do.*

"Tell me what?" Wynona demanded. She was starting to get frightened. Everything was happening so fast and she wasn't quite sure why Lusgu was on the floor or why he'd been hurt. Surely her shield couldn't have done this to him. "Why is Lusgu hurt? Did my shield break and I passed out or something?" Wynona frowned and rubbed her forehead. Something was terribly wrong.

Rascal changed back into his human form and held out his hand. "Come on," he said softly. "Let's get you some tea."

Wynona took his hand and stood up. "I don't want tea," she said petulantly. "I want answers."

"Trust me," Rascal said over his shoulder. "You want both." He paused at the kitchen threshold. "What do you have to help alleviate fear or anxiousness?"

"Are you serious?"

He nodded soberly.

Sighing, Wynona wiggled her fingers and prepped herself a cup. Two minutes later they were seated on the couch, though Violet never left Lusgu's prone body. "Now what?" Wynona didn't touch the tea. She wanted to know what was going on.

"You…" Rascal cut off and looked to Violet. "I can't do it."

The sting of tears pricked the back of Wynona's eyes. "Rascal," she whispered. "You're scaring me."

He grabbed her hand, rubbing his thumb over her knuckles. "Do you really not remember anything from the last few minutes?"

Wynona wiped at her eyes and shook her head. "I remember starting to let Lusgu out of the bubble and then you were a wolf, he was on the ground and Violet was angry."

Rascal muttered a couple of curse words under his breath. Standing, he prowled in front of her as if he couldn't bear to stand still. "You…became someone…some*thing* else," he stated finally.

Wynona frowned. "I don't understand."

"Do you remember how Granny Saffron said if left unchecked, she had seen the type of creature you were going to be?" Rascal asked, plopping himself back down at her side.

Wynona nodded.

"I think you…became…her for just a few moments."

Wynona reared back. "That can't be right."

Oh, it is, Violet added. *Why do you think I had to bite you?*

Wynona looked down at the tiny marks on her leg and rubbed away the small bit of blood. "That…you *bit* me? You were trying to wake me up?" she whispered hoarsely. A heavy feeling, like a lead cauldron, was settling in her stomach. Rascal and Violet wouldn't lie to her. Not about something like this. Trying to hide a gift or a surprise party, sure, but saying she had been some kind of evil being? No…surely they wouldn't.

I was, Violet said, her regret nearly palpable. *I'm sorry for that.*

Wynona kept her eyes on her leg and shook her head. "Don't be," she said softly. "Apparently, I needed it." It took every bit of courage in her system to meet Rascal's eyes. "How bad was it?"

Rascal scratched under his chin, behind his ear and then slapped his hands on his knees. "You…were…not yourself."

"Would someone just tell me?" Wynona cried. She felt as if she couldn't take it anymore. "What did I do? Did I hurt someone?" Her voice trailed off and she looked at Lusgu. "Oh, no…"

"Wy—" Rascal tried, but Wynona ignored him.

"I hurt him, didn't I?" she asked. She wrapped her arms around her chest and folded inward, as if she could hide her shame from the world. "I hurt him. Just like I did once before." Wynona buried her face in her hands. "What's wrong with me?" she whispered thickly. "Why am I like this? Why was I ever allowed to live?"

Rascal's warm hands landed first on her shoulders, giving her a little shake, until Wynona looked up, then they cupped her face, forcing her to meet his gaze. "Don't. Ever. Talk. Like. That," he growled in a menacing tone. His eyes were flashing in his anger. "You were made for me. Do you understand that? You were made for me. No one is allowed to take that away. Not your stupid dad's plans, or your sister's sarcasm, or even the flip side of your unlimited powers." His eyes softened just the slightest amount. "I've never known anyone who fights so much for what's right," he continued, his voice continuing to drop and soften the longer he spoke. "You follow your heart. You help those no one else wants to touch. You do *so* much good," he said, his eyes growing misty. "You do so much good." Slowly, Rascal shook his head and leaned back, his hands falling as he cleared his throat. "Don't let one bad situation ruin everything you've done and become."

Wynona wiped at her wet cheeks. She hadn't even realized she was crying until she saw Rascal struggling with his emotions as well. "I love you," she whispered.

One side of his mouth twitched. "I love you."

Wynona grabbed his hand and held on tight. "You're sure you aren't afraid of me?"

Rascal scoffed. "Like you could ever hurt this." He flexed and Wynona laughed a little through her tears.

It didn't last long. They both knew she could most definitely hurt him, but she was grateful for his show of confidence.

You aren't likely to hurt him, Violet pointed out.

Wynona turned and fornwed. "Why do you say that?"

Because scary witch only seems to come out when those you love most are in danger. Violet scrubbed at her face. *You were protecting Rascal. That's why you snapped. Even the far side of your powers recognizes what he is to you.*

Rascal gave her a hand a squeeze. "And you thought you could get rid of me so easily."

She smiled softly and shook her head in denial. "I would never want to."

Okey, dokey, love pups. We need to address the real issue at hand here.

Wynona pinched her lips together. "Did I hurt you, Violet?"

Violet shook her head. *No. But I'm sorry I had to bite you.*

Wynona rubbed her ankle. "Thank you for waking me up."

Violet nodded and tapped her foot on Lusgu's chest. *Up and at 'em, Lusgu. We need to get this party started...but this time with a lot less violence.*

Lusgu blinked and stared at Violet as if he understood her.

Wynona frowned. She thought only she and Violet had a connection, because Violet was her familiar. Rascal had been able to understand because of their connection to being animals, and having Wynona between them. It was supposed to be a very unique situation. So how was it possible that Lusgu shared it as well?

Violet glanced up, but didn't address Wynona's thoughts. *So you're going to take on the case?*

Wynona stiffened. "Excuse me?"

"You said you would." Lusgu groaned as he slowly pushed himself up from the floor. His face was pale and he looked like he had aged fifty years in the last ten minutes.

"I did not," Wynona argued. "I don't even know what all was being said. You just kept saying I was the one. What did you mean by that?"

The brownie stood and rubbed the back of his neck, stretching it from side to side, causing his long ears to shift and flop. "You're the only one I trust to help save Rayn."

"Who is Rayn to you?" Rascal asked, leaning in slightly. His body language was wary, though Wynona wasn't sure if it was from her own scare or because of Lusgu's tantrum only a few minutes before.

Lusgu shook his head. "I can't."

"Can't or won't?"

Lusgu shrugged. "In this case, it doesn't matter. I can't."

Wynona sighed and leaned back against the couch. "So you want me to help clear her name?"

Lusgu nodded. He scowled when he spotted some of the broken table against the floor. "Sorry about breaking your thingy."

"That thingy was an expensive electronic device," Rascal said bluntly. "I think you owe her more than an apology."

"Rascal—" Wynona began.

Lusgu held up his hand. "No. He's right. Sorry isn't enough." Straightening himself, he marched up until they were toe to toe. "I'll pledge my servitude forever in repayment and if you agree to take on the case."

Wynona's eyes widened. "Lusgu," she breathed. "I would never want to do that to you."

He spread his hands to the side. "I have nothing else to offer."

"What about magic lessons?" Rascal inserted slyly.

Wynona's head snapped from one man to another. "Magic lessons? You think he can teach me?" She peered at Lusgu. "Is our magic too different for something like that?"

Lusgu turned away and rubbed his bald head. "I...could help...but it would be difficult."

Wynona didn't even hesitate. "Lusgu, you're my friend. I'm more than happy to help you just because of that. But if you'd be willing to offer me any help magically, I'd welcome it with open arms."

He sighed, his shoulders deflating before he nodded. "I suppose it *would* come to this," he muttered. "Curse you, Saffron."

Wynona gasped. "Lusgu!"

He shook his head and his face was almost back to normal when he looked up and glared. "This was never meant to be my job," he stated bluntly. "But yes. I'll do it."

Wynona almost didn't want to make the commitment. Something about it felt off, like she was still missing a piece, but after nearly killing Lusgu, she didn't feel like she had much choice. "Thank you," she said softly. "I'll do everything I can to help you, friend."

Snorting, Lusgu began to walk away. Snapping his fingers, the broom and vacuum both burst into life and the brownie went right back to keeping the cabin clean, ignoring Rascal and Wynona on the couch.

"Are you sure this is a good idea?" Rascal asked Violet.

Violet shrugged. *A little late now.*

Rascal growled. "I don't trust him."

You should.

Leaning forward, Rascal got right in Violet's face. "He tried to destroy her," he said darkly. "Tell me why I should."

Violet gave Rascal a sad look. *Is my word not enough?*

"You said to let him out of the bubble. See where that got us?"

Violet nodded. *I know. But it's all over now. All we can do is move on.*

Wynona tucked a loose chunk of hair behind her ear. "Can we please stop talking about me like I'm not here?"

Rascal clenched his jaw, then nodded. "Yes. Sorry."

Wynona took a sip of her now cold tea. Pressing her fingers against the side of the cup, she warmed it back up and tried again. *Much better.* "Now. What all do I need to know before jumping into this fully?"

Rascal glanced at his buzzing phone, not answering her right away as he punched out a reply and shoved the device in his pocket. He stood and offered his hand. "What you need to know is that Thathion woke up. I say we start with him."

Wynona let the wolf pull her from the couch. "Wow. He was out for a long time."

Rascal nodded. "Yep."

"And they're sure it was from the lightning strike?"

"Yep."

Wynona nodded. "Okay. Let's go see where he got the box from." She looked to Lusgu momentarily before following Rascal outside. Violet didn't move from her spot on the coffee table and Wynona raised her eyebrows.

The purple mouse shook her head.

Wynona could feel her familiar's worry and was grateful she would be staying with Lusgu. He shouldn't be alone after the debacle they just had, even if Wynona did heal him.

His body is the least of my concerns, Violet said.

Wynona nodded and closed the front door behind her. She was beginning to understand why some people were so frightened of her. The more she thought about what had just happened in her house, the more she was frightened of herself.

Rascal grabbed her waist and lifted her into the passenger side of the truck. After setting her down, he leaned in for a quick, but fierce kiss.

Wynona watched him walk around to the driver's side. If she was going to survive any of this, it would be because of him. Because he wasn't willing to give up on her. Even Violet had a divided loyalty with her connection to Lusgu. But not Rascal. He was all Wynona's, all the time.

"What?" he asked, when he caught her staring.

Wynona shook her head. "Nothing," she assured him. Moving to the middle seat, she buckled in and rested her head on his shoulder. Fate knew exactly what it was doing in sending her the most loyal animal possible. Wolves mated for life. Wynona might have had a lot of hard knocks growing up and even now, her life wasn't full of rainbows and sparkles, but she had Rascal. Steady, true, wonderful Rascal. And right now, that was all she needed.

CHAPTER 10

Rascal flashed his badge at the front desk. "We're here to see Mr. Thathion. I understand he's been moved."

The nurse's eyes widened and she turned to her computer, clicking away for a few moments before nodding nervously. Her nose twitched, giving away the fact that she was some kind of shifter, more than likely a prey type. "He's been moved to room Two-Four-Five," she squeaked.

"Thank you," Wynona said with a soft smile as they left the desk. She held tight to Rascal's hand. "I've never met any of the Original Five. Have you?"

Rascal shook his head. "Nope."

"Aren't you nervous?"

Rascal raised an eyebrow at her. "You grew up in the palace. Why would this guy make you nervous?"

Wynona grinned. "Maybe because I'm meeting a celebrity."

Rascal shook his head. "He's not a celebrity. He's a nerd who made it big."

Wynona's gentle laughter continued as they went down the hallway. "That device in your pocket is all due to that nerd," she teased as they reached the door they wanted.

"Deputy Chief," an officer said with a respectful nod.

Rascal nodded in return. "Has anyone else been inside?"

The officer shook his head, his eyes darting questioningly to Wynona. "I spoke to Chief a bit ago and he said you would handle it."

Rascal put his hand on the door. "He's right. Ms. Le Doux and I are to have full access to this room, and no one else. Is that understood?"

"No one?"

"Chief excluded, but otherwise, no. No one."

The officer's brows furrowed, but he nodded. "What do you want us to tell the media when they come sniffing around?"

"Not your job, officer," Rascal snapped. "We have people who handle the precinct's statement. Let them do their job." He put his hand on Wynona's lower back and pushed the door open, gently guiding her inside.

"Yes, sir," the officer said, snapping to attention.

Rascal snickered as the door closed behind them.

Wynona whacked his arm. "You're horrible. Be nice to the new ones."

Rascal shrugged. "I went through it. It's his turn now."

"Do you mind telling me why you're in my room and what's ssssso funny?" a voice hissed from the far side of the space.

Wynona instantly sobered. "Forgive us, Mr. Thathion," she said pleasantly. If she closed her eyes, Wynona could still see the creature's wild look of terror as he ran into her shield and demanded entrance. Today, he looked only slightly better put together. His hair was recently washed and at least sort of combed, though his skin was still paler than normal.

His second set of eyelids was working properly now, Wynona noted, as they blinked separately.

White eyebrows rose high, but the gorgon stayed quiet, waiting.

"I'm Wynona Le Doux," Wynona said, stepping forward and extending her hand.

His eyes widened even further. "Le Doux?"

Wynona nodded and folded her hands primly together after their greeting.

"The President's daughter?"

Again she nodded.

The gorgon tilted his head. "You were the one in the sssstreet. The one with the purple bubble."

Wynona pinched her lips together. Would he still be willing to talk to her when he realized she could have saved him?

"I'm sorry if I frightened you," Mr. Thathion continued. He rubbed his hands over his face. "I…wasn't exactly myself in that moment."

Rascal's hand landed on her lower back and Wynona relaxed into it. "I'm sorry you were hit," Wynona continued. Her eyes went to his leg, but it was covered by a blanket. "Is the wound repairable?"

Mr. Thathion moved the limb. "Good as new," he declared, then winced. "But the inner healing is still sore." He sighed and leaned back against his pillow. "Tell me, Ms. Le Doux. Why did the President ssssend his daughter to talk to me?"

Wynona hesitated and looked to Rascal.

"Deputy-Chief Stronglcaw," he said in his authoritative voice. He stepped forward and shook the tech mogul's hands as well. "Ms. Le Doux is with me."

"You're her bodyguard?"

Wynona tried to keep from smiling, but there was no helping it.

Rascal huffed. "No. She's helping us work the case. Ms. Le Doux has been instrumental in a number of murder cases in the last couple of years and we wanted her insight on this one."

"Murder." Mr. Thathion shook his head. "It's such an ugly word." His chin drooped. "Still, I don't suppose there's anything to do but call a spade a spade." His green eyes came back to Wynona's. "With Arave dead, I don't ssssuppose there's anything else to call it, issss there?"

"Arave?" Wynona asked. "Was that the name of the woman with you?"

Mr. Thathion nodded. "Arave Smouldons. She was my fiancee."

She had to have been hundreds of years younger than him, Rascal sent to Wynona.

Age doesn't mean anything, she scolded him. In the paranormal world, age was completely relative. There were creatures who didn't reach their primes until they were in their hundreds, while some only lasted fifty years at most.

Would you be willing to marry me if I was old and white haired?

If you had the fortune he has, she teased, enjoying the flash of retribution in the wolf's eyes. Wynona forced herself away from their flirting. It was time to be serious. "I'm sorry for your loss, Mr. Thathion. That must have been a difficult revelation when you woke up."

The gorgon shrugged. "She was wife number five and wassss only looking forward to the credit card. I think I'll ssssurvive."

Wynona's jaw just about hit the ground while Rascal tried desperately to cover his howling laugh with coughing. It didn't work.

Mr. Thathion smirked. "I'm a self-made creature, Ms. Le Doux," he said. "It means I'm also very self aware." His eyes trailed over her from head to feet and back. "But if it makes you feel better, you could sssssertainly help heal my broken heart."

Rascal growled in a warning.

The smirk grew. "So it's like that, isss it?" Mr. Thathion tilted his head. "Does your father even know you're here?"

"Like you, I'm a self-made creature," Wynona said in a tight tone. "My life is no concern of my father's."

"Hmmm…"

"What we are concerned about, is you," Wynona said, trying to sound as authoritative as Rascal. "Can you tell me what you and Ms. Souldons were doing on the street that day?"

The gorgon frowned. "Are you going to tell me it'ssss illegal to take a walk in Hex Haven?"

"No…but why were you taking a walk?" Wynona asked. "It seems odd for a man as well known as yourself to randomly be strolling the streets of a town where he hasn't been seen in years, just as a storm is coming up."

A low chuckle came from the tech mogul and grew into full laughter. He waggled a finger at Wynona. "You're a thinker, Ms. Le Doux… or can I call you Wynona?"

"Ms. Le Doux is fine," Rascal snapped.

Mr. Thathion ignored the officer. "Look…Wynona…I wassss in town. My fiancee wanted to look around." He spread his hands to the side. "I wasss entertaining her the best I could. I swear."

"And where did you find the weather box?"

"Weather box?" Mr. Thathion's white eyebrows pulled together. "I don't understand."

"The box that the lightning came from," Rascal inserted.

He was practically breathing down Wynona's neck, but she didn't allow herself to step away. She knew it made him feel better to be close when Mr. Thathion didn't seem to do a good job obeying boundary lines. Wynona had learned during her growing up years that that was a common trait among wealthy, powerful men…and women.

"I sssstill don't understand." Mr. Thathion folded his arms over his chest. "Arave and I were walking and the wind started to pick up, followed by dark skiesss. We were trying to find someone to shelter, but most of the doors I pulled on were locked." He rubbed a hand over his hair. "I don't know why. Maybe they were all closed down for the sssstorm or something, but anyway, I was trying to find ssssomewhere for us to wait it out when the lightning began to ssstrike the ground right next to usss."

Rascal's hands stiffened on her back.

"There was nowhere to hide," Mr. Thathion choked out. "Everytime we moved, it followed." His eyes were wide and much different than the shrewd looks he'd been giving Wynona since they entered the room. "I could ssswear that the lightning was coming directly for us. As if it was *trying* to hit ussss." He shook his head and blew out a shaky breath. "But even in the paranormal world, that's crazy, right?"

"Have you ever seen one of these before?" Rascal dropped his hand from Wynona and pulled out his phone, until he had the picture of the box up and handed it to Mr. Thathion.

The gorgon pursed his lips. "Sort of. An old co-worker of mine built ssssomething similar to that ages ago. It was meant…" He trailed off, all the blood draining from his face.

"It was meant?" Rascal demanded.

"It wasss meant to control the weather," Mr. Thathion finished hoarsely. He leaned forward intently. "But not like thissss. The designsss were never meant to attack or personally direct lightning."

"Who was the designer?" Rascal asked, though Wynona knew he was only doing to be sure.

Mr. Thathion leaned back again, looking tired. "Does it really matter? We haven't spoken in years. *Hundreds* of years."

Rascal simply raised an eyebrow.

Mr. Thathion sighed and looked out the window. "Most people knew her as Dr. Rayn," he said softly. "But her full name wasss Zullorayn Brownhide."

"Do you know where we might find her?" Wynona asked. They still hadn't managed to pry that information out of Lusgu despite his wanting her to help.

Mr. Thathion shook his head. "Somewhere in the Grove of Secrets last I heard."

"No one lives in the Grove of Secrets," Rascal said sharply.

Mr. Thathion smirked, looking much more like himself. "She did." His green eyes widened and grew excited. "She wassss brilliant. Beautiful, commanding and everything you could ever want in a creature." His excitement dimmed. "Her dragon form wasss something else as well…" He sighed. "But it doesn't matter now. Ssshe's been in hiding for ages."

"So you've never seen that box before?" Rascal said, returning to the previous subject.

Mr. Thathion shook his head. "No."

"Do you know why you and your fiancee might be targeted? Why would someone want to kill you?"

Mr. Thathion pinched his lips together. "Money? Bitternessss? I've spent and taken billions of dollars in my lifetime, Deputy Chief Strongclaw. There's always a healthy dose of risk when working in such elite sssspheres."

"Any threats lately? Or odd messages?"

Mr. Thathion started to shake his head, then stopped.

"What?" Wynona asked.

"Well, there was a message with my personal ssssecretary," Mr. Thathion muttered. He scrunched his face and shook his head. "But I didn't think anything of it at the time." He looked up. "Now I'm not ssso sure."

"What did it say?" Rascal asked. "Do you still have it?"

Mr. Thathion waved away the notion. "No. I threw it away, of courssse, like I always do. I get junk mail all the time. But…"

"Mr. Thathion," Rascal growled.

The gorgon looked like he would be stubborn for a moment before he finally relented. "It ssssaid, 'Meet me at the bridge'."

"And what did that mean?"

"I had no idea at the time." Mr. Thathion huffed a laugh. "Funny thing wasss, it was something Rayn and I used to say to each other at work." The smile on Mr. Thathion's face was of a man who was remembering the past. "She called her lab the bridge. Ssssaid her work was a bridge between yesterday and tomorrow. She was always coming up with new and better ways to do things and her goal wasss to better sssociety for everyone, whether they had magic or not."

"When did you get the note?" Rascal asked again.

"A week or so ago," Mr. Thathion said, coming back to himself. He leaned back in his pillows. "Look, Officer, Wynona. I'm worn out. I know I've been sssleeping for days, but my second lidsss are stinging. Perhaps we could finish this discusssion another time?"

"Of course," Wynona said. She smiled placidly and pressed a hand to Rascal's arm. "Thank you for your time, Mr. Thathion."

"Meldaeon," he corrected with that flirty smile again.

Wynona didn't bother to correct him. She simply took Rascal's hand and led him out of the room.

"What was that all about?" Rascal said in a growly tone once they were in the hallway. "That guy was hitting on you and you didn't even care?"

Wynona continued until they were away from prying eyes and tugged him close. "It was him," she whispered so only he could hear.

"Him?"

"He killed her," Wynona stated with finality. She could feel it in her bones. This man was more than a snake shifter, he was a snake in all aspects of his life. She felt slimy from simply being in the same room as him.

"Whoa…now wait a minute," Rascal said, putting up his hands. "How do you know?"

"Can we take this discussion elsewhere?" Wynona asked, pointedly looking around.

Rascal followed her gaze and noted the new officer staring at them. "Yeah. Come on." Taking Wynona's elbow, he led her back outside and into the truck. "I hope you have some good proof," he said. "Because everything I saw is still pointing to our missing dragon."

"I don't have proof," Wynona said calmly. "But I'm going to find some."

CHAPTER 11

"We're going to the precinct?" Wynona asked as Rascal merged in the direction of downtown.

Rascal nodded. "I think we should talk this over with Chief." He glanced toward Wynona. "That way we don't have to repeat anything."

Wynona nodded. She knew she was right about Thathion. The man was a complete fake. She wanted to take a shower just to wash off his presence, but Wynona was a little more logical than that. Instead, she sat quietly while Rascal drove. They would still need to speak to Dr. Rayn. She was a key player in all this, but Wynona had to agree with Lusgu.

The dragon was being set up.

They parked and Rascal hurried around to help Wynona down. "Thank you."

He smiled, took her hand and led her inside. The place was bustling with activity and they were able to slip into the back without causing too much of a fuss. Rascal took them straight to the chief's door. "Chief?" Rascal knocked, then opened and poked his head inside.

Chief Ligurio held up a finger. "I don't care what certificate the press has, they aren't allowed to talk to him," Chief Ligurio said sharply. "If Deputy Chief gave you an order, then you follow it, Officer, or I'll find someone who will." He slammed down the phone and turned to the door. "Speak of the devil."

Rascal grinned as they walked in.

"You two are horrible," Wynona said, tsking her tongue.

Chief Ligurio gave her a rare smile. "The newbies have to learn."

"That's what I said," Rascal tossed in. He chuckled when Wynona gave him a look.

"I'm assuming you just came from the hospital," the vampire said casually, leaning back in his office chair.

Wynona nodded and sat down across the desk from him. "We did."

"And what do we have?"

Wynona took a deep breath. "On the outside, all signs point toward the mysterious Dr. Rayn."

"On the outside?" Chief Ligurio leaned forward, folding his hands together. "Why do I get the feeling, Ms. Le Doux, that I'm about to hear your hunch that all that evidence is incorrect?"

She sat a little straighter. "Because it is."

"Maybe you should tell me what he said," the chief said wryly.

Wynona nodded and proceeded to share their findings. "The creature was as slimy as his namesake," Wynona concluded. "He was lying through his teeth!"

"Do snakes have teeth?" Rascal muttered.

Wynona glared.

Rascal chuckled again. "We understand that you think he's lying, but again, I ask…where's your proof?"

Wynona threw her hands in the air. "I don't have any…yet." She tapped a fingernail against her knee. "But don't you think it was just a little too convenient that he said he hadn't spoken to Dr. Rayn in centuries, only to get a mysterious note…a note he *forgot* to mention… until we brought up the dragon in conjunction with the weather box? And everyone seems so intent on saying it's similar to hers, but not quite. Like we're supposed to not quite suspect her, but can't quite put her off the list either."

"All the mounting evidence is convenient," Chief Ligurio said easily. "But some cases are like that."

"If she's truly as brilliant as everyone is saying she is," Wynona pointed out, "she wouldn't have left so much evidence behind."

Chief Ligurio pursed his lips. "I'll give you that one. It's inconsistent with what we're hearing from her admirers."

"Admirers," Wynona scoffed. "It almost seems as if Lusgu and Mr. Thathion are both in love with her."

Chief Ligurio appeared nonplussed. "I'm failing to see what this has to do with anything."

Wynona gave a short shake of her head. "I'm not sure. But something about it doesn't sit right. Lusgu has never shown a preference for anyone, but for Dr. Rayn? He can barely control himself, yet he admits he hasn't spoken to her in ages and tries to pretend he doesn't care. Then there's Mr. Thathion. He also spoke of her as if he had feelings for her, yet he's been marrying willy nilly for years, just lost a fiancee, already invited me to take her place…" Wynona's head shake grew harder. "No. Something's off with that. I just don't buy it."

"You don't think the men like her?"

"What I think is that we don't have a clear picture on how they feel about her. Lusgu is trying to pretend he doesn't. Mr. Thathion is trying to pretend he does." Wynona raised her hands in the air. "Why?"

Chief Ligurio rubbed at his chin, looked up at his deputy chief who was standing next to Wynona's chair, and back down. "I don't have any answers, Ms. Le Doux." He smirked. "Although, I'm guessing from your barging in here and from the vomit of information that you've decided you want to be part of this case."

Wynona sighed, deflating a little in her seat. "I suppose I am," she said. She wasn't about to tell Chief Ligurio about everything that had happened with Lusgu. She was enough of a freak as it was, no need to add more horror stories to the mix.

Rascal gave a low growl and she looked up to see him glaring at her. "Don't."

Wynona relaxed and gave him a small smile. "Sorry."

Nodding firmly, Rascal straightened back up.

Chief Ligurio watched the scene with barely covered patience. "Right. Well…what do you plan to do next?"

Wynona chewed on her lip. "I…I think we need to find Dr. Rayn. But no one wants to give us her address. We keep running into, 'Last I heard she lived in the Grove of Secrets.'"

Chief Ligurio snarled for a split second. "No one lives in the Grove of Secrets."

"That's what I keep saying," Rascal inserted. "But it's the only clue we've got."

Wynona tapped her fingers against the arm of the chair. "Chief Ligurio…is Daemon available?" An idea was percolating, but she'd need the black hole to put it into use.

"I can make him available," the chief responded. He narrowed his eyes. "What did you have in mind?"

"Have you ever walked the perimeter of the grove?" Wynona asked. Neither man answered as she looked back and forth between them. "Me either," she said when they still didn't respond. "But I wonder if there are…pockets, per se…of forest that aren't quite what we think they are."

"Are you saying the magic doesn't extend to the edge?" Rascal asked, frowning.

Wynona shrugged. "I'm saying it's possible. Two creatures, both intelligent and powerful, have mentioned she lives there. If you were looking for isolation and to get away from the world, there's no better place than the Grove. Especially since everyone thinks it will kill you if you go near it." Wynona tilted her head. "It sounds like the perfect place for a dragon to me."

Chief Ligurio frowned. "It sounds like a waste of time. I've been around a long time, Ms. Le Doux. Do you really believe that I wouldn't have heard by now if there were pockets of the grove that were safe for entrance?"

"Do you really think anyone would want the Chief of Police to know something like that?" Wynona challenged.

"I haven't been the chief my whole life."

"No," Wynona agreed. "But still, you run in the circles, and have run in the circles of those who uphold the law, Chief Ligurio. I don't find it impossible that those who want to disappear keep the secret very well."

Chief Ligurio snorted. "You can have this afternoon. That's it. I won't waste my resources any more than that."

Wynona stood, knowing it was time to say goodbye. "Thank you, Chief. You won't regret it."

"I already do," he muttered, waving them away.

Wynona held back the urge to roll her eyes. *Who spit in his blood?* she asked as she and Rascal walked into the hallway.

Rascal choked on a laugh. "Someone's been spending too much time with Violet lately," he said through the laughter.

Wynona sighed. "No, sorry. I just…I'm on edge I guess. Mr. Thathion really gave me the creeps. I'm positive he killed his fiancee, though I'm not sure why. If he didn't want to marry her, he doesn't seem the type that would care about her feelings. Why not just break off the wedding?"

Rascal shook his head and held open the door for her. "I have no idea. Prenup of some kind?"

"It's possible…" Wynona let the idea roll around in her mind, but it didn't ring true. "Oh. Wait. We need to grab Daemon."

"I texted him," Rascal said before closing the truck door. He came around to the driver's side. "He'll meet us at the house."

"My house?"

Rascal started the engine. "I assumed it was the best place to start," he said. "It's a point we're all familiar with and can get back to easily."

"Do you know how big the perimeter of the forest is?" Wynona asked.

Rascal shook his head. "Nope. Can you look it up on a map?"

Wynona looked it up on her phone while Rascal drove and her heart fell. "Oh my word…the grove is huge. We'll never cover it all today."

Rascal grunted.

Dropping her phone in her lap, Wynona huffed. "How are we

going to do this? Both of them said she was in the grove. There has to be a way to find her."

"We can talk to Lusgu again," Rascal suggested. "See if he's willing to give us more information."

"We can try," Wynona agreed, though she didn't feel very confident in the outcome. Still…it was better than nothing. Maybe with the odds stacking against Dr. Rayn, Lusgu would be more willing to open up a little.

One could only hope.

"Lusgu?" Wynona called once they were inside. Daemon wasn't here yet, so she and Rascal could grab a snack and a drink before they began scanning the entirety of the forest. There simply had to be a better way than to try and case hundreds of miles of border.

Violet?

You guys are back?

Yeah, Wynona responded. *Can you please bring Lusgu out here? I know he probably doesn't want to see me, but it's important.*

I'm pretty sure he'll do anything you ask now that you're trying to help Dr. Rayn. Give us a minute.

Wynona began brewing some tea, knowing that Rascal had heard her conversation with Violet and didn't need to be told what was going on.

He groaned as he landed on the couch, pushing his hands into his hair. "I feel like we haven't even begun to scratch the surface of this case," he muttered. "We've only got one suspect, who you're sure is innocent, a wounded gorgon we can't trust, a violent brownie who has said more in the last twenty-four hours than his entire life combined and a grumpy mouse who won't leave the brownie's side." He blew out a breath. "It makes us sound nuts."

"Don't forget the fact that we're going to go looking in the most dangerous place in our region for something that might not exist."

"Oh yeah…that too," Rascal added, a small grin tugging at his lips. "Thanks," he said when Wynona handed him a teacup. He took a sip. "Hot."

"It usually is," she said wryly. "You'd think you'd learn."

Before Rascal could tease her back, Lusgu and Violet came through the broom closet door. "You needed me?"

"Yes." Wynona set down the teacup on the coffee table. "Lusgu, I know you want us to leave Dr. Rayn out of this as much as possible, but we need to speak to her." She held up her hand to stop any arguments. "We really need to speak to her, Lusgu. If you want us to clear her name, then you have to let us get her alibi. Chief Ligurio feels certain that the evidence all says she's guilty of something. We can't prove otherwise if she stays in hiding."

Lusgu snarled and Rascal was in front of Wynona in a heartbeat. "Back down, brownie," he said tightly. "You might have caught me off guard last time, but if you think I'm allowing you another chance to attack the one person on your side, you've really lost it." Rascal's lip was curled. It was evident that any and all camaraderie between the two creatures was gone. Lusgu had never exactly been friendly to Rascal, but Rascal had used the opportunity for some teasing fun.

No one was teasing now and neither side was willing to back down either.

Wynona leaned around Rascal. "I know you want to protect her," she said softly. "But she needs a chance to protect herself."

Slowly, Lusgu's anger dissipated. "You're right," he whispered. "In fact, she'd skin me alive if she knew I was doing this. She always told me she could handle herself." He chuckled darkly and without humor. "Fate save us from strong women."

"So?" Wynona pressed, deciding not to get offended by such an archaic notion.

Lusgu hung his head. "If she hasn't moved, which I can't guarantee, you'll find her home due east of here. Three miles in."

"That's it?" Rascal barked. "That's all you'll tell us?"

Lusgu glared up, not the least bit intimidated by the wolf. "That's all you need, pup. Make of it what you will." Spinning on his heel, Lusgu walked straight back into the door just as someone knocked on the front.

"That must be Daemon," Wynona murmured, quickly going to

answer it. "Hello," she greeted the officer. "Are you ready to do a little investigating?"

"Not sure there's anything little about what we're attempting, but yeah, I suppose I am," Daemon said with a smile.

"Then let's get to it," Rascal said from behind Wynona's shoulder.

She smiled at him, trying to put the last couple moments behind them. "Lusgu gave us a clue, but we're not quite sure how to use it yet."

"What did the little guy say?" Daemon asked.

Rascal laughed, but Wynona ignored the dig. "Due east from here. Three miles in."

Daemon looked at the forest behind Wynona's home and nodded. "Okay, then. At least it's a direction."

Wynona nodded. "You know what to do?"

His eyes went completely black. "Let's give this a try."

CHAPTER 12

"So...do we just head east?" Rascal asked as they closed the door to the house.

"That's the best plan I have," Wynona said. "Daemon, I'd like you to look for pockets of non-magic, but otherwise, let's just start walking and see what we find."

Daemon grunted his agreement and the three began walking. They crossed the distance between the house and the grove and the closer they came to the treeline, the slower Wynona's steps.

She could feel the power dancing along her skin and she didn't like it. The power wasn't as dark and heavy as what she'd felt on the grimoires in her closet, but it certainly wasn't as warm and friendly as her granny's had been either. More than anything, it simply felt...alive.

"What's wrong?" Rascal asked, though his eyes never left the trees.

Wynona rubbed her hand up and down her arm. "The magic is really strong," she said softly, almost afraid that if she spoke louder someone would hear her. But who? The grove wasn't sentient...she hoped. "Daemon?"

"Hmm?"

"What color is the magic?"

Daemon's black eyes were solemn as they met hers. "It isn't."

"What does that mean?" Rascal demanded.

Daemon shook his head. "There's no actual color. As if the magic is completely neutral."

Wynona nodded. "That makes sense."

"For who?" Rascal argued. He folded his arms over his chest. "I realize I'm just a lowly, magic-less shifter, but what's going on?"

Wynona gave him a look. "That's not what I meant, sweetheart. I'm sorry I made you feel that way, I'm mostly…thinking out loud I guess."

Rascal's stiff stance diminished. "No, I'm sorry. I'm not sure why I'm so on edge." He scrubbed his hands over his face. "I just can't seem to fully calm down from Lusgu. I always thought he would protect you and now I'm terrified of leaving you in that house with him. It puts my wolf on high alert."

"He won't hurt me," Wynona assured him. "But I understand why you're upset and we'll do our best to work things out." She looked back at the forest. "I don't think the magic is good or bad here. It simply is. The grimoires were slimy and heavy and dark. The magic here is heavy because there's so much of it, but it doesn't feel one way or another. So I suppose not having a color makes an odd sort of sense." She turned to Daemon. "I think, then, our goal is to find a place where there *is* color. Then we'll know another creature put it there."

"Right." Daemon looked down the line of trees. "Hope you have good shoes on," he said. "I think we should move a little faster." Leaves crunching and sticks breaking, the three broke into a slow jog, the men catering to Wynona's physical capabilities.

One of these days I need to start doing cardio, she puffed.

If you can stop solving murders long enough, I'm sure you can fit that right in, Rascal sent back.

Wynona laughed breathlessly as they moved along. Actually, looking for color instead of something else should make their job easier…in theory.

"Up ahead!" Daemon called, pointing.

Wynona wanted to ask more, but she'd have to wait until they were there and she could catch her breath. Daemon's eyes must have been very good because it still took several minutes for them to arrive at the spot he was indicating.

"Right here," he said, sounding only slightly out of breath. He turned to the side. "And I can see several more patches down the row."

"What color is it?" Wynona panted.

Daemon grinned. "Red."

Wynona straightened. "The teapot."

Daemon nodded. "Exactly my thought."

"What colors are down there?" Rascal asked with a chin jolt.

"Not sure if it's blue or gray," Daemon said, squinting. "It's too far to know for sure."

"I think this is the right one," Wynona said. "The leftover magic on the tea caddy was red and Lusgu identified it as Dr. Rayn's."

"I didn't ask before, but why didn't you just use your own powers?" Daemon asked, tilting his head. "You're learning to control them."

"Exactly," Wynona responded. "I'm learning. I didn't want to risk our lives on my learning. Though…" She took a couple of seconds to change her own sight. "I should probably be practicing as we go."

"Your eyes are so bright," Rascal said with a laugh. "It's odd how much they change."

She stuck out her tongue at him and he kissed her cheek.

"I didn't say I didn't like it," he teased in her ear.

Wynona began to blush, but Daemon's throat clearing made the heat in her neck grow even faster. "Come on, gentlemen. We have a dragon to talk to." Wynona could see the red that Daemon had been referring to, but it made her slightly uneasy. The color was a small trail that went into the forest, surrounded by the colorless magic from the grove itself. "Daemon, would you please lead, just in case my sight doesn't continue to work properly?"

"Actually," Daemon hedged, "I think you should lead. Deputy Chief needs to be in the middle so he doesn't step somewhere not safe and I should bring up the rear in case of any danger behind us."

Wynona didn't completely agree with his assessment, but she understood the idea nonetheless. "Rascal, right behind me please. The path isn't very wide."

"Then how does it accommodate a dragon?" the wolf muttered. Without warning, he landed on all fours, turning into the very animal Wynona had just been thinking of.

"Warn a guy," Daemon snapped.

Rascal grinned, his tongue lolling out of his mouth.

"He'll be more agile this way," Wynona said, realizing why Rascal did it. It would keep him safer for sure. She took a deep breath, pushing down the fear wanting to bubble up in her stomach. "Okay. Let's go."

She unconsciously held her breath as she stepped over the forest line for the first time. The Grove of Secrets was known for letting people in, but not letting them back out. No one knew what happened to those inside because no one ever lived to tell the tale.

Wynona was very much hoping to come back. She had too many things she still wanted to accomplish for this to be the end.

"Lusgu said three miles?" Daemon clarified.

Wynona nodded. "That's what it sounded like anyway. Three miles in." She paused. "How far was it from my house to here?"

Daemon shrugged. "Maybe two?"

"Okay, so yeah, I'm guessing the distance is the first part of the instructions." She blew out a breath. She definitely needed to get in shape. Walking as swiftly as she dared, Wynona kept herself on the yellow path, occasionally checking on Rascal and Daemon.

To her shock, they didn't encounter any creatures or danger at all, though Wynona could feel the power of the forest surrounding them on all sides. It was an odd sensation, like swimming through gravy. Thick, but fluid. She still didn't like the feel of it on her skin, but she was growing used to it and it didn't bother her quite so much.

I don't like how quiet it is, Rascal sent through their mental connection.

Wynona nodded. "I know. You'd think there were animals or something."

"What was that?"

Wynona paused to look over her shoulder. "Oh, sorry. Rascal was just saying it was too quiet."

"Could be because of that." Daemon pointed ahead.

Wynona turned and squealed, nearly jumping off the path.

A large red and yellow dragon stood in the path, not a hundred yards from where they had stopped.

Rascal began growling and trying to push past her, but Wynona held out her arm. Now that she wasn't jumping out of her skin, she realized that the dragon didn't seem upset or threatening. It was simply staring and blinking, as if the intruders were specimens under a microscope.

"Um...hello!" Wynona called out loudly. She cleared her throat when the dragon didn't respond. "I'm Wynona Le Doux. This is Deputy Chief Strongclaw and Officer Skymaw. We're looking for Dr. Zullorayn Brownhide."

The dragon's eyes narrowed and Wynona panicked.

"Lusgu sent us," she said quickly, hoping desperately it would help the situation and not make it worse.

The dragon stilled.

"Lusgu is my...friend," Wynona said carefully. "He's been working for me for a couple of years and now he lives in my house."

The dragon bristled and a brilliant flash of fire filled the sky, causing Wynona to cover her eyes. "Lusgu is *living* with you?" a feminine voice demanded.

Wynona blinked until she could see the absolutely lovely older woman in front of her. Mr. Thathion had been right. Dr. Rayn was magnificent. Tall, strong and statuesque, she didn't look like someone who had lived centuries or would be plowed over by her own company. And the smoke coming from the woman's nostrils told Wynona she was truly dealing with a *dragon*.

"I believe that came out wrong," Wynona said, putting her hands in the air. "His portal entrance was attached to the tea shop I own and he worked at. When that was burned to the ground last month, he moved the entrance to my house. He's simply staying there until the shop is rebuilt. That's it."

Rascal growled in agreement.

Dr. Rayn, or at least who Wynona was assuming was Dr. Rayn,

looked them over with suspicious eyes. "What did you say your name was again?"

"Wynona Le Doux."

The woman immediately softened. "Wynona," she whispered almost reverently. She walked forward. "Is it really you?" She cupped Wynona's cheeks and Wynona was too shocked to move. "Lusgu found you? Saffron said he would."

"You knew my grandmother?" Wynona blurted out. Just who was this woman? And when was someone going to explain the relationship between Lusgu and Dr. Rayn?

"Knew her?" Dr. Rayn snorted. Her eyes shifted when movement sounded from behind Wynona. "Ah...I forgot. We aren't alone." She smiled one more time at Wynona, then dropped her hands and stepped back. "Welcome, all of you." Her grin grew self-deprecating. "I'm sure Wynona told me your names, but when the flames are burning, I have a hard time hearing."

Rascal shifted back. "Deputy Chief Strongclaw," he stated, not budging from Wynona's side.

Dr. Rayn's eyes widened. "Ah...I see." She nodded. "I wonder if Saffron saw that one coming."

Wynona frowned, but didn't get a chance to ask a question.

"Officer Skymaw," Daemon said from the very back.

"A black hole," Dr. Rayn said consideringly. "I haven't had access to one of those in a very long time." She tapped her chin. "It's no wonder you found my path so easily." She clapped her hands together. "But where are my manners? Come! Come inside. We have much to discuss."

The woman turned and began walking, but Wynona hesitated. Where were they going? There was nothing but forest. As soon as she had the thought, Wynona's vision was opened and a large meadow with a castle in the middle of it flashed into being.

"Oh my word," Wynona breathed. "How is this possible?"

"My assistant is a deft hand at illusions," Dr. Rayn called from halfway across the meadow. "Come in. You can meet her!"

Wynona looked wide-eyed at Rascal. "I feel like we're in some kind of fairy tale," she whispered. "And yet I'm terrified I'm about to find out how it all ties in with my own life."

"I guess the question is whether or not you want the answers," Rascal murmured, his eyes glued to their host, who was waiting patiently. Whether she could hear their conversation or not was unknown, but she wasn't pressing them one way or another.

"We can interview her without you," Daemon added.

Wynona shook her head. "No…I think I need to hear what she has to say. After all…nothing she knows could be worse than hearing that Granny was the one who cursed me…right?"

Rascal looked uneasy, but nodded. "Right."

Wynona tried to take a step forward, but found herself struggling. Inside that castle were possible answers, but also possible heartache. Would she get both? Or would Dr. Rayn clam up like everyone else who had information on Wynona? Maybe Wynona would come away with nothing more than she came with.

A warm hand slid into hers and she felt her stiff body relax.

"It doesn't matter," Rascal said. "We know who you are. And just in case you've forgotten, that's the woman I love. Anything else about your history or your family is all clutter. We can throw it away at any time. It doesn't define you unless you want it to."

She gave his hand a squeeze. "Thank you."

"Always."

They took the first step together.

CHAPTER 13

The inside of the castle was cool and a little stark. Wynona wasn't quite sure what she'd been expecting, but this wasn't quite it. What little furniture was lying around was slightly haphazard and had been purchased nowhere near the last century.

"Excuse the mess," Dr. Rayn said breezily, waving her hand in the air. "I've never been one for guests…or even socializing." She laughed at her own comment, but Wynona was too anxious to join in the joke.

"Thank you," Daemon said as he wiped his feet, then stepped through the door. His eyes stayed black and Wynona was grateful he refused to let down his guard.

"I don't have a gathering area," Dr. Rayn said. "Please, just come into the kitchen."

Wynona kept a hold of Rascal's hand and followed their host. "Just to be clear," Wynona began, "you *are* Dr. Zullarayn Brownhide?"

Dr. Rayn paused her walk. "Didn't I say that?" She laughed and smacked her forehead. "I'm so sorry. I assumed I already introduced myself." Shaking her head, she continued on. "Yes. I am she, though you can simply call me Rayn. No one calls me 'Doctor' anymore."

"Well, that's not true," another voice added to the conversation.

Wynona and the men turned to see a small woman with extra large glasses standing in the doorway of the kitchen. "Hello," she said in a soft, breathy voice. She tilted her head to the side. "Who are you?"

"Oh, Quinin," Dr. Rayn cried. "I'm glad you're here." She began slamming through cupboards. "We have guests and I don't know what refreshments I have in stock."

Quinin pushed her glasses up her nose and walked across the room. "Not much if you plan to feed two hulking men of that size," she muttered.

Wynona bit her lips between her teeth, trying not to laugh at the woman's bluntness. "I'm Wynona Le Doux," she said, holding out her hand.

Quinin hesitated ever so slightly. "Le Doux? The president's family?"

Wynona nodded. "Yes. Though, I don't live with my family."

"Oh?" Quinin tilted her head again, her eyes large behind the frames. "I didn't realize anyone was allowed to leave the palace."

"You'll have to excuse my assistant," Dr. Rayn said, giving Quinin a slight nudge. "She gets out even less than I do and she doesn't care for people…at all." Dr. Rayn finished the end of the sentence in a whisper.

"I can hear you," Quinin said dryly. "Owls have excellent hearing, Rayn."

"Maybe so, but we dragons aren't always good at remembering," Dr. Rayn shot back. The two women smiled at each other.

It was clear there was a bond there and Wynona wondered about it. Quinin had mentioned an owl, meaning she must be a shifter. It would explain her little mannerisms, like the large eyes and the head tilting.

Dr. Rayn looked at Wynona, her assistant doing the same. "She looks like her mother, doesn't she?" the doctor said to Quinin.

Quinin narrowed her gaze, then nodded. "She does."

Wynona held her ground. This entire situation was a little ludicrous, but she wasn't to blame for her genetics, and she definitely wasn't like her mother in anything but appearance. "Dr. Rayn, Lusgu told us how to find you. We need to ask you some questions." Not the least of which were about Granny Saffron and how Lusgu and Dr.

Rayn knew each other. But the murder would need to come first. "Are you aware that the police are looking for you?"

Dr. Rayn stilled. "It would appear they found me," she said, her eyes growing shrewd. "But the question is...why?" She directed the question to Rascal. "And why bring Wynona with you? I had assumed your presence was merely to assure her safety. Was I wrong?"

Rascal cleared his throat, looking slightly uncomfortable. "It's two-fold," he responded. "We were here to keep her safe, but she's also helping us with a case and we've been searching for you in regards to that case."

Yellow eyes shot to Wynona. "You're helping the police? Does your father know?" Quinin asked.

Wynona fought the urge to roll her eyes. If she had a nickel for every time someone asked that, she'd have paid for the tea shop a long time ago. "What I do is none of my father's business."

A slow smile crept across Dr. Rayn's face. "Saffron was right. Good girl."

Wynona frowned. "How did you know my grandmother? And what are you to Lusgu?"

Dr. Rayn's eyebrow rose up. "Are you sure those are the questions you want to ask? Somehow I doubt the case has to do with my relationship with either of those individuals."

Wynona swallowed down a retort. The dragon was right. While she truly did want those answers, that wasn't what they'd come to ask. "Forgive me," Wynona said in a softer tone. "You're right. I got carried away."

"Too many questions, not enough answers," Dr. Rayn mused.

Wynona nodded. That was her life in a nutshell.

"Tell me about this case," Dr. Rayn said, her tone giving away her curiosity. "I haven't heard any news from the outside world in many years."

"I thought we were going to test the new adapter," Quinin offered, causing Wynona to remember the owl shifter was still hanging around.

Dr. Rayn waved her assistant off. "There will always be time for that. Our guests, however, are on a different timeline than us." She stared at Rascal and nodded encouragingly.

"Two days ago, Meldaeon Thathion was injured and his fiancee killed in a freak storm," Rascal said in his official tone.

Dr. Rayn sucked in a breath through her nose, followed by a trail of smoke. "Why should I care what happens to that serpent?"

"Because a box was found in the area," Rascal said carefully. "A box that we've been told by multiple creatures resembles one of your inventions."

The smoke grew stronger and Dr. Rayn's eyes flashed red. "So you came to ask if I murdered my old business partner?" she hissed. "Was it not enough that I left society? Turned my back on all I held dear and stayed isolated for the last several hundred years? Why would I choose now to murder that backstabber? Why wait so long?"

"Rayn," Quinin said sharply. "Pull it back. They're only doing their job."

Wynona held her breath, truly terrified of the absolute loathing that was choking the room from the dragon's emotions. Rascal's hair was standing on end and Daemon looked as if the veins in his arms were about to burst, so tightly was he coiled. The doctor seemed unpredictable and Wynona didn't want anyone to get hurt. Her fingers began to tingle and purple sparkled in her vision the longer the tension sat in the room.

"Their job," Dr. Rayn spat, tiny sparks floating into the air. "I'm not the only inventor in town." She growled and more smoke poured into the room.

"Rayn..." Quinin warned.

Wynona noticed the sweat beading Daemon's brow. He was trying to pull down the magic, but he wasn't strong enough. Rascal's nails were growing and he growled back at Dr. Rayn, but Wynona knew the wolf would be no match for a dragon.

Dr. Rayn huffed, her face growing red, and her nails began to shift, leaving Wynona with no choice.

"STOP!" Wynona shouted, putting out a hand and creating her purple shield over her and her companions. It occurred to her a second too late that she'd left Quinin out of the protection. Just as she was trying to figure out how to include the owl, there came a tapping on her bubble.

"What *is* this?" Gone was the smoke, the nails and the flashing eyes. In fact, Dr. Rayn didn't look the least bit threatening at all as she studied Wynona's shield.

"I…" Wynona dropped her hand. "I don't really know," she admitted. "I use it for protection."

"How strong is it?" Dr. Rayn asked.

"Really, Rayn?" Quinin drawled. "They were scared for their lives and you want to run experiments?"

Dr. Rayn turned to look at her assistant. "Isn't that how we learn things, Quin? Have I taught you nothing?"

"How about we make a deal?" Wynona offered, quickly ridding herself and the men of the protection bubble.

Rascal growled, stepping closer to Wynona. *We should go. I don't like this.*

I don't think she wants to hurt us. But we got off to a rough start. Mr. Thathion is obviously a sore subject.

One that we need answers on, Rascal returned. *But we should have her come into the precinct where we have the advantage.*

Wynona reached to the side, taking his hand.

Dr. Rayn folded her arms over her chest. "I'm listening."

"A woman has been murdered," Wynona said, watching for any signs of a temper again. "We, the police, need some answers from you since there is evidence that suggests your invention might be involved."

Dr. Rayn snorted. "You mean, that *I* might be involved."

Wynona shrugged. "The point is we need to speak about the situation *without* you flying off the handle."

"You mentioned a deal," Dr. Rayn said with a twitch of her lips. She was obviously amused at Wynona's leading of the conversation.

"When all is said and done, I'd be happy to let you do some experiments on my magic," Wynona responded. "I'm still learning about it myself and Lusgu has agreed to do some tutoring, but truly, I can use all the help I can get. If you have some insights that might help and that interest you along the way, I'd love to hear them."

Dr. Rayn's shoulders dropped. "Lusgu is helping you? Why isn't Saffron doing it?"

Wynona couldn't say it. Her heart pinched and her eyes grew misty, followed by the shame she felt every time she spoke of her grandmother. It was Wynona's fault that Saffron was gone, at least permanently, and though Wynona had tried to move on, the pain seemed to sit in the background, never truly leaving.

"Saffron passed away a couple years ago," Rascal said, his warm hand landing on Wynona's lower back.

She leaned into his support, grateful he had only mentioned the first death.

"I know that," Dr. Rayn said hurriedly. "But she should still be here."

Wynona's eyes nearly bugged out of her head. "How did you…? I mean, what?" She swallowed hard. What was going on here? What did this woman know?

Dr. Rayn sighed and rubbed between her eyebrows. "Nevermind. That's a topic for another time." She looked up, appearing tired and older. "It seems that there are more pressing matters, like putting my ex-coworker in his place once more. I don't know why someone had my invention," the dragon said snippily. "Many of them are on the market and easily accessible, though I'll admit the weather one isn't mainstream. Only a few were ever purchased and I stopped selling the design ages ago. I also don't know why anyone would want to hurt people with it. The point of the invention was to allow creatures the ability to take care of crops, or to build storms to enhance spells. It was never meant for attack." She raised an eyebrow. "But the point is…*anyone*…could have used my work."

"Where were you two days ago at ten in the morning?" Rascal asked.

Dr. Rayn snorted again, the tiniest stream of smoke rising into the air. "Here. Same place I always am. I don't leave the forest, Deputy Chief Strongclaw." She turned away. "I have no reason to."

The words struck Wynona wrong. They weren't true. Wynona wasn't sure why, but she had a suspicious thought that it was Lusgu. Had the two been an item? Why had they broken up? It was hard to imagine Lusgu having those types of feelings for anyone and a brownie and a dragon together were even more strange.

"All the same, we'd appreciate it if you came down to the precinct," Rascal said, still using his authoritative voice. "The chief would like to speak to you and we'd like to clear this whole thing up."

"You mean you'd like to have a chance to make sure I wasn't involved."

Rascal shrugged. "Call it what you will, Dr. Rayn, but we need to speak to you in a more official capacity."

Dr. Rayn folded her arms over her chest. "You do realize that you don't have authority over me here. The Grove of Secrets is out of your jurisdiction."

Rascal's jaw clenched. Wynona hadn't even considered that. Technically, Rascal only had authority over Hex Haven and the Grove of Secrets was just outside the city boundaries. If she wanted to, Dr. Rayn could refuse to cooperate and there would be nothing Rascal or anyone else at the precinct could do about it.

Before anyone could respond, Quinin stepped forward, pushing her glasses up her nose. "Rayn," she said soothingly. "Why don't you go along? We both know you had nothing to do with this, but these creatures don't know you. Answer their questions, clear the air and then come back and we'll get back to work."

Dr. Rayn pursed her lips. "Why do you always have to be so logical?"

Quinin grinned. "One of us has to be, or we'd never get anything done around here."

Dr. Rayn waved a dismissive hand through the air. "Logic is overrated. A little imagination…or passion…never hurt anybody." She sighed, long and loud. "Fine. I'll come into town with you and give you my alibi, though I doubt it'll do much good. The only witnesses to anything out here are Quinin and myself. You are the first to actually be brave enough to cross the tree line." Her eyes narrowed and landed on Daemon. "And I'm guessing your black hole friend is the reason why."

Daemon didn't respond, just stood tall and strong, his eyes bottomless pits of black.

Wynona was grateful to her friend, but she had to wonder what was going on in his head. He wasn't as chatty as herself or Rascal, but he was a good man. Still, he didn't look ready to relax any time soon and she wondered what he was seeing that she didn't know about.

If Prim could ever calm down her flighty personality, she'd have a man worth holding onto.

Rascal's hand landed on her back again. *Do I need to prove something?* he teased.

Wynona rolled her eyes mentally. *You know where my heart lies,* she sent back. *But he's a good man. I just wish Prim saw it as well.*

I don't think she doubts his qualities, I think she's struggling to find her feet. Prim has been proving herself her entire life in a community that thought she was less than them. It's hard to give up the kind of determination and pride it takes to climb to the top. If she would stop trying to prove herself to Skymaw, they'd get along just fine.

Wynona turned to give him a look. *Since when did you become so philosophical?*

Rascal grinned. *I suppose I've been hanging out in your head enough to look a little deeper at the creatures you surround yourself with.*

Wynona laughed softly. *Well, get out. It's my head.*

Too late, I've already laid claim.

A clearing throat caught their attention and Wynona realized just how rude she was being. *Shoot. Sorry.*

Dr. Rayn was looking back and forth between the two of them. She nodded slowly. "I'll bet Saffron did *not* see that coming." She shook her head harder. "Nonetheless, let's get this over with. I shall be in town first thing tomorrow morning. I have things to wrap up today before I can leave the house." She smirked. "Believe it or not, it's not that easy to simply walk out of the grove whenever I wish."

Wynona allowed Rascal to take the lead.

He nodded. "Fine. We'll see you then." Ushering Wynona back toward the door, Rascal guided her outside.

"Thank you!" Wynona called over her shoulder, sending a wave to the two creatures still standing in the kitchen.

Quinin gave a small wave back, but Dr. Rayn just stared. It was a little disconcerting, but Wynona shrugged it off. There were secrets there, and it was more than how a dragon came to live in the grove. Somehow, it all tied back to Granny Saffron, which meant it was also tied to Wynona.

How and why remained to be seen, but Wynona was determined to get some answers…right after they solved a murder.

CHAPTER 14

The entire group breathed a sigh of relief when they finally stepped out of the tree line and back into Hex Haven.

Rascal shook his head hard. "I don't ever want to do that again."

Wynona nodded her agreement. "I don't know how Dr. Rayn can live in there. The magic from the forest was like a living entity and everything felt…heightened because of it." Her eyes strayed to the forest. Just like her life, there were secrets in the forest. But this time, Wynona didn't want to know what they were.

Finding Dr. Rayn's house and the pocket of non-magic let Wynona know that others knew the secrets of the grove, or at least some of them, but the whole situation still felt incredibly dangerous to her. Maybe more so than she'd thought before. There were creatures who manipulated the magic in the grove and that made Wynona afraid. Very afraid.

"Come on," Rascal said, pulling her farther away. "I want some distance between us and it."

Daemon's eyes finally went back to normal and he pushed a long breath out of his lungs. "That was…interesting."

"And stressful," Wynona added. "How did Dr. Rayn discover the pocket, do you think? Or did she create it?"

"I don't even want to think about the amount of power it would take to create something like that," Daemon said with a visible shudder. "The magic was oppressive in there as it was and I have no doubt that the forest influences her work, whether she knows it or not."

"What did you see while we were standing there?" Wynona pressed.

Daemon paused before answering. "I saw a lot of red," he said carefully. "But there were also hints of brown, green, blue, and yellow."

Wynona frowned. "Red has to be Dr. Rayn, right?"

Daemon nodded. "As far as I could tell. Isn't that what was on your teapot as well?"

Wynona nodded. "Yes. Broken red, but red." She squished her lips to the side. "Maybe the brown is Quinin?"

"She's a shifter," Rascal pointed out. "We don't have our own magic."

"Right." Wynona huffed. "Is the green the forest?"

Daemon nodded. "My thoughts as well."

"So someone else has been around her home."

Neither creature answered her. They didn't need to. If there was other magic around, there were other creatures around. Which meant Dr. Rayn was either lying to them, or didn't know that she wasn't as alone as she thought.

"Can we go talk to Mr. Thathion again?" Wynona asked.

Rascal paused. "You have more questions?"

She nodded. "Yes. After listening to Dr. Rayn, I want to clarify a few things."

He shrugged. "As long as he doesn't hit on you again, we can do that."

Wynona rolled her eyes. "I can't say whether he will or not, but you know I'm not interested, so it really doesn't matter. The guy gives me the creeps."

"There's a ring on your finger," Rascal muttered. "The creature should respect that."

"Somehow I doubt he got to the top of the food chain by

respecting boundaries," Daemon muttered. "Do you want me along for the interview?"

Wynona nodded. "Yeah. I want you to see if you can see his magic."

"Again, he's a shifter," Rascal remarked. "We don't have magic."

"But he builds technology with magical components," Wynona pointed out. "He must know how to use it at least indirectly."

Rascal pursed his lips. "Interesting theory. I suppose it doesn't hurt to check it out." They were coming up to the house. "We'll take the truck."

Wynona smiled to herself. "Of course." Rascal's obsession with being the driver cracked her up. She let him help her into the passenger seat and buckled up while he walked to the other door.

"Next stop, Hex Haven Hospital," he said, putting the truck into gear.

The ride was quiet, but Wynona didn't mind. Her brain seemed to be running on overdrive at the moment and she was having to work to separate her own troubles from those of the case. After talking with Dr. Rayn, they all seemed to be intertwined, yet they truly weren't. The people, however, were mixed up in both and Wynona needed to get one out of the way before she could address the other.

Lusgu would help her with her magic, Dr. Rayn wanted to study it, but she needed answers from both of them in order to have her life make any sense. Putting Lusgu and Dr. Rayn in the same room together might be the best way to push that envelope a little.

"Until she blows his head off," Rascal muttered. "Although, at this point in time, I'm not sure I'd care."

"Rascal," Wynona scolded. "Not nice."

Rascal grunted but didn't say anything more. She knew his protective side was bringing the anger to the surface. Wolves took care of their own, and Lusgu had broken Rascal's trust with his latest escapades.

Rascal pulled up on the sidewalk in front of the hospital and parked the truck.

Wynona tsked her tongue. "This isn't an emergency."

"This is a perk." He grinned unrepentantly and hopped out,

coming around to help Wynona down. "You still sure he's the guy?" Rascal asked as they headed inside.

Wynona nodded. "Yes. There's just something about him that doesn't sit right."

"Dr. Rayn might have been lying to us and her magic is worth taking note of."

She nodded. "Agreed, but I didn't walk away from her feeling slimy."

"Thathion's a snake," Rascal said dryly. "Slimy is part of the territory." He paused before opening the door to the creature's room. "We have no evidence that he's involved."

Wynona pinched her lips together. "Then I suppose it's our job to find it." Without waiting for another argument, she pushed on the door, forcing Rascal to open it and let her in. A nurse was standing next to Mr. Thathion's bed and her face was beet red. By the way she wouldn't meet Wynona's eyes, Wynona had a good idea that Mr. Thathion had been pushing boundaries…again. "Hello, Mr. Thathion," Wynona said pleasantly, though her skin rippled with disgust as she grew nearer.

Mr. Thathion didn't look amused. He turned to the nurse, who appeared to want to be anywhere but there. "Thank you, Evaeline. We'll speak later." His finger ran across her knuckles where she was holding onto the bed rail.

The red on her cheeks flushed even deeper until Wynona was sure the woman would faint. Nodding, the nurse fled.

Rascal growled. "There are laws against that type of thing."

"Only if it's unwelcome," Mr. Thathion shot back. He sighed and settled against his pillows. "Now…what can I do for my friends at the police force today? I thought I gave you all the information you needed when we last spoke, but it would appear I was incorrect." He smirked. "That rarely happens, so take note."

Wynona wanted to roll her eyes, but her desire to remain cool and in control kept it from happening. "We visited Dr. Rayn, and now have some more questions."

Mr. Thathion jerked upright. "You spoke to her? Did she mention me?"

Wynona hesitated. Why did it feel like she'd made a mistake in mentioning their meeting?

Mr. Thathion fell back against the pillows. "That bad, huh?" He sighed and rubbed his forehead. "I had hoped bygones would be bygones by now."

"Why are you so interested in speaking to her?" Rascal asked. He stood at attention near the end of the bed, his legs spread and his arms folded, showing off his physical power. The slight man in the bed should have been intimidated, but Mr. Thathion showed no sign of caring.

"I wanted…" Mr. Thathion pushed a hand through his hair. "We all make mistakes," he said in a softer, more reflective tone. "Well over a hundred years ago, I made one of the biggest mistakes of my life." His eyes went to the window, looking at something no one else in the room could see. "I wasn't always a leader. When we first built our company, I tended to be the quiet one. The follower."

Wynona scoffed mentally.

You don't believe him? Rascal asked.

Why should I?

Why shouldn't you indeed? Rascal retorted. *We have no evidence to say he's lying, yet we walked out of the grove with evidence that Dr. Rayn is lying.* He sighed. *I think your desire to help Lusgu is coloring your opinions, Wy.*

Wynona didn't respond. Firstly, she wasn't sure Rascal was wrong. Secondly, she really had no way to prove that wasn't true.

"Once we got big, the…egos…if you will, began to show themselves," Mr. Thathion continued.

Wynona forced herself to focus. "Were you in love with Dr. Rayn?" Wynona blurted out unceremoniously.

Mr. Thathion narrowed his green eyes to mere slits and chuckled without humor. "Who wasn't?" he demanded. "Dr. Zullarayn was the envy of every man, woman and child of the era."

"Yet you pushed her out of the company."

Wy... Rascal scolded.

Mr. Thathion's demeanor softened again. "I wasn't the one to push her out," he corrected. "But I also didn't stop it."

"And now you think she's out for…what? Revenge?"

Wy! Rascal said loud enough to make Wynona wince.

We need to know, she shot back. *Evidence or not, this man is not honest and has made a living on the backs of others. We need to know what he's hiding.*

Are you upset because he reminds you of your father?

Wynona stilled.

"No, no," Mr. Thathion responded, completely oblivious to Rascal and Wynona's inner arguments. "She's not the type." He paused. "Or at least she wasn't the type." He shrugged. "Dragons are funny creatures. Brilliant and passionate. I suppose after this amount of time, I can't say what she is or isn't."

Wynona put her hands on her hips. She was going to ignore Rascal's implication for now. She knew this man wasn't her father, but any creature who abused others for their own gain was never going to be on her good list. This man was dirty. And she was going to prove it.

Mr. Thathion chuckled. "If I didn't know any better, Ms. Le Doux," he said slowly, "I'd say you want to trip me up. As if you think you can prove something against me." He leaned forward. "Just in case you forgot…I'm the one who was attacked. It was my fiancee who was killed and my leg that was hit with lightning."

Wynona didn't budge. She wasn't normally quite so aggressive, but this creature rubbed her the wrong way. She could feel the hairs on the back of her neck standing up, and for someone who tried to give everyone the benefit of the doubt, this was new for her. "That doesn't mean you're not hiding something," Wynona said softly.

Mr. Thathion continued to chuckle, the smirk on his face growing. "I'm finding you more and more interesting, Ms. Le Doux." His eyes darted to a very still Rascal. "Perhaps we could get a drink when I'm finally out of the hospital."

Rascal growled.

Mr. Thathion put his hands in the air. "Strictly as friends, you understand. Her father and I are friends, I wouldn't ever wish to cause troubles in the family."

"My father has no say in my life," Wynona said automatically. It proved to be the wrong thing to say when Mr. Thathion's eyes flashed.

"Really? How interesting." The older creature tilted his head. "Does that mean you accept my invitation?"

"No," Wynona said bluntly. "I'm afraid my time is already spoken for."

"Pity," Mr. Thathion said, completely ignoring Rascal's warning growls. "I think our conversation could have been…very enlightening."

Wynona felt sick to her stomach. How dare he try to dangle information in front of her like that? Who did he think he was?

A man who has never been told no, Rascal snarled in her mind.

Do you believe me now? she asked.

I don't necessarily believe he's guilty of anything except being an egomaniac and hitting on unavailable women, Rascal said. *But I don't like him. And I don't think anything will change that.*

Frustration filled Wynona. How could Rascal not feel the aura spilling from the gorgon? It practically oozed from every pore.

I think you might be mixing up entitlement with evil.

One and the same, she shot back.

Rascal snorted. "If you'll simply answer Ms. Le Doux's question," he said sharply, "we'll be on our way so you can rest. I'm sure creatures of your age need more than their fair share."

Mr. Thathion was anything but amused, but Wynona couldn't find it in her to care. "And what question was that?" he hissed.

"Why do you wish to see Dr. Rayn?"

Mr. Thathion scoffed. "I wanted to offer her a job," he said, sticking his nose in the air. "Letting her go all those years ago was a mistake and our company has felt the hole she left ever since."

"But you're not on the board anymore," Wynona pointed out.

"No, but I still advise," Mr. Thathion said, his smirk emerging once again. "I have some new ideas I wanted to sell back and with her backing..." He spread his hands to the side. "I can't lose."

"So you're saying that you've been looking for her when you were attacked with one of her inventions?"

The gorgon shrugged. "I'm not claiming anything of the sort. I'd like to speak to her. Whether the invention is hers or not remains to be seen. I have yet to see it myself. I only know of what she's done in the past."

"Thank you," Rascal said through clenched teeth. His claws were out as he put his hand on Wynona's back. "We'll let you take that nap now."

Wynona held back a snicker when Mr. Thathion glared. "Tell her I said hello, will you?" Mr. Thathion called out as they left the room. "And let her know that I'd welcome her back with open arms."

"I'm sure you would," Wynona muttered.

"I'm not sure I've ever seen you so harsh," Daemon whispered once they were in the hallway.

Rascal took a few steps away, shaking his hands until he had control of himself again.

"I totally forgot you were there," Wynona admitted to Daemon.

He smiled. "It's amazing what happens if you just stand and listen."

"So what did you discover?" she asked.

Daemon's eyes turned black for the briefest of moments. "Mr. Thathion has magic."

Wynona and Rascal both stilled.

"And it's green."

CHAPTER 15

"Have a seat and I'll fix something for you to eat," Wynona said as they entered her cottage. She walked directly to the kitchen and began putting a meal together.

Their time in the grove had taken most of the day and now they were looking at the dinner hour, but no one seemed to want to go home yet. Their minds were all still churning with the information they'd gathered, though no one quite knew what to do with it.

"So a snake shifter, who shouldn't have magic…does," Rascal clarified.

Daemon nodded. "Though, I'll admit that something about it looks different."

"How so?" Rascal pressed.

Wynona directed the stone to turn on and pulled a couple of steaks out of the freezer. They were becoming commonplace for her to keep on hand since she fed the men so often and Rascal much preferred a meal with meat, meat and more meat. Even while she worked, she kept her ears tuned in to the conversation.

"I'm not sure," Daemon mused. He tapped his fingers on the table. "It sort of…oozed from him, where most creatures have a…aura…for lack of a better word, about them. Plus, I can mostly see a creature's magic only when they're using it. For instance, I can't see Wynona's purple until she puts it to work. Like she's doing right now."

Wynona looked over her shoulder. "So it came from him constantly? Like a liquid?"

Daemon shrugged and tilted his head back and forth. "I suppose that's one way to put it."

"Could it have been a spell?" Rascal asked. "Or a curse?"

Daemon shook his head. "No. A spell or curse is like a blanket laying over someone. It's clearly not part of them. But this…this was inside, but behaved differently."

"I wish I'd known," Wynona murmured as she set the table. "I should have used my sight while I was there."

"Next time," Rascal assured her.

"I'm afraid I can't communicate in your mind to be able to tell you when it would be helpful," Daemon said with a chuckle.

"Thank heavens for that," Wynona shot back. "My brain is full of enough voices as it is." Though, lately, it had been quieter than normal. With Violet spending all her time with Lusgu, Wynona had felt slightly bereft, though she was glad someone was helping the brownie.

Daemon's chuckle grew a little louder. "But like Deputy Chief said, you can look at him next time."

"I'll do that." She put the steaks on the hot pan, the sizzle immediately causing the room to smell savory.

"Mmm…" Rascal took a deep breath. "Have I said lately that we need to have a short engagement?"

Wynona walked over and kissed his cheek. "Only every day."

Daemon cleared his throat. "Anyway…"

Wynona smiled at her friend just as the front door burst open.

"NONA!"

Daemon stiffened in his chair.

"Come on back, Prim," Wynona called, keeping an eye on the black hole. "We're just about to eat dinner."

Prim flounced into the room, only hesitating a moment when she spotted Daemon. "Good evening, everyone."

"Prim," Rascal said with a small smirk. "How goes the flower business?"

"Three weddings this week," Prim said as she slid into the chair farthest from Daemon. "It would appear that romance is in the air." She paused and frowned. "Though, I did have a cancellation as well."

"Oh? A broken engagement?" Wynona asked.

Prim shrugged. "Not sure. I was just told the wedding was off. It was for a woman named Avare Smouldons." Prim leaned forward with a grin. "I heard she was marrying someone high and mighty, so.."

Wynona's jaw dropped. "Prim. She died."

Prim blinked. "What?"

"The creature you're talking about. She died. Her fiance is in the hospital, but Ms. Smouldons didn't make it."

"Oh, wow." Prim fell back against the seat. "That's terrible." She shivered, then jerked upright again. "This has to do with the Dr. Brownhide case, doesn't it?"

Rascal growled. "How in the world do you know about that?"

Prim looked a little too smug. "Do you really think that the gossip chain hasn't picked up on Meldaeon Thathion being in the hospital? I didn't realize that was the fiance of Ms. Smouldons, but no celebrity ends up hurt without us hearing about it."

Daemon knocked on the table agitatedly. "The ghost reporters need to mind their own business."

"It's their business to share it with the rest of us," Prim shot back. She stared at Daemon for a moment before clearing her throat and looking back at Wynona. "And since I figured you'd be involved in the case, I've got some information for you."

"Are you hungry?"

"Is it too much of an imposition?"

Wynona smiled and shook her head. "Never."

Prim jumped up. "I'll grab myself a bowl of greens."

"There's some quinoa in the back as well," Wynona told her. They might be meeting for a sad reason tonight, but Wynona loved this. These were her people. Now if she could just help Lusgu as well.

Once they were all settled with their respective meals, Prim continued. "Okay, I was at the Curl and Die today and Sulanara from Don't Imp On Your Nails was there."

Daemon snorted and Prim sent him a withering glare.

"Anyway…" she said slowly, before turning her gaze back to Wynona. "Word on the street is…Dr. Brownhide is in trouble."

"What kind of trouble?" Wynona asked for clarification. She knew that there was mounting evidence against the dragon, but what exactly were the gossipers talking about?

Prim's pink eyes practically glowed. "Financial trouble."

Wynona looked at Rascal, then at Prim. "Do you have more than that?"

Prim danced in her seat. "Of course! They're saying that some of her inventions are showing up on the underworld market because she's looking for money to pay some debts." Prim leaned in conspiratorially. "She's about to be bankrupt and is trying to make some quick cash."

Wynona's eyes flared. "She didn't mention anything about finances."

Prim's pink eyebrows shot high on her brown. "You *spoke* to her? I thought Dr. Brownhide was hidden somewhere. No one's heard from her for a hundred years!"

Wynona rubbed her forehead. "Yes. We spoke to her this morning." She looked up. "And I struggle to think she's in that much trouble. She lives in a place where she wouldn't need much in the way of worldly goods."

Prim folded her arms over her chest and pouted. "You're not going to tell me, are you?"

Wynona put her hands in the air. "Not my place. If Dr. Rayn wants to share her whereabouts with the world, that's her choice, not mine."

Prim rolled her eyes. "Sometimes your sense of justice works against me."

Daemon grunted again, earning another glare.

"Guess you would know about that, wouldn't you?" Prim asked a little too sweetly.

Daemon's eyes narrowed. "Guess you wouldn't," he retorted.

Wynona slapped the table as Prim's face turned bright red. "Children," she scolded. "Let's stick with the topic at hand, shall we?"

Rascal choked on a laugh, but got himself under control quickly.

"We're all helping in our own way," Wynona said, making eye contact with each of her friends. "So please don't make fun of or be sarcastic about the ways in which a creature offers information."

Prim pouted, but nodded. "Fine."

Wynona looked at Daemon and raised her eyebrows.

He shrugged. "I have no problem with that."

Wynona held back the urge to roll her own eyes. Sometimes she just wanted to smack some sense into her friends. Usually Prim was the flighty one, but something seemed to be pushing Daemon to follow suit. It was ridiculously stupid.

Hear, hear! Violet called out as she and Lusgu came through the doorway.

Wynona pushed her way up from the table. "Are you two hungry?"

Violet purred her agreement, but Lusgu shook his head. "Did you see her?" he asked Wynona.

Wynona grew somber. "Yes."

Lusgu opened and closed his mouth a few times. "How did she look?"

She gave him a small smile, realizing her thoughts were correct. "Like a magnificent dragon." She leaned over slightly. "She's beautiful, Lusgu."

His eyes relaxed slightly. "Was she happy?"

Wynona shrugged. "I can't truly answer that, but she didn't appear to be *un*happy."

He nodded. "Thank you."

Sniffling from the direction of the table drew all their attention and Wynona turned to see Prim wiping her eyes. "Sorry," Prim said. "I just…I had no idea that you two had been an item. Whatever happened?"

Lusgu sniffed as well, but it was in disdain. "Never said we were," he grumped, turning to the kitchen and snapping his fingers at the broom.

The room grew quiet as they watched the brownie busy himself in his work.

"Lusgu," Wynona said, drawing his attention. "I think that can wait."

He grunted.

"We have a few questions and you might be able to help us."

Lusgu paused.

"Dr. Rayn is coming into the precinct tomorrow to tell the chief her alibi," Wynona continued. "But Prim has heard some…information…that says the doctor might be having financial trouble. Do you have any idea if that could be true?"

Lusgu spun. "Who was saying that?" he snarled.

Wynona immediately encased Lusgu in purple. "Lusgu," she snapped. "I won't put up with another tantrum. We're all on your side, but we can't do our job if we're constantly fighting you as well as trying to solve the case."

Lusgu closed his eyes and hung his head.

"Can I take down the shield?" Wynona asked. She was actually surprised at how quickly she'd managed the magic. Usually, it took some conscious effort on her part to bring it into being, but she had reacted without thought.

Progress, Violet said with a grin as she waited on Lusgu's shoulder inside the shield.

Wynona gave her familiar a smile.

Looking up, Lusgu nodded. "Take it down," he said.

Wynona did as he asked, noting Rascal's presence at her back. He wasn't quite as ready to let down his guard as she was. "Are you under control?"

His black, narrowed eyes met hers. "Yes."

"Can we talk about Dr. Rayn without you losing it?"

Lusgu rolled his eyes. "I said yes, Wynona. Enough already."

Rascal growled low in his throat. "Her questions aren't out of bounds," he snapped. "You nearly killed her last time."

"It wasn't quite that bad," Wynona said softly. "In fact, we all know I…" She suddenly remembered there were creatures present who had no idea about her good witch/bad witch moment. Best not to bring it up. "But ever since this case came up, you haven't been yourself, Lusgu. I can't keep helping if you don't keep yourself out of trouble."

The brownie relaxed a little. "Understood." One side of his lip curled. "I don't like her being gossiped about and I don't like creatures assuming things."

Wynona squatted down so she was on the brownie's level. "Were the two of you together at some point?" she asked softly, even knowing the whole room could hear. "I've never seen you get so upset and she definitely had a reaction when I mentioned your name."

Lusgu snorted. "It couldn't have been good."

Wynona shrugged. "It wasn't bad. She reacted strongest when she figured out who I was. Lusgu…how did Dr. Rayn know Granny? Were you all friends together? Did you go to school together? I just…how are you all connected?"

Lusgu stared at her, taking several heartbeats before responding. "That's a story for another time," he replied in a tone that was far from his usual snark. "Maybe someday…" He shook his head and stepped back. "It doesn't matter. Rayn and I haven't seen each other in a century. That's all you need to know." Rascal moved and Lusgu hurried to speak again. "Nothing else is relevant to the case," he clarified.

Wynona nodded and stood up. "Prim heard that Dr. Rayn is in financial trouble. That she might be marketing her inventions on the underworld market to save herself from ruin. Do you believe something like that is possible?"

Lusgu's thin lips disappeared as he pressed them together. "Never," he said vehemently. "She wouldn't do such a thing."

"You just said you haven't spoken in a century," Rascal offered.

Lusgu gave a decisive nod. "I know. But she wouldn't. Rayn never cared for money, so I can see her having little. Her mind was always on her inventions. But she created and built with the idea of making life better for all creatures, particularly those who didn't have magic of their own. She would never sell her things on the black market. If she was struggling that badly, she would turn to her family's hoard."

Wynona put her hands on her hips. "I forgot about dragon hoards. Is her family well off?"

"Enough that if she chose to live differently, she could."

"You truly believe that? Even though you haven't seen her in a long time?" Rascal asked again.

"Dragons don't change their stripes, wolf," Lusgu said curtly. "She never used the hoard because she didn't care about it. Rayn's treasure was her mind and what she created with it. She left her family for that exact reason, but she's the only one left. If she needed money, she had a way to get it."

Wynona nodded. "Okay. Thank you for clearing that up." She turned to Prim. "I've got an assignment for you."

The fairy preened. "Anything."

"Find out where the rumors are stemming from." Wynona held up a finger. "But not to the point where you put yourself in danger, please."

Prim made a face. "I can handle a little danger."

"Well, I can't," Wynona shot back, but softened the command with a smile. "Please don't do anything that might get you in trouble, okay?"

Prim smiled back and nodded.

"I simply would like to see where the rumors began, or at least in the direction they began. If Dr. Rayn doesn't truly need money, why would someone say she did? And what would they gain from such a rumor?"

Prim clapped her hands and rubbed them together. "On it."

"I'll go with you," Daemon said.

Prim bristled. "You will not."

Daemon leaned over the table. "You need someone with actual authority to do this. Since you're not hired by the chief, I'll go along to make sure you don't push the limits of the law."

"Spoilsport."

"Following the rules is the only way to stay safe." Daemon leaned back. "And it's how to keep your loved ones safe as well," he finished in a quieter tone.

Prim's retort stopped short and she pressed her lips together. "Your loved ones?"

Daemon didn't move.

Prim's cheek turned pink enough to nearly match her hair. "You want to keep me safe, Officer?"

He hesitated only a second before nodding.

A slow smile crept across Prim's face. "Well, then...what are we waiting for?"

"You're waiting until the morning," Wynona pointed out. "It's too late to speak to people tonight."

"Not people." Prim pushed back her chair and stood up to her full height in her human form. She grinned wickedly. "I get much more information from plants than creatures." She winked. "We'll check in soon."

Daemon scurried to follow the fairy who was headed out the door.

"You're on duty in the morning," Rascal hollered at his officer.

"Yes, sir!" Daemon called out.

Lusgu snorted as the front door opened and shut.

Rascal turned to Wynona. "Why do I get the feeling he's going to fall asleep on the job tomorrow?"

Wynona patted her fiance's chest. "Maybe this is just what they need to stop acting like toddlers around each other and hash out their troubles."

"Talking with plants?" Rascal raised a single eyebrow. "Doesn't sound very helpful to me."

Wynona rolled her eyes. "Spoken like a true carnivore."

He growled playfully at her.

Wynona grinned. "Come on, handsome," she said. "We need to figure out our next steps, because the deeper we get into this, the more I think someone is setting Dr. Rayn up for disaster. But the question is why...and who?"

CHAPTER 16

Wynona took her helmet off her head and attached it to the side of the Vespa. She had managed to convince Rascal this morning that she could drive herself to the precinct, though he didn't like it...at all. His protective side seemed to be getting stronger and stronger and Wynona had to wonder if it was because they were getting married. *Maybe his wolf is just getting antsy,* she mused as she pulled open the door to the police station.

"Good morning, Amaris," Wynona said cheerily, even knowing the vampire officer wouldn't return the greeting. Amaris had once been her friend, but ever since Wynona's powers had emerged, the front desk secretary had been afraid of Wynona and their friendship had slid by the wayside. Still...Wynona tried.

Amaris's red eye met Wynona's and she nodded. "Ms. Le Doux."

Holding back a sigh, Wynona walked past the desk and down the hallway to Rascal's office. She didn't have to wait at all, as he stepped into the hallway before she got the chance to knock.

"Morning, beautiful," he said, kissing her cheek.

Wynona smiled up at him. His hair was standing on end this morning. It was always a little messy, but today he'd either been electrocuted or he'd run his hands through it a thousand times already.

He patted his hair. "Sorry," he said, obviously having read her thoughts. "Rough night."

"Oh? Are you okay?"

He nodded. "Fine. Just trying to figure out all this nonsense. I know we're trying to catch a murderer, but I can't help but feel that things are also stacking up against you. Everywhere we turn, someone knows something we don't." Rascal blew out a breath. "And your father has been far too quiet lately. It makes me worried."

Wynona patted his chest. "I get it. But we can only handle so much. Let's worry about the case and then we'll see if we can get Dr. Rayn to share the other information she has."

Rascal nodded and pushed a hand through his hair, bringing it right back up. "Right. Case first." He glanced down the hall. "I don't think she's arrived yet." He glanced at his watch. "But she should be here any moment."

Taking her hand, Rascal led her to the chief's door and knocked.

"Enter."

Rascal guided Wynona inside.

"Ms. Le Doux," Chief Ligurio said with a nod. "How are you this morning?"

Wynona sat down in the chair across the desk. "Fine, thank you." She studied the vampire's dull eyes. "You have another migraine?"

He gave her a small smile. "How do you do that?"

Wynona shrugged. "I'm not sure. I guess it comes with the healing gift." Narrowing her gaze, she studied him and waited for a moment. "Green tea, rooibos and turmeric," she murmured. Shaking her head, Wynona came out of her slight trance. "I don't think we're going to find that around the office."

Chief Ligurio picked up the phone. "Say it again?"

Wynona repeated the ingredients while Chief Ligurio ordered Amaris to go grab what he needed at the store.

The chief put the phone back in its cradle. "I guess we'll see how that turns out," he muttered.

Wynona smiled. "I believe it's turned out just fine all the other times."

He snorted. "True enough." Leaning back in his seat, he turned to his second in command. "You said Dr. Brownhide was going to be here this morning?"

Rascal nodded, but before he could speak, there was another knock.

"Enter," Chief Ligurio called out, raising an expectant eyebrow at Wynona before turning to the door.

Wynona spun on her hip so she could see who was outside.

"Chief. We've got a Dr. Rayn and a Ms. Greik out here to see you," the officer said.

Chief Ligurio nodded. "Put one in interrogation room two, and the other in number three."

"Yes, sir."

The door closed and Wynona turned. "Are we all going together?"

Rascal hummed in thought. "Probably. Otherwise we just have to share all the info later."

Chief Ligurio shook his head. "Except that this time I'd like to utilize Ms. Le Doux." He turned his eyes her way. "I'd like you to speak to the assistant. You seem to have the ability to get creatures to open up and share their stories with you, and I'd like some insight on the doctor from someone who didn't know her a century ago."

Wynona nodded. "Okay. I'll see what I can do." The order made her a bit nervous. What if Quinin didn't want to talk about it? Wynona hadn't even realized that the owl shifter would be coming and had no idea what she would ask her. But Chief Ligurio was right. The perspective from someone who was around the doctor all the time would go a long way in helping them know whom to trust.

Wynona desperately wanted to trust Lusgu, but it was difficult when everyone and everything said the exact opposite.

Once out in the hall, Wynona squeezed Rascal's hand and headed to room number three. After a short knock, she went inside, giving a small smile to the officer at the door. "Hello, Ms. Greik," Wynona said pleasantly.

The owl pushed her glasses up her nose and blinked. "Good morning."

"We're so glad you came in today," Wynona continued, sitting across the table.

Quinin's eyebrows rose high. "Did we have a choice?"

Wynona smiled. "Dr. Rayn was asked to come in, yes, but I don't think anyone realized that you would be coming with her."

Quinin looked away. "The doctor...doesn't really go anywhere by herself." She turned back to Wynona. "She's brilliant in the lab, but in normal life?" The owl shifter shrugged. "She doesn't always get it."

"So tell me...what do you do for the doctor?"

Quinin chuckled. "Everything you can possibly think of," she admitted. "I help her with her inventions and testing, but I also do laundry and make sure the garbage can is where it needs to be."

Wynona jerked back a little. "Garbage? You two get your garbage picked up? From the grove?"

Quinin's cheeks flushed. "Well...I don't think the company actually knows where we live, but the can is on a nearby street."

"I don't think anything is truly nearby where you live," Wynona teased.

Quinin smiled in return. "Everything's faster when you have wings."

"True enough." Wynona leaned forward. "How long have you been working with Dr. Rayn?"

"Nearly twenty years."

"Wow." Wynona nodded slowly. "That's a long time. And you haven't dated or met your significant other during those years? Or maybe wanted to move on to something less isolated? You seem pretty young yet."

The owl shifter blushed again. "I've never been good with social graces," she said in a soft voice. "While a partner would be nice, it doesn't ever seem to happen for me."

Wynona smiled. "You're a beautiful young woman, Quinin. I have no doubt that if you spent time with other creatures your age, you'd do just fine."

Quinin shrugged. "Men my age don't seem to be as interested in a woman with a brain."

Wynona made a face. "I think that's the age-old problem, isn't it? Males being intimidated by a woman who can think?"

"Obviously, not all of them," Quinin replied, tilting her head and studying Wynona. "You found your partner."

Wynona nodded, not bothering to mention that she and Rascal were soulmates. That bit of information was something they didn't offer unless it was warranted as both were afraid the information would be used against them, especially when it came to Wynona's family. "I did," Wynona agreed. "I was lucky."

Quinin snorted and folded her arms over her chest. "Doesn't really matter," she said. "I'm happy where I'm at." She smiled widely. "Dr. Rayn is brilliant, even if she can't keep track of the days of the week. Working with her is a dream."

Wynona grinned back. "So science has always been your thing, huh?"

Quinin nodded. "Yes. I love it. It's like having magic for those of us without it."

"I can see the draw," Wynona continued. "I don't have a lot of experience with science, but I've read a lot of books. Some of the things they do in the human world are utterly fascinating."

Quinin's eyes began to glow with excitement and she leaned forward. "Seriously!" she cried. "Did you know they're creating robots that can do everything from go into space to play basketball?"

"Pretty incredible."

Quinin nodded eagerly. "Someday I'm going to go to the human world," she said, her words spilling out faster than Wynona had ever heard her. This was obviously a topic the owl shifter felt strongly about.

"Is that on your bucket list? Or something you've already got planned?" Wynona asked.

Quinin's excitement dimmed and she leaned back in her seat. "No plans," she said dully. "I…can't afford it."

Perfect entry, Wynona thought. She rested her arms on the table and leaned forward a little. "Quinin," she said softly. "There are some rumors that Dr. Rayn is in financial trouble. Do you know if they're true?"

Quinin blinked, the emotion completely gone from her face. "How would I know?"

"Well…does Dr. Rayn pay you fairly for your work?"

Quinin frowned. "I guess that depends on what you mean by fair. I get paid…most of the time. But I also get free room and board, so when Dr. Rayn forgets to write a paycheck, I don't usually worry about it too much."

"So Dr. Rayn does all her own finances?"

Quinin's eyes dropped. "Mostly."

"Have you ever helped with the books?" Wynona pressed.

Quinin took a second to respond, then jerked her head from side to side. "No."

Either she's lying, or this is getting us nowhere. "So you've never heard Dr. Rayn mention a struggle to pay the bills? How do you get groceries out there? Or the supplies for all her experiments?"

Quinin pursed her lips. "I do the grocery shopping for the most part. I have it delivered to a certain spot and then pick it up."

"And how do you pay for those?"

Quinin chuckled. "Dr. Rayn has an account with the grocer, and since I keep getting food, I assume she keeps paying the bill."

"But you do the ordering?" Wynona frowned. That seemed an odd set up.

Quinin nodded. "Yeah. Rayn can't really be bothered to leave the house if she doesn't have to."

Unless she's scaring intruders out of their wits, Wynona thought wryly. "So, as far as you know, Dr. Rayn is doing just fine financially?"

Quinin shrugged one shoulder. "I can't offer information otherwise," she said, though Wynona didn't miss how carefully the sentence was structured.

Quinin was obviously just as smart as her employer and Wynona knew she would have to watch herself around the young woman.

"Thank you for clearing that up," Wynona said, brushing the topic aside. "May I ask you a few more questions?"

Quinin blinked and pushed her glasses back up her nose.

"Have you had any visitors to the house lately?"

"Just you," Quinin said.

"What about in the last couple of years?" Wynona asked. "Surely people are interested in Dr. Rayn's inventions? Don't they ever come to find her? Would anyone be willing to kill for her inventions, or who would profit from her death?"

Quinin shook her head. "No. Once in a while, Rayn will send something to other inventors in Cauldron Cove or Witch Wharf, but as far as I know, no one has ever come checking on her. And her inventions are all willed to Para University, so killing her wouldn't do them any good."

"Do you know what happened between Dr. Rayn and Meldaeon Thathion?"

Quinin snorted and folded her arms over her chest. "Doesn't the whole world know?"

"It was before your time," Wynona said. "So it would be easy not to know."

Quinin rolled her eyes in a rare show of emotion. "I've heard enough rumors and been with Rayn long enough to know that Paratech treated her like garbage. They wanted to use her inventions to build an empire." She huffed. "I suppose that's what they did anyway. It was her inventions that led the company to the top."

"So why would she leave them?" Wynona asked. "She got to invent and they got to sell. It sounds to me like everyone should have been happy."

"You'd think, wouldn't you?" Quinin asked. "But Solarspike, Toleus and Guanaco all wanted to take their profit to the next level. They wanted Rayn to send certain inventions out before they were ready for public use."

Wynona spread her hands to the side. "That's hardly a good reason to break up such a successful company."

"I suppose that depends on your perspective." Quinin tilted her head. "If your invention could possibly hurt or kill people and your bosses refused to let you fix it, would you want to stick around?"

"What invention was it that finally broke the contract?"

Quinin pursed her lips and squished them to the side. "I believe it had something to do with creating rainstorms. It was supposed to be used for the farming dwarves."

"And what was deadly about it?" Wynona asked.

Quinin frowned. "I seem to recall something about flooding? Or maybe it was lightning?" She shook her head. "I can't recall for sure, but it needed more work, three of the board wanted to sell it right away and Thathion sat somewhere in the middle." Quinin sighed. "When they continued to press, Rayn finally took her stuff and left, but then she lost most of her plans in the lawsuit that followed."

"So if Mr. Thathion came back and wanted to work with Dr. Rayn again, what do you think she would say?" Wynona asked, though she knew her own thoughts on the matter.

Quinin scoffed. "I'm pretty sure he'd be lucky to escape with his skin intact," she said wryly, then smirked. "Dragon fire can be a nasty beast."

CHAPTER 17

Wy!

Wynona jerked upright in bed. "What?" she asked, rubbing her eyes.

Wy? Where are you? Rascal demanded.

"I'm at home," she muttered, swinging her legs over the bed. "Why are you waking me up at…" Wynona glanced at her clock. "Three o'clock in the morning?"

The pounding on her front door had her grabbing her robe and rushing to open it.

"What are you doing?" she asked as Rascal rushed in and wrapped his arms around her.

"There's been another killing," he said through heavy breathing.

From the windblown scent of him, Wynona was sure that Rascal had run the whole way to her house in his wolf form. She reached around him and let his protective wolf hold on. "Who died?" she asked softly.

"Eve Guanaco."

Wynona gasped and leaned back. "Another one of the Original Five?"

Rascal nodded and pushed both hands through his hair, tugging tightly. "No one was sure about the first death. Whoever left the device could have been after the fiance or Thathion, though he was the more likely suspect. But now we're certain." His eyes flashed gold. "Someone is killing The Five."

Wynona tugged her robe tighter around her, suddenly feeling chilled. "It was Mr. Thathion."

"Wy…" Rascal let his head drop back. "He was in the hospital. A dozen nurses and staff can vouch for him."

Wynona shook her head and waved a finger at Rascal. "I'm telling you, he's involved! There is something *wrong* with that man. I don't know how you can't feel it."

"Okay, okay." Rascal put his hands up in a placating manner. "I hear you. But Wy…I have no proof. Do you have any idea what the chief would say if I showed up at the hospital to arrest Thathion? Chief would think I was completely out of my fur."

Wynona sagged into his chest. "I know," she muttered. "But I still think he's evil."

Rascal chuckled and Wynona bounced against him. "You don't like him. Understood. I don't like him either. But that doesn't make him a killer."

Wynona huffed. She raised her head. "Why were you so afraid? You don't usually wake me up for every call in the middle of the night."

Rascal sighed. He didn't answer right away and it gave Wynona long enough to come up with an idea.

"You thought I wasn't safe with Lusgu," she said softly.

Rascal hesitated, but ultimately nodded.

Wynona stepped away. "I can't believe you think he would hurt me," she cried.

Rascal scowled. "Think? He already hurt you. Do you not remember how your magic reacted to him? It was completely defensive!"

"He's promised to train me," Wynona argued. "Is that the actions of a person who would hurt me?"

"He's not himself at the moment," Rascal insisted. He took

Wynona's hands and held them tightly. "Only a couple of weeks ago I wouldn't have believed him capable of it, but I've watched him nearly kill us all." Rascal shook his head. "I don't trust him."

"He's hurting," Wynona whispered hoarsely. "He's hurting and it's causing him to lash out."

"He's an adult," Rascal snapped. "And if what we've gathered is correct, he's an adult several centuries over. He has no excuse to act like a two year old being denied his favorite toy."

Wynona's bottom lip began to tremble. She hated fighting with Rascal. It was completely understandable that he was concerned. Logically, she knew this. But she couldn't bring herself to turn her back on Lusgu. There was something there. Something just beneath the surface that called to her, let her know there was more to him than meets the eye. She could *feel* that he needed help and it was more than just the case with Dr. Rayn.

Just like her intuition was screaming that Mr. Thathion was guilty, it had declared that Lusgu was a mystery worth solving. And part of that mystery was coming to light with the most recent case.

"He asked for my help," Wynona said, forcing her voice to be soft, though she couldn't help the tremble. "He promised he'd behave."

Rascal closed his eyes and hung his head.

"I have to give him the benefit of the doubt." A couple of tears trickled down her cheek and Wynona sniffed, wiping at them with her palm.

Groaning, Rascal reached out and pulled her to his chest once more. He kissed the top of her head. "I'm sorry," he whispered against her forehead. "I shouldn't have been so harsh."

"I'm sorry that I argued with you."

Rascal chuckled. "Your loyalty is gonna kill my wolf, but it's also one of the things I love most about you." Leaning back slightly, he cupped her face. "But please...promise me that if you ever feel unsafe or your witchy powers say something's amiss, you'll protect yourself no matter the cost."

Wynona nodded. "Okay."

He leaned forward, giving her a sweet kiss that quickly turned into something more as their volatile emotions got the better of them.

Just as Rascal tilted his head to deepen the kiss, the buzz of his cell phone broke through their moment and Wynona had to reluctantly pull back.

"What?" Rascal growled into the device. It was clear he wasn't any happier about being interrupted than she was.

Wynona wrapped her arms around his chest and nestled her forehead into the crook of his neck.

"I don't have my truck," Rascal snapped into the device. "I'll be there as soon as I can." He ended the call and sighed. Pocketing the phone, he wrapped his arms around her waist. "I need to go to the crime scene."

Wynona nodded and yawned. "Do you want me to come?"

"I guess that depends on if you want a firsthand look, or just reports."

Wynona's shoulders slumped. "Looks like I'll be needing a nap tomorrow."

Rascal kissed the top of her head again and stepped back. "Grab the keys to the Vespa, but I'm driving."

"I can do you one better." Wynona grinned. "How about I port us?"

His eyebrows shot up. "I thought that didn't go so well last time?"

She shrugged. "I have to practice, right? This is a good time for it."

"Without Violet?"

Wynona chewed her bottom lip. "Yeah…that does make it harder, but I still think I can do it."

He rubbed his hands up and down his face. "Why do I have the feeling I should be worried about ending up in the middle of the Spell Summit?"

"Hey!" Wynona whacked his chest with the back of her hand.

He laughed and held on. "Teasing. Only teasing…mostly."

She scowled, but he simply gave her another kiss, then wrapped her up tightly in his embrace.

"Okay. We need to go to Moonbeam Park."

Wynona took in a deep breath and nodded. "Got it." She refused to acknowledge how anxious she was. Teleporting wasn't something she was very good at yet, but she'd done it before…once. But how was she supposed to learn a skill if she never practiced it? And they needed to get to the crime scene quickly.

Closing her eyes, she called her magic to her and let it thrum through her body. She felt her hair begin to lift up as the power filled the room. Wynona squeezed her eyes tighter, imagining the park in her mind. She put together the leaves, the smell of the grass and the flowers that dotted the walkways. She imagined the moonlight shining on the benches and bushes, creating shadows that danced with the breeze, the very picture that gave the park its name.

Her body felt tight, like her skin was shrinking, but Wynona pushed on. Rascal's hold tightened and Wynona gripped his shirt in her fists, chanting the name of the park over and over again in her head.

Just as she felt like her head would burst with the pressure, there was a light popping noise and several loud shouts that shouldn't have been there.

Cracking open one eye, Wynona jerked and automatically threw up her shield when she noticed the taser aimed in her face.

"Stand down, Officer Aldor," Rascal said in a deep voice, the hint of a growl making it extra dangerous.

The officer blinked several times, then lowered his weapon. "Deputy Chief," the wizard said. "I didn't see you arrive."

Rascal smirked at Wynona. "That was the point, I believe." He kissed her temple. "Well done, sweetheart."

Wynona swayed slightly, her body still coming down from the magic induced high. "Thanks, I think." She looked around. Several other officers were eyeing them suspiciously. "I didn't mean to put us right in the middle of the action. No wonder they're all staring."

"It's fine," Rascal assured her. "But do you mind?" He tapped the purple bubble still surrounding them.

"Oh. Yeah. Sorry." Wynona pulled the magic back in, tucking it away for later use. It didn't give her as much trouble as usual. Either she was getting better, or she was simply tired. Since her sleep had been interrupted and she'd just used a great deal of her powers, it could go either way.

"Strongclaw!"

Wynona and Rascal spun to see Chief Ligurio headed their direction. His red eyes were anything but welcoming.

"Was that necessary?" he growled.

Wynona gave him a sheepish grin. "Sorry. Rascal was checking on me and I wanted to practice porting. It got us here faster," she offered.

Chief Ligurio sighed and rubbed his forehead. "True enough. But maybe a warning next time. Some of these men are a little trigger happy this evening."

"Tell us what's going on," Wynona said, stepping up next to the vampire as he turned to walk back the way he came.

"Almost an exact replica of last time," he stated bluntly. "An odd storm brewing, lightning and darkness. Victim was hit by lightning multiple times."

"Did you find another device?"

Chief Ligurio shook his head. "Not yet. But we're still searching."

"Last time it was almost a block away," Wynona reminded him. "Perhaps the search area is too small."

Chief Ligurio gave her a sideways glare. "I'm aware, Ms. Le Doux."

Wynona snapped her mouth shut. The grumpy chief was even more grumpy in the middle of the night.

The group slowed as they reached a tarp-covered body and Wynona gulped. She hated this part.

Chief Ligurio squatted down and pulled the tarp back. An older woman with sharp features and a hawk-like nose that gave away her heritage lay peaceful on the ground. The look on her face was at odds with the carnage down the side of her neck and upper torso.

"What a horrible way to die," Wynona whispered. She got down on her knees and studied the wound. The flesh and fabric had been burned, just like Mr. Thathion's fiancee. "How many times was she struck?"

"As far as we can tell...three," Chief Ligurio stated, his voice growing slightly softer at the end. "The coroner should be here any minute and then we'll know for sure, but there are three distinct burn areas on her."

Wynona shook her head and rose up, stepping back slightly. "The true question here is why. Why is someone targeting the Original Five?"

Rascal grunted. "You realize this only implicates Dr. Rayn even more?"

Wynona shook her head harder. "Do you really think she's a killer?"

"I don't know," Rascal said honestly. "I think she has a lot of secrets, I think she was kicked unfairly out of her company and we know she lost millions of dollars in the break up." He shrugged. "That kind of bitterness can drive people to do crazy things."

"Agreed," Chief Ligurio said, recovering the woman's face. "We'll have to bring her in for more questioning."

Wynona sighed, then yawned. "Sorry," she said, covering her mouth. "I'm not used to being up all night."

Chief Ligurio huffed.

"CHIEF!"

They all turned to watch an officer run in their direction. He was panting heavily by the time he arrived at their sides.

"We found it, sir."

"A weather device?" Chief Ligurio clarified.

The troll nodded. "Yes, sir. It was tucked under a hibiscus bush at the far end of the park."

The trio walked quickly toward the area and Wynona's heart fell as they got closer. She could see the yellow box with all the strange markings on it, just like they'd seen before. Including the silver encasing the edges.

Chief Ligurio held out his hand and the troll slapped some gloves in the chief's palm. After putting them on, Chief Ligurio picked up the box. He turned to Wynona. "See anything?"

One of these days, I'll remember to try that.

Rascal gave her a commiserating grin.

She blinked a few times, bringing her magical sight into focus. An odd haze enveloped the box. "It's not red," she murmured, walking around to get a better look. "In fact, it sort of looks…rainbow." She swallowed hard.

"What does that mean?" Chief Ligurio snapped.

Wynona shook her head. "I don't know, but it's not quite right."

"A little more information would be helpful, Ms. Le Doux," he grunted.

Wynona sighed and closed her eyes. "There are holes in the magic," she whispered. She looked up at Rascal, feeling the weight of her next words. "Just like with my teapot."

CHAPTER 18

Chief Ligurio stared her down. "You realize what this means?"

Wynona nodded jerkily, her heart thudding against her chest. "I realize what this *looks* like," she corrected.

The vampire sighed. "The evidence is mounting, Ms. Le Doux."

Wynona spread her hands. "But again, I ask…why now? Why wait so long before taking revenge? And you didn't arrest her yesterday, so you obviously didn't have enough evidence to hold her."

The chief nodded. "I know, but that could mean many things. She simply hasn't slipped up enough. She's been biding her time until all her ex-coworkers weren't watching over their shoulders."

"She's a brilliant doctor," Wynona butted in. "Something like this is too messy for her."

"She's an absent-minded inventor," Rascal said softly. "She's also a dragon. Their passionate natures could lead to many mistakes."

Wynona forced herself to stand down. "I don't believe it," she said. "I see the evidence and I understand where you're coming from, but I don't believe it."

"You still think the gorgon lying in a hospital bed is responsible," Chief Ligurio said, rather than asked.

"I do."

"And how do you propose he accomplished such a thing?" the vampire pressed. "He has no magic."

We need to fill the chief in on that...as soon as we know what it means.

"But these are science," Wynona said, an idea forming. "How do we know it isn't controlled by remote? Maybe he's been able to do the whole thing from his bed simply by pushing a button."

Chief Ligurio sighed again and pinched the bridge of his nose. When he finally looked up, he appeared to have aged fifty years. "I will hold off arresting her until morning," he said in a dull tone. "Bring the device back to the precinct and you can study it. If you can find evidence of remote control, then we'll look into the possibility."

"Thank you," Wynona said sincerely. She had no idea what she was going to be looking for. How could a creature tell if something was controlled remotely? Especially if they didn't have a remote?

But she was determined to find something. There *had* to be something. Dr. Rayn was quirky, quick to temper and her head got lost in the clouds, but she was no killer. Wynona was willing to bet her life on it.

"Don't thank me yet," Chief Ligurio said as he began to walk away. "I follow evidence, Ms. Le Doux. And everything I have points to your dragon." With that parting shot, he slipped into the darkness.

Wynona knew she wouldn't see him again until the next day. She was actually a little surprised the chief had shown up in the middle of the night at all, normally he left his officers to do this kind of work.

"It's because it's another high profile creature," Rascal muttered. His hands were on his hips and he was staring at the device that sat innocently on the ground.

"Makes sense," Wynona replied. She stepped forward and started to bend down, but Rascal stopped her with a hand on her arm.

"I don't think you should touch it," he said.

"Oh...right." Wynona shook her head. She was a mess. Wiggling her fingers, she caused the device to float and started walking toward the parking lot. "How are we getting to the precinct? I'm a little worried about porting with this thing." She glanced over her shoulder. "I'd hate to risk setting it off while we were traveling."

Rascal nodded and grabbed his phone. "Skymaw? We need a ride back." Rascal grunted a few times. "Right. See you there." He shoved his phone in his pocket. "Skymaw will meet us in the parking lot when he's finished scanning the scene for more residue."

"Did he say if he'd found anything yet?"

Rascal shook his head. "No. We can ask him on the ride over."

They waited impatiently near Daemon's car. Wynona rubbed her hands up and down her arms and suddenly realized she was still in her robe and pajamas. Her head hung back. "Kill me now," she muttered to the dark sky.

Rascal chuckled.

She glared at him. "Why didn't you say something?"

The wolf shrugged. "Why? You look cute."

"No wonder they were all staring at me like I was an apparition," Wynona muttered. She put her hands on her hips. "I can't believe you let me wander around like this."

Rascal simply wrapped his large hands around her waist and tugged her close. "Easy, Wy. You might crush that little device if you get too mad."

She scowled at him, but let him keep his arms around her. They protected her slightly from the nighttime elements, for which she was grateful. There was something about wolves that was always warm and she couldn't deny how much she needed his body heat right now.

The crunch of gravel caught their attention and Daemon's large figure emerged from the dark. He paused, giving Wynona a look. "In a hurry, were we?" he teased.

Rascal gave a warning growl, but Wynona laughed. "I suppose I was," she said. She looked over her shoulder. "You didn't get mad at anyone else who saw me tonight."

"They had the good grace not to say anything," Rascal said with a sniff.

Wynona shook her head. "If you don't want creatures seeing me in my robe, don't let me leave the house in it."

He squeezed her waist slightly before ushering her inside the car.

Wynona brought the device in with her, setting it on the seat next to her.

Rascal climbed in the front seat and they drove away from the park.

"Did you see anything around the park?" Wynona asked as they drove along. The night was dark and there were almost no cars on the road. The weight of the night felt heavy and the presence of the weather device tugged at Wynona.

She tried to study it, but the car was too dark for her to see well. *There's probably a spell for that, but I don't know it.* She sighed. She needed those lessons from Lusgu…pronto.

"Not much," Daemon said in answer to her question. "I kept feeling like there was magic out of the corner of my eye, but every time I turned to look at it, there was nothing there. The only thing that stood out was the box and the spilled magic on the bush the box was hidden under."

"Hmm…" Wynona tapped her bottom lip. "So magic was present, but not visible."

Daemon's large shoulder shrugged. "I suppose you could say that."

"Have you and Prim done any sleuthing yet?"

Daemon shook his head. "No. We were supposed to go tomorrow." He sighed. "I might need to put it off until I can take a nap. Everything was asleep the night we left your house together."

Rascal grunted and Wynona leaned back in her seat. "Be careful, please," she said softly.

"Of course," Daemon replied. They pulled into the precinct and the trio walked inside. The place was quieter than during the daytime hours, which was probably a blessing since they had a dangerous piece of equipment with them. If something went wrong, there would be fewer creatures around to possibly be hurt.

"How about we take this into the interrogation room?" Rascal asked. "There's more room in there."

Wynona nodded and directed the box into the room with them. She set it down on the table with a small sigh of relief. Sustained magic was still new to her. She loved seeing her powers grow, but her endurance to hold the levels necessary was still a work in progress.

"Thank you," she said as Rascal pulled up a chair and offered it to her. Sitting down, Wynona stared at the box. It was green this time, just right for blending into the environment it had been planted in. "Is there some kind of on/off switch?" she murmured, turning her head one way and another.

Rascal sat next to her and Daemon took the seat across the table. "Not that I can see."

Daemon's eyes flashed a solid black. "Whoa."

Wynona nodded. "Odd…isn't it?"

He nodded in return. "I'm not sure I've ever seen rainbow before."

Wynona called her own magic into usage again. It took a little extra effort since she'd already expended so much tonight. The light colors of magic came into view and she narrowed her eyes. "It's a rainbow…but it's not."

"Would someone please explain that statement?" Rascal grumbled.

Wynona reached out and patted his knee. "The colors are sort of… random. There are multiple colors, but they aren't banded together like an actual rainbow."

"And you said there are holes in the power?"

Wynona nodded. "Yes. Like something's wrong with it. It's not quite..natural."

"Exactly my thought," Daemon murmured, his eyes still glued to the box. "Does anyone know what the symbols mean?"

Wynona reached out, stopping just short of touching the device.

"Wy…" Rascal warned.

Holding her breath, she put one finger on the box, then relaxed when nothing happened. "We touched the first one," she reminded Rascal.

"Yes, but that was before we knew better."

Wynona shrugged and turned the box around. "The precinct doesn't happen to have a book on dragon writing, does it?"

Daemon snorted out a laugh. "I don't think so."

"The only dragon I actually know besides Dr. Brownhide is

Gendyl," Rascal admitted, scratching behind his ear. He was referring to the manager of a gas station. The elderly dragon was well known for her ability to gossip and scare away thieves, but no one knew much beyond that.

"I suppose we could try asking her?" Wynona suggested.

"If all else fails, that's fine," Rascal said. "But her eyesight is so bad at this point, I'm not even sure she's capable of reading."

"What type of dragon is she anyway?" Daemon asked. "Is she that much older than Dr. Brownhide? Why has one of them aged so much and the other not?"

Wynona blinked until her sight cleared and leaned back in her seat. "That's an excellent question. Dragons can live for centuries, but I have no idea how old Dr. Rayn or Gendyl is. Gendyl has looked old as long as I've known her, but that means little in dragon years."

"How old is Lusgu?" Rascal asked.

Wynona opened her mouth, but paused. "I have no idea," she admitted. Yet another question to put in the mystery jar that was her janitor.

"He's been around a while," Daemon said. "He has to have been. We know Dr. Brownhide is at least three centuries old, if not more, and Lusgu has known her since the beginning of the Original Five."

Wynona nodded.

"That leaves us two creatures that have lived far past their normal age ranges," Rascal muttered with a frown, referring to their victim in the hospital. His dark brows were pulled together. "I can't help but feel like this is all tied together somehow."

Wynona pursed her lips. "What *is* the average span of a gorgon?" she asked.

Rascal and Daemon both shook their heads. "What about a brownie?" Daemon asked.

"Rascal, can we use your computer please?" Wynona asked. Her eyes strayed to the box. It was certainly a mystery, but they didn't seem to know enough about other topics to try and solve this one. The layers in this case just seemed to be getting thicker, rather than revealing anything. Would they ever catch a break?

"On it." Rascal slipped out the door and returned a moment later with his laptop tucked under his arm. He handed it to Wynona.

She opened it and waited for him to enter his password before getting on a search engine. Her eyes scanned the files provided. "It looks like the average gorgon lives to be one hundred," Wynona said. "Though, some have been recorded as high as a hundred and fifty."

"So, Mr. Thathion is at least a hundred and seventy years over that."

Wynona nodded. "Yes."

"And brownies?"

Wynona punched in the question. "It looks like brownies are about the same. The oldest ones are a little over a hundred years old."

"So Lusgu is three times what he should be."

Wynona nodded. "I suppose so." She looked around. "But what does that mean? Is it just good genetics? Or something else?"

"The only thing the two have in common is Dr. Brownhide," Daemon said softly.

"And her goal with her inventions is to bring magic to those without it," Rascal added.

Wynona rubbed her forehead.

"I don't know how long we can keep fighting this," Rascal pointed out.

Wynona nodded. "I get it, but Chief said I could have a little time." She looked up. "I think we need to figure out what the writing says."

Daemon picked up the box and turned it this way and that. "Maybe we need a screwdriver," he said. "We could try taking it apart."

"Oooh, I hadn't thought of that."

Rascal stood up again. "I have some tools in the truck." He paused. "But the truck's not here."

Wynona bit back a yawn. "Tell you what. How about we all go get some sleep. Then tomorrow we can tackle the writing and the taking apart." She rubbed her eyes. "I can barely see straight and right now, this thing seems to be dead."

"How do we know it'll stay dead?" Rascal asked, though the lines around his eyes said he was as tired as she was.

Wynona pinched her lips in thought. "Do you have a hag's thread on you?"

Rascal shook his head and they both looked at Daemon.

Daemon pulled one from the pocket of his uniform and held it out.

Carefully, Wynona picked up the thread, then wrapped it around the box and tied it in a bow. "There. That should keep the magic from doing anything weird and we can undo the thread whenever we're ready to try again."

Daemon's eyes went black and he nodded. "It seems to have worked. The colors are gone."

Rascal rubbed his hands down his face. "Fine. But I want it down in the locker before we leave. I don't trust it." He gave Daemon a meaningful look.

Daemon nodded and stood, taking the box with him. "I'll see you both tomorrow. Ms. Le Doux…Deputy Chief." With a nod, the black hole was gone.

Wynona yawned again and stood up, stretching her arms. "I'm gonna try to port home," she said.

Rascal came up and put his arms around her waist. "I'll sleep on your couch."

She frowned. "Why?"

"Because my wolf demands it."

Wynona sighed but didn't bother arguing. Until her life was back to normal, she knew her soulmate would be taking more precautions than ever. "Hold on tight," she warned. "I don't have as much energy as I did."

Closing her eyes, Wynona took them home. By the time she was done, her knees were shaking and she could barely stay awake. She didn't even remember Rascal's kiss goodnight as she stumbled to her room. One way or another, she needed a break and sleep was the closest thing she was going to get right now.

CHAPTER 19

Wynona wiped her mouth and stood from the table to put her dishes in the sink. A grunt from behind her let her know Lusgu had arrived for the morning and the dishes she was holding floated out of her hands. She turned. "Thank you, Lusgu." She was suddenly glad that Rascal had left early this morning. She definitely didn't need a clash between the two men first thing as the sun rose.

Lusgu scowled, but nodded.

How are you doing? Wynona asked Violet, who was steadfastly sitting on his shoulder. Wynona didn't want to admit how much she missed her little familiar. The mouse's connection to Lusgu was helpful and Wynona didn't want Lusgu alone, but it was hard having a piece of herself away so much.

I miss you too, Violet sent back.

Wynona smiled. *Thank you for taking care of him. Is there anything more I should be doing?*

Violet shook her head. *No. The best thing we can do is clear Rayn's name. He needs her safe.*

Wynona frowned. *They were lovers, weren't they?*

It's more than you think, but not my story to tell.

Wynona sighed. She closed her eyes for patience. If just one person would finally speak up, she had a feeling they'd have this all solved. But every person in this case was drowning in secrets and until some of them were unearthed, they would continue to have a mess on their hands.

Violet shrugged.

Wynona cleared her throat. "You should know, Lusgu, that Eve Guanaco was killed last night."

Lusgu paused in his cleaning. "How did she die?"

"The same way Mr. Thathion's fiancee did. A weather box."

Lusgu's head hung and he slowly shook it back and forth. "Why?" he croaked. "Why are they targeting her?"

"They?" Wynona pressed. "What do you mean, *they*?"

Lusgu spun. "I meant it in general," he spat. "But it's obvious someone wants Rayn in jail. But why?" His black, beady eyes looked misty and it caught Wynona off guard. "She hasn't hurt anyone," Lusgu continued. "She does so much good for the world and someone is setting her up."

Wynona dropped to her knees. "Who? Who would want to do such a thing?"

Lusgu ran a large hand over his face. "I-I'm not sure," he stammered.

"But you have a guess?"

He stilled.

"I'm fighting for her," Wynona whispered. "But I need help. The evidence is mounting and soon the chief won't listen to my complaints. He's only given me a little more time."

One side of Lusgu's lip curled, but he pulled it back. "Her only enemies are the Original Five," he spit out.

"But they're the ones dying."

"Meldaeon didn't die."

Wynona nodded. "I know. And truthfully, I feel like he's as twisted as his animal, but he was in the hospital last night, surrounded by guards and nurses. There was no way he was the one setting out that box."

"Another, then," Lusgu argued. "Ebux or Ceraon."

Wynona nodded. "We're going to talk to them for sure. We weren't positive Mr. Thathion was the actual target before, since it was his fiancee that was killed. But now I think it's safe to say The Five are all in danger."

She stood and brushed down her skirt, eyeing Lusgu from her peripheral vision. His face showed heavy disdain at her mention of the Original Five, which made sense after the breakup with Dr. Rayn, but did Lusgu really think they were guilty of murder?

Probably, Violet added.

I've believed Mr. Thathion was hiding something from the beginning. But it's really hard to pin anything on him when he's got a rock solid alibi.

"Lusgu?"

He grunted.

"Do any of Dr. Rayn's inventions work on remote?"

His brows pulled together. "Not that I'm aware of."

"Like the weather thing? Have you ever seen it before?"

"Only when you showed me the first one."

Wynona squished her lips to the side. "And you said it wasn't Dr. Rayn's."

"That model wasn't."

"How can you tell?" Wynona argued. She felt like they'd been over this before.

His scowl deepened. "I just know. It's not hers."

Wynona rubbed her forehead. "Fine. I'm going to go to the hospital and talk to Mr. Thathion. Maybe I can get something out of him." She grabbed her keys and headed to the garage. A nice long ride sounded good right about now.

Wynona was usually pretty level-headed, but right now she wanted to give Lusgu a hard shake. Why wouldn't he just tell her what he knew? What was Lusgu hiding? What was Violet hiding? What was Mr. Thathion hiding?

Wynona growled under her breath. She was doing her best to solve this murder, all while keeping an innocent doctor out of prison and putting her own life back together. Why wouldn't anyone throw her a lifeline? Lusgu was so sure that Dr. Rayn was innocent, yet he clamped up every time Wynona questioned him.

Clipping on her helmet, Wynona pushed her way out of the garage, then turned the key and took off. After a few minutes, she began to relax. The cool breeze helped calm her ire the same way it brought down the temperature of her cheeks. The twenty minute ride was exactly what Wynona needed in order to get herself under control before dealing with Mr. Meldaeon Thathion.

After parking on the street, Wynona headed up to the hospital doors and walked inside. She knew exactly where she was going, and even greeted the officers outside of the shifter's door, but she paused momentarily before going inside.

"Is everything alright, Ms. Le Doux?" Officer Heskill asked. The vampire's white brows were pulled together. Wynona had met him on previous cases and gave him a small smile.

"Fine," she assured him. "Thank you." *Except that I'm terrified of the man inside and don't want to talk to him, but I need to if I'm ever going to figure out who's trying to frame Dr. Rayn.* She turned the handle and walked inside. "Knock, knock," she said by way of greeting.

Green eyes snapped to hers, and a second lid twitched, keeping them moist. "Misss. Le Doux," the gorgon hissed in a low tone. "What a welcome sssurprise." His smile was nothing short of malicious. "And without your bodyguard. How delightful."

Wynona held back the desire to rub her skin free of the warning tingles she was getting. Being near this man was almost as bad as being near the dark grimoires. "Mr. Thathion," she said in a cool, but polite tone. "I came to ask you a few questions."

He raised a single eyebrow. "Oh? Can't quite get enough of me?"

Wynona kept her face clear. "Are you aware of the passing of Eve Guanaco?"

Mr. Thathion's cheek twitched. "Yesss."

"Do you have any idea as to why someone would want to kill her?"

He shook his head. The smug demeanor gone, it was replaced by the sharp businessman. He was almost as terrifying as the perverted flirt. "How should I know? I haven't ssspoken to Eve in several yearsss."

"You don't keep track of your old business partners?"

"Why should I?" Mr. Thathion challenged. "We parted waysss when we sold our shares. Each took their money and ran."

"But some of you never left the limelight."

Mr. Thathion shrugged again. "Doesn't mean we remained friendsss. Too many witches at the cauldron, you might sssay." He smirked. "We all had strong personalitiesss, Ms. Le Doux. Our working relationship was anything but sssmooth."

"Yet it lasted years." Wynona knew she was probably pushing his buttons, she was secretly hoping it would drive him to make a mistake. Someone would have to, or Wynona feared that she'd never make any progress at all.

His green eyes grew very narrow. "What are you really trying to asssk me?" Mr. Thathion hissed in a low tone.

Wynona straightened the front of her shirt, trying to buy time. "I'm trying to understand whether all original five are targets. Or if one of you is trying to get Dr. Rayn framed and in jail for a murder… two murders…she didn't commit."

Mr. Thathion chuckled and lay back against the pillow. "Can't figure it out, can you? You're ssstuck. You believe Rayn's innocent, absent-minded professor act, ssso you're looking for other waysss to clear the crime." One side of his mouth quirked up in a tiny smirk. "But you can't find it. None of it makes sssense without Rayn."

Wynona clenched her jaw. "You once told me that you had feelings for her."

"I did."

"Then why are you so ready to believe her capable of murder?"

Mr. Thathion huffed. "Any of us are capable of murder, Ms. Le Doux. Any creature you walk by on the ssstreet, or brush against in the grocery store. Every sssingle one of them is capable of murder, if given the right incentive."

Wynona shook her head. "You're wrong. There are some of us who would rather give our own lives than take another's."

"Murder isss murder, isn't it?" he pressed. "If it came down to killing sssomeone or allowing yourself to die, and you chose the latter, you'd ssstill be allowing a death." He shrugged. "Tomato, tomahto."

This might have been the first time in her life that Wynona could understand why someone would want to hurt another creature. Mr. Thathion would drive anyone…any criminal…to extreme measures. If someone was after his life, the murderer probably had a very good reason for his behavior.

"I'm afraid I can't subscribe to your way of thinking, Mr. Thathion," Wynona said tightly. She studied his thin, but able body and had a thought. *He's old. How is he in such good shape? Oh! And the magic!*

Daemon had mentioned that the magic was wrong. Gorgons shouldn't have magic at all and they shouldn't live to be hundreds of years old. But the only way for Wynona to see Mr. Thathion's magic was to use her sight and he would see her purple eyes.

"You know…" Wynona hedged, forcing herself to walk a little close to the bed. "I've been discovering that I had a bit of a healing gift." She blinked a few times, causing her vision to turn purple.

Mr. Thathion narrowed his eyes, interest flickering like a flame. "Just what are you suggesting, Ms. Le Doux? Are you asking if you can heal me?"

Wynona tilted her head back and forth, trying to appear innocent. Daemon had been right. Instead of a green brush of smoke, Mr. Thathion's magic appeared to ooze from his pores, like some kind of disease. It looked wrong, like it didn't belong, yet he didn't appear to be in any distress. "I have to practice sometime," Wynona said, clasping her hands in front of her. "Would you like me to give it a try? It seems to me that you've been in here a long time. Perhaps the doctors aren't up to the challenge?"

Mr. Thathion leaned back, looking slightly uneasy. "No, thank you," he said carefully. "I believe I'll keep my health in the care of the professionalsss. You'll have to experiment on sssomeone other than myself."

Wynona blinked away her magical vision. "Are you sure? It probably wouldn't hurt much for me to try. Creatures used to come from all over for my Granny Saffron to heal them."

"Your grandmother had centuries of experienssss," Mr. Thathion snapped. "I will not be your guinea pig."

Wynona sighed, feigning being put out. "How am I going to learn if no one lets me try?"

His cheek twitched again. "You're welcome to try…on sssomone elssse."

Wynona scowled to hide her relief. She had no idea what she would have done if he'd actually wanted a healing. Not that she couldn't have helped, but she had no desire to touch the snake. Getting two steps closer to him had already been difficult enough. She was slightly afraid that her magic would react badly with whatever powers he had. *Though, the only way to know would be to try…*

A battle ensued in Wynona's mind. Should she try to touch him anyway? What if her magic hurt one of them? She'd set off small explosions more than once when her magic took offense to something untoward.

She did notice that when her purple vision cleared, Mr. Thathion relaxed a little. "I mussst admit…" he said. "It would be interesssting to sse what a healing from sssomone like yourself would feel like," he continued with a smirk. "Though you're not trained, there'ssss no denying your power."

Wynona automatically stepped back. There was something distinctly proprietary about his words, as if he intended for that power to be at his disposal.

"Your father isss a lucky man," Mr. Thathion muttered under his breath.

"My father isn't involved in my life," Wynona argued.

The infuriating snake only smiled.

Sticking her chin in the air, Wynona backed up. "I think we're done here. Thank you for your time. We'll keep in touch."

Mr. Thathion put up his hand. "Now, now…don't leave in sssuch a tizzy, Msss. Le Doux." He offered his hand for a shake. "Let us depart as friendssss."

Wynon hesitated. Everything in her was screaming for her to tuck tail and run, but the very opportunity she'd been debating about had just opened up. *Just do it*, she scolded herself. *What's the worst that could happen?*

Snorting inwardly at her thoughts, she pushed stiff legs toward the bed. Grasping his cold, clammy hand as lightly as possible, she gave it two hard shakes, then stepped back and forced herself not to wipe her palm against her skirt. "Again, thank you."

Spinning on her heel, she marched out, ignoring the dark chuckle behind her and the low, "Delicioussss..."

After the door closed and she was in the hallway, Wynona closed her eyes and leaned against the back of the door, taking a moment to catch her breath.

"Ms. Le Doux?" Officer Heskill asked. "Are you alright?"

Wynona held up a finger to ask for a moment, and nodded. "I will be," she whispered. She finally stood, having gained enough control over her rioting emotions to move forward. "Bathroom?" she asked.

Officer Heskill looked worried, but pointed down the hall.

"Thank you." Wynona nodded and marched away. She was going to wash her hands until the slimy feeling of Mr. Thathion's magic was gone. Then she was going to go home and figure out why his magic felt as gross as it looked. There was definitely something wrong with it. But why? And how did he get it in the first place? It was high time Wynona found out.

CHAPTER 20

After finishing in the restroom, Wynona hopped on her Vespa and headed for the police station instead of her house. Rascal was already there and maybe she could spend some time going over what they knew, there was nothing for her back at her home. Sometimes the clues were already in front of her, but she simply needed to take the time to lay them on the table.

Traffic was heavy for the morning and Wynona was grateful for her small vehicle, which allowed her to weave in and out of areas quickly. Parking in front of the station was much nicer with such a small ride.

"Hello, Amaris," Wynona said, determined to remain kind and polite no matter how the vampire felt about her.

Instead of the tight smile Wynona had been receiving for almost a year now, Amaris looked a little less disgusted and gave a small wave. "Wynona," the vampire secretary said softly.

Wynona almost missed a step, but kept her shoulders up and smile in place. *Is she starting to forgive me?*

Don't you dare, Rascal scolded through their mental link. *You don't have anything to be forgiven for. The problem has always been her. Not you.*

Wynona agreed…logically…but it still hurt when a creature's

friends turned on them. She didn't even want all the power that was supposedly flowing through her brains. Thus far it had brought nothing but trouble, but like it or not, Rascal was right. This was who Wynona was and she couldn't help that. Amaris's decision to be frightened was her own.

"Is Rascal...Deputy Chief Strongclaw...in his office?" Wynona asked, wondering just how far she could push the conversation.

Amaris nodded and watched Wynona walk by, but didn't say anything else.

It's a start, Wynona thought as she walked down the all-too-familiar hallway. She knocked before entering Rascal's space and smiled when she spotted her fiance rising from behind his desk. "Hey, handsome," she said, greeting him with a sweet kiss.

Rascal wrapped his hands around her waist and pulled her close. "Have you figured out that date yet?" he asked.

Wynona's smile widened. She loved how eager he was to get married. What woman wouldn't want their significant other to be chomping at the bit to claim them? She reached up and tried to smooth down his wild hair, but it was to no avail. "No. I'm trying to get the shop finished and I think we ought to have this mystery out of the way first, don't you think?"

Rascal shrugged. "Who cares about the case? I'm just tired of having to be separated from you."

"You'll still have to go to work even after we're married," she reminded him with a laugh.

"Maybe so, but it means my time spent with you will last much longer," he teased back, pumping his eyebrows. "Maybe that'll make the separation less painful."

Wynona shook her head and patted his chest. "Impatient."

"In love," he corrected with a kiss on the tip of her nose. He stepped back. "So...what did you learn at the hospital? Which..." He glared at her. "I'm not happy you did without me, by the way."

Wynona's eyes widened. "How did you—?" She snapped her mouth shut and shook her head. "One of these days you need to learn to ask permission before you go invading my thoughts."

His smirk was positively wolfish. "Where's the fun in that?"

"Fun has nothing to do with it," she said primly, making herself comfortable on his couch. "It's about manners."

Rascal snorted. "Better get used to it, sweetheart. You're stuck with me."

Wynona rolled her eyes, but laughed quietly. "If you were listening in, surely you know what he said?"

Rascal glared. "I wasn't focusing that hard. I just knew where you went."

"Hmmm..."

"I could subpoena you for it."

Wynona's jaw dropped and she jumped to her feet. "Rascal Strongclaw! Are you threatening me?"

He stepped forward, his hands sliding around her waist. "Would it work?"

"Not if you ever want me to cook for you again." Rascal made a considering face and Wynona smacked his chest. "Be nice."

He laughed and kissed her forehead. "I'll back off...for now."

Wynona huffed in feigned annoyance and plopped back down on the couch. "I wanted to see his magic," she said, changing the direction of their flirtatious conversation.

Rascal stilled. "And?"

She shook her head. "It's just like what Daemon said. The magic is...off. It oozes from his pores, like some kind of liquid, rather than shifting around him like an aura of smoke."

Rascal went to his own seat and sat down hard, groaning. "But does it have to do with the case, is the question. Mr. Thathion is a powerful man. He didn't get to where he is by being gentle or easy to get along with. He's intelligent and ruthless and has obviously made some choices over the years that have been questionable." Rascal raised an eyebrow. "Like where he got magic in the first place."

Wynona nodded. "Right."

"But that still doesn't make him a killer."

"It makes him more capable of being a killer than a reclusive inventor who minds her own business."

Rascal sighed and scrubbed his hands over his face. "We've been over this, Wy. Mr. Thathion was in the hospital. Now, I'm all ears if you gave a suggestion as to how he managed to not only kill his fiancee when he was being chased by lightning, but to then kill an old colleague while he was lying wounded in bed, but until you do…I can't put him on the suspect list."

Wynona threw her head back, staring at the ceiling. There had to be a way to get around this. "We live in a magical world," she muttered. "Maybe there was something paranormal involved."

"Did you or Daemon see anything that would suggest that?"

Wynona shook her head. "No. I mean, there's magic in the weather box, but it's not the same as what Mr. Thathion has." She paused, then pulled her head up. "Can we see the box again? And did the department ever get someone to translate the dragonese?"

Rascal snorted. "Dragonese. Very nice. And no. We're still coming up empty handed."

"We could try Gendyl."

"We could," Rascal said, grabbing the phone on his desk. "But I don't know how reliable she would be. She can barely see at this point."

Wynona pinched her lips together and squished her lips to the side. If only dragons weren't quite so rare, it would make things much easier at the moment.

Rascal put down the phone. "Evidence will bring it up in a minute."

"We could have gone down and gotten it," Wynona offered, hiding a grin.

Rascal rolled his eyes. "That's all we need is an hour long conversation with Oozog."

Wynona let her smile through. "He's sweet."

"He's also so chatty you never get any work done," Rascal grumbled.

Wynona laughed and shook her head. "Since when did you get so cranky?"

"Since I had to put off my wedding to solve a murder that is putting my fiancee in danger," he snapped back.

Wynona's humor fled. "I'm sorry," she said. "I'll keep working on the wedding plans."

"No...I'm sorry." Rascal scratched behind his ear. "My frustrations are my own. Guess I need to start acting like an adult or something."

"Or something," Wynona teased.

Just as Rascal gave her a playful glare, there was a knock on the door. "Evidence," the officer said, coming through.

"Just set it here," Rascal said, indicating his desk. "Thank you."

"Anytime, Deputy Chief." The officer nodded at Wynona, then slipped quietly back out.

"Such service," Wynona said, standing and walking toward the device. She blinked a few times to bring her magic vision to the forefront. Immediately she saw those strange rainbow-like lines of magic. Pulling up a chair so she was closer to the desk, Wynona began to tilt her head and really look at every part of the box.

She raised her hand, wondering if the magic would feel the same way it looked, but Rascal cleared his throat.

"Are you sure you want to do that?" he asked.

Wynona paused to think about it. "Yes. I touched Mr. Thathion while I was in his hospital room and his magic felt thick and slimy. I need to know if this is similar."

"WHAT!" Rascal bellowed, standing up so fast he almost knocked over his chair.

Wynona dropped her chin to her chest and groaned. "That totally came out wrong."

"You bet it did," Rascal growled. His teeth were elongated and fur was starting to sprout on the back of his hands. "Now, please explain before I have to go kill a snake."

Wynona put her hands in the air. "I played it off, but I wanted to see if I could feel his magic. Mr. Thathion has always given me the creeps, but I was curious how my magic would respond to his."

"Well, you're not dead," Rascal muttered, his ire starting to fade. "And I didn't hear anything about explosions at the hospital, so I'm going to assume it went alright."

Wynona shrugged. "I suppose so. But like I said, the magic was kind of slimy. Just like how it looked. I'm curious if this is the same."

"And if it isn't?'

She shook her head. "Then, I guess I'm still at square one."

Rascal's voice dropped. "Please don't hurt yourself."

Wynona nodded solemnly. "I don't feel the same as I did with the grimoires," she assured her fiance. "Those were giving off terrible, dark vibes. This isn't the same malicious feeling."

"I hope you're right."

Wynona turned back to the box and gently put her finger against the color. She frowned. She couldn't feel it. Flattening her palm, she rubbed over the entire box, but there was nothing there. Not like there had been with Mr. Thathion. Huffing in frustration, she leaned back, folding her arms over her chest.

"You don't look happy."

"I can't feel anything." Rascal paused, waiting for more, but Wynona didn't know what else to say.

"Nothing?"

Wynona shook her head. "Nope. Nothing." She glared at the device. "It's like there's no magic at all." She leaned forward. "Wait… what if I can't feel it because it's not turned on?"

"Don't even think about it," Rascal growled.

"But…"

Rascal shook his head. "No, Wynona."

She gave him her best stink eye. "We'll never learn anything if we don't give it a try."

"In my office? In the precinct where a hundred people are working?" Rascal growled. "You're asking for trouble."

"I'll put up a shield first."

Rascal's growl grew louder. "It's too dangerous."

"I promise I'll be careful."

He threw himself back in his seat. "You're determined to kill yourself, aren't you? Do what you want," he finally ground out. "But don't expect me to like it."

Wynona stood and walked over, sitting on his lap and wrapping her arms around his neck. "I've got too much to live for," she murmured into his uniform collar. "I don't have a death wish, but I do have a driving need to solve this case."

He was slow about his response, but finally Rascal's arms came around her back and he squeezed her until she could barely breathe. "I don't like you doing dangerous things on purpose."

Wynona tilted her head back so she could look him in the eye. "I know, but there's no other way to figure this out. My magic can see things others can't. As far as I know, Daemon can't feel magic like I just did with Mr. Thathion. I have to use my gifts. If I don't…then they'll continue to control me."

Rascal's shoulders dropped. "I still don't like it."

"I know, but I'm grateful you understand."

He snorted but dropped his hold on her. "Put up your shield. I suppose if you're going to risk your life, I'll have to come along."

Wynona stiffened, but forced herself to relax. He wasn't asking anything unfair and it wouldn't be right of her to demand different rules for the two of them. If anything, having Rascal inside the shield would make her more cautious, which probably wasn't a bad thing.

She wiggled her fingers and brought up a purple bubble, careful to make it as thick as she possibly could. Then, her trembling knees took her to the front of the desk, where she rested equally trembling fingers against the device. Keeping the jolt as small as possible, Wynona sent a little bit of magic into the device.

At first, she didn't think anything had happened, but she waited, listening intently for the sounds of life. Slowly, she increased the flow, hoping to kickstart whatever engine or motor was running inside.

A whirring sound began to hum and Wynona's eyes widened.

"Steady," Rascal said, stepping up behind her.

Her body relaxed slightly at his proximity, but Wynona kept her eyes glued to the box. The colors had begun to intensify and were spilling out of the device at an increasingly alarming speed.

"Rascal…" she hedged.

"Yeah?"

"DUCK!" Wynona screamed, throwing herself back to try and

knock Rascal to the ground just as a bolt of lightning and a splash of rain exploded within the bubble.

Breathing heavily, Wynona picked up her head after noise stopped ringing in her ears.

"Are you okay?" Rascal asked, panting.

Wynona nodded and sat up, pushing her hair out of her face.

"Whoa." Rascal touched the purple wall that was encasing them. "I didn't know you could do a bubble within a bubble."

"Neither did I," Wynona said hoarsely. Clearing her throat, she dropped the smaller shield she'd used to keep them safe, examined the burn stain on the inside of the large bubble, then dropped that too. "That thing has a real kick," she whispered.

"Is it off?" Rascal asked warily.

Wynona nodded. "Yeah. It's back to what it was. It simply spit out the magic I pushed in."

"So, is that how it works? Someone puts in magic and it spits it out in the form of weather?"

Wynona shook her head. "No. I think it was simply reacting to my pushing magic at it." She rubbed her fingers together.

"So we didn't learn anything," Rascal huffed. He shoved his hands through his hair. "At least your shield held, right?"

"Actually…" Wynona continued to study her fingers. "I think I might have learned something important."

Rascal raised his eyebrows.

Wynona looked up. "That rainbow of magic? It's just as slimy as Mr. Thathion's green stuff. It's not real magic."

CHAPTER 21

"What do you mean, it's not real magic?" Rascal asked, his thick brows furrowed. "Magic is magic...isn't it?"

Wynona wiped her hands on her skirt. She didn't like the residual sensation. "I thought so, but now I'm not so sure."

"Wy..." he warned.

Wynona took in a long breath. "I'm learning here too, Rascal. Please be patient with me."

He pushed both hands through his hair again. "Sorry. Sorry... you're right. I need to calm down, but I'm still confused."

Wynona walked back to the couch. She didn't want to be next to the weather thing anymore. Sitting down, she groaned slightly. Apparently, throwing herself on the ground wasn't exactly the type of exercise her muscles enjoyed. "I'm not quite sure how to explain it," she began. "Because I've never encountered it before."

Rascal leaned against his desk, arms folded over his broad chest, and tilted his head. "Give it your best shot."

Wynona's mind churned as she tried to think of the right thing to say. "I've never actually tried to *feel* someone's magic before today," she explained slowly, buying herself a little time. "But like Daemon and I described, this magic appears to flow like a thick liquid, rather than something airy and smoke-like." Wynona couldn't suppress the shudder that ran down her spine. "When I tried to see if it was tangible, it felt just like it looked." She stared at the box. "When I pressed my magic into it, trying to turn it on, it took a moment to react, but then the colors began to bleed out of it, just like the green magic does in Mr. Thathion. When I heard the whirling inside, I could feel a pressure building behind the edges and the magic grew brighter until I knew it was going to explode." She rubbed her hands on her upper arms. "But the lightning strike was from my own magic," she said confidently. "I could feel its familiarity. The magical rainbow oozing from the box, however, *was not*."

"So Thathion and the box are related," Rascal declared.

Wynona shrugged. "They at least came from similar places. Mr. Thathion had to have gotten his magic somewhere, since we know it's not natural. And that…" She waved at the box. "Is a creature-made weather device. Technically, it's not natural either, so it probably shouldn't surprise me that the magic is similar."

"Can you tell where it came from?" Rascal asked, sounding tired and defeated.

Wynona gave him a sympathetic look. "No. Not that I know of. I'd know it again if I felt it, but I have no idea where something like this would have originated."

Rascal's phone rang before they could say anything more and he twisted to grab it from its cradle. "Strongclaw." His eyebrows shot up. "Yes, sir. We're on our way." The phone landed with a *crack*. "We got a tip," he said, only glancing at Wynona for a moment.

"I'm not going to like it, am I?" she asked, her stomach turning sour at his expression.

Rascal shook his head, stuffed his cell phone in his back pocket and walked over, holding out his hand. "Come on."

"Please tell me," Wynona said softly as he walked out of the office.

There's a safety deposit box at Shade Banking and Loan that holds the plans to the weather device.

Wynona pulled him to a stop in the middle of the hallway. "Whose is it?" she croaked.

Rascal looked like he was sucking on something sour. It was evident in every line on his face that he didn't want to tell her. "It's just a tip. Let's go check it out. It might not be true."

"Rascal," she warned.

He sighed and closed his eyes. *Dr. Rayn.*

Wynona felt like the air had been pulled from her lungs and she followed Rascal in a blind haze. She couldn't have told anyone what they passed on their way to the bank or how long the ride took. How had this happened? How could yet another piece of evidence show up against the scatter-brained inventor? It was as if every clue was very neatly being put in their path to guide the police exactly where the criminal wanted them.

"Come on, Wy," Rascal said gently, lifting her down from the truck. "Let's make sure it's legitimate before we jump to conclusions, alright?"

Wynona nodded and followed Rascal up to the front. There were no doors at the bank, making it impossible to rob. It was run by shades and a creature had to be accompanied by one in order to be pulled through the walls of the great stone monument.

"Deputy Chief Strongclaw," Rascal said in his office tone, as they approached the guards out front. "I believe Chief Ligurio called ahead and told you what we need?"

The troll nodded sagely. "Yes, sir, Deputy Chief. We have two shades waiting for you and Ms. Le Doux on the backside of the building. They'll take you directly to the vault." He began to walk. "If you'll follow me, please."

Wynona didn't say a word as they walked, but she clung to Rascal's hand, striving to stay grounded in reality. *The tip was anonymous, wasn't it?*

Rascal glanced sideways at her. *Yes.*

"Figures," she muttered.

Rascal gave her a warning look, then they stopped. He watched the security guard who had led them.

"Deputy Chief," the troll said gruffly. "This is Ethae." Black eyes glanced at Wynona. "And Ms. Le Doux, this is Shaydo."

Wynona nodded at the barely there spirit. "Hello," she said, trying not to sound as frustrated as she was.

"You'll take us directly to the vault?" Rascal clarified.

There was an odd buzzing sound, then a voice became clear. "Yes, Deputy Chief. The security boxes are in there."

"Thank you." Rascal stiffened slightly, but a moment later he was gone.

Wynona didn't have time to blink before a coldness washed over her and she found herself floating. The sensation lasted about ten seconds before she stumbled to her feet inside a dark, cold room.

"Apologies, Ms. Le Doux," the shade murmured, the sound barely audible.

Wynona nodded as she straightened her skirt. "It's fine. Thank you," she said. She swallowed hard when she realized they were far from alone in the space.

"Deputy Chief Strongclaw," one of the shades said, floating forward. This one was much easier to see, though like all shades, the figure was of undetermined shape. "I'm Guya Remane, the President of Shade Banking and Loan."

Rascal nodded. There was no point in shaking hands since shades weren't corporeal enough for that. "Thank you for allowing us to come so quickly. We appreciate your discretion in the matter."

"As do we," Mr. Remane replied. "We wouldn't want to cause a frenzy if people believed there was a chance a crime happened here."

"Is there a chance?" Wynona asked, hoping desperately the answer was yes.

"I'm afraid not," Mr. Remane replied, though his tone didn't sound very sorry. "No corporeal being could have gotten inside without our consent and knowledge. Dr. Rayn's box has been here for many years and is rarely touched."

"When was she last here?" Rascal asked.

There was a slight pause. "I believe it was two years ago," the shade stated. "But I will double check to be sure my information is correct."

"We appreciate it." Rascal waved at the wall of drawers. "If you please?"

The three shades plus Wynona and Rascal walked over until one of the spirits floated high, toward the ceiling.

Wynona nearly lost track of him before she noticed a drawer open and a box slide out. *So they knew Dr. Rayn was still around,* she sent to Rascal.

It appears so. I wonder why she needed to have a safety deposit box? And why would she risk coming into town in order to put things in it?

Her hoard?

Rascal subtly shook his head, his eyes glued to the shade slowly coming back to the ground with the box in its indistinct hands. *Unless Lusgu was wrong, he said Dr. Rayn's family wasn't around here and her hoard was where her family was from.*

Wynona sighed.

"If you will?" Mr. Remane said softly, leading Rascal and Wynona to a table.

The shade who brought down the box set it on the table in front of the president, then handed the president a key.

Wynona watched as the key went into the lock and turned, causing a clicking sound. She blinked, bringing her magic vision to the forefront, and noticed a gray magic floating around. She also realized that she had the ability to see the shades much more clearly this way. *Oh my word...you won't believe what type of paranormal the president is.*

I want a full report, Rascal sent back. *But right now let's take care of the box's contents.*

Wynona nodded, but left her magic in place. She wanted to be able to see if anything inside the box contained magic. When the lid lifted with a puff of air, Wynona almost sneezed at the dust it disturbed. The president was right. It had been a long time since someone had opened this box.

She rose up on tiptoe, peering inside as Rascal reached inside. His hand brought out several manila folders and Wynona's eyes widened. "That one," she whispered shakily as she watched small amounts of rainbow magic dance around the envelope.

Rascal gave her a questioning look, but obediently opened the top and pulled out the papers inside.

Wynona's heart was in her throat. She knew exactly what Rascal had found before he ever said a word.

"It's the plans for the device," Rascal muttered. He looked to the president. "This room is officially closed off for police business until further notice. Please have your creatures remove themselves without touching anything so we can gather any other evidence that may have been left behind."

The president grumbled, but obeyed, taking his entire staff with him. Soon Rascal and Wynona were the only two left in the cavernous space.

"Chief?" Rascal said into his phone. His eyes met Wynona's and he looked torn, but resolute. "Put Skymaw in charge of a team to go to the Grove of Secrets." Rascal's golden eyes went to the documents and back up to Wynona.

Her hand went to her stomach where she tried to keep breakfast where it belonged.

"Arrest Dr. Zullorayn Brownhide for murder and attempted murder in the case of Eve Guanaco, Arave Smouldons, and Meldeaon Thathion." He paused. "Yes, sir. We have everything we need."

Rascal didn't speak as he shut down his phone and put it in his back pocket.

"She's being set up," Wynona whispered thickly, trying to keep the tears at bay.

Rascal closed his eyes. "The evidence says otherwise, Wy. And I can't present a case in court based on your gut feelings, no matter how much I want to believe you."

Wynona clenched her jaw and stepped forward, getting nose to nose with her fiance. "I don't know how and I don't know why, but someone has been planning this coup on Dr. Rayn for a very long time." Her chest was heaving as she tried to control herself, but there was nothing for it. "And I will prove it."

Rascal's face was tired and resigned. "I hope you do," he said softly. "I don't like this any more than you do, no matter how frustrated I am with Lusgu at the moment. But it's my job to follow the evidence."

"So you're saying I'm on my own?"

Rascal shook his head. "No. I'm saying I have to follow this through. If you happen to go a different way for the next little bit, you aren't obligated the same way I am."

Wynona stepped back. This was huge. Rascal hated putting her in danger and giving her permission to dig around while he did his job was akin to throwing her into the griffin's den.

"Please be careful," he begged.

Wynona nodded. "I will," she promised.

Rascal's eyes darted to the front of the cavern. "You better go now. When Chief gets here, he'll want you to stick to what we have."

Wynona felt her bottom lip tremble, but nodded again, then turned and marched to the door. "President Remane?" she asked.

"Yes, Ms. Le Doux?"

"I need to be taken back outside, please."

"Of course."

Twenty seconds later, Wynona blinked at the sunlight hitting her face and she quickly made a beeline for the street. Time was ticking and there was no time to waste. Dr. Rayn would be arrested within the hour and Wynona was determined that the dragon would spend as little time behind bars as absolutely possible.

She also put up a conscious wall between her and Rascal's line of communication. It was better that he didn't know where she was headed, though she would keep her promise to be careful.

But with Daemon headed out to get the inventor, Wynona knew that *now* would be her only opportunity to take a good deep look through Dr. Rayn's office without anyone watching. And if she used a bit of her magic to figure out what was going on, or what *wasn't* going on…then there'd be no one to stop her.

CHAPTER 22

Wynona ported herself home, taking the chance to practice her ability. She planned to use it to get into Dr. Rayn's lab, but wanted to grab a couple of things first.

Once inside, she headed to her room and changed her clothes. She needed something a little more breathable than a pair of slacks and a blouse. She also took the opportunity to pull back her hair.

Wynona rarely kept her hair restrained. It was one of her features she enjoyed the most and tried to use it to her advantage, especially since her mother often had a slick hairstyle every time she went out in public.

By allowing her waves and light curls free rein, it was just another way for Wynona to celebrate her freedom. But today, if she was going to be sneaking around…she needed it contained.

Glancing in the mirror, she nodded. "Okay. Here we go."

She went outside, not wanting anything to distract her from what she was about to do. Porting home or to a park she had been to a dozen times was one thing, but this time, Wynona was a little more unsure. She'd only been in the lab for a moment and Dr. Rayn's house was in the middle of the most magical…and deadly…piece of land in the entirety of the paranormal world.

Wynona sent a quick thought to the fates that they would protect her, then closed her eyes and tried to imagine the lab. She imagined the pieces of machinery, the microscopes, the wall full of small bits of metal and pieces for building. Another wall had tools, which had been neatly put away, but seemed to have no rhyme or reason to where they had been put away.

"Dr. Rayn's lab," Wynona muttered. "Dr. Rayn's lab." Over and over again she chanted the words, then finally, when she felt she was sufficiently focused, allowed her magic to come out.

It poured down her limbs and through her body as if it had been held back too long, though the thought was ridiculous. It had been used more in the last few days than it normally was in weeks.

But despite that fact, her magic was hungry and eager and Wynona felt herself struggling to keep it under control. She needed quite a bit of power to port, but too much could leave behind devastating circumstances, like taking out Wynona's house when her power sent her through the ether.

She felt herself begin to feel weightless, a sure sign that the port was working, and then Wynona gave one final push of power, keeping her focus on Dr. Rayn.

She hated the sensation that seemed to accompany the travel. It always felt like her head was being squeezed in a vise and her skin was too tight, but each time Wynona traveled, she found the pain was shorter and shorter.

She landed with a thud and spread her arms for balance, only to whack something before her eyes cleared enough for her to see.

"What the—" a deep voice shouted.

Ah crud. Wynona held her eyes closed a little longer than she should have. She had no idea where she had landed, but from the voice and the distant sounds of shouting and scuffling, it wasn't in Rayn's lab.

She cracked an eye, only to gasp and have them both open wide as saucers. "Daemon!"

The black hole was standing with his hands on his hips, giving her an evil glare. "Hello," he said conversationally, though the thread of steel in his tone told her his real feelings. "And just what are you doing here?"

Wynona looked around to get her bearings. Well...she'd gotten close. Instead of landing in Dr. Rayn's lab, Wynona had managed the front of the house. But she'd been a little too early in her arrival. The police were still in the process of arresting Dr. Rayn and the entire squad of officers were staring at her as if she'd grown a third head.

"Um..."

"Wynona!" Dr. Rayn cried, rushing to her side. Smoke was trailing out the dragon's nostrils and her eyes were fiery red. "Tell these men that I'm innocent. They're trying to arrest me!"

Wynona could see the tightness in Dr. Rayn's jaw and instantly grew afraid for the officers. If Dr. Rayn freaked out, she could hurt some creatures or possibly get herself hurt as the police tried to restrain her.

"Dr. Brownhide," Daemon said in a calm tone. "We aren't looking for trouble, but some evidence has come to light and we've been asked to bring you in."

Dr. Rayn stomped toward the officers, the smoke becoming more pronounced. "I don't care," she growled.

Wynona spotted a lick of fire dancing among the doctor's fingers. She had to do something...and now. "Dr. Rayn," Wynona said in a soothing tone, coming up behind the woman. "Please listen."

"I'll listen," Dr. Rayn snapped, her teeth growing longer. "As soon as these men get off my property. I'm not under their jurisdiction. They have no power here."

Daemon held up his hands. "I understand that. Which is why we aren't taking you by force." He raised his eyebrows. "I'm asking you to come with us."

Dr. Rayn snorted. "No."

Daemon shook his head. "Two creatures are dead," he said. "Evidence is mounting in your direction. Wouldn't you rather clear your name than remain a fugitive the rest of your life?"

Dr. Rayn folded her arms over her chest, the fire still dancing along her skin. "I'm already a fugitive," she declared easily. "Or haven't you read up on my history?"

"Rayn," a soft voice said from behind Wynona.

She spun and sighed in relief at the sight of Quinin.

"Not happening, Quin," Rayn said without looking back.

Quinin had guts, Wynona had to give her that, because the shifter walked up and put her hand on Dr. Rayn's arm. "Please, calm down. These officers are only doing their job."

Dr. Rayn snorted once more, but there was less vitriol behind it. "I understand that, but they've got their eye on the wrong creature."

Daemon nodded. "Then come show us. Because everything we have says it's you."

"Then look again!" Dr. Rayn shouted.

"Rayn." Wynona stepped up to the dragon's other side. "Please." She waved at the men. "These are my friends." Taking a cue from Quinin, Wynona put her hand on Rayn's other arm. "And you're my friend. I don't want to see anyone hurt. But Officer Skymaw is right. We need you to explain away the evidence." She waited until Dr. Rayn looked at her. "I'm on your side," Wynona said softly, trying to make her words for the dragon only, though with so many paranormals, it was a difficult task. "I'm working to find evidence of your innocence, but I need help. I don't like the idea of you being arrested, but if you would go willingly, you can work on proving your innocence along with me."

Rayn's shoulders drooped. "You really think I should go in?"

Wynona hung her head. "I don't *want* you to go in, but I don't think a fight is a good idea." She squeezed lightly on the doctor's arm. "I won't give up until you're freed."

Rayn studied Wynona, her red eyes penetrating clear to what felt like Wynona's soul. Finally, after what seemed an eternity, the doctor nodded. "I'll go in," she declared. Her eyes never left Wynona's. "But I'm counting on you. Saffron said we wouldn't regret it. I'm holding you to it."

Questions enough to talk the entire day away became blocked in Wynona's throat. If for no other reason than to figure out more about herself, Wynona needed this woman free from jail. *Though, I should probably consider the fact that she's innocent the most important reason.*

Rayn surprised Wynona by reaching over and giving her a hug. "Follow the magic," she whispered before pulling back and turning to Daemon. "No hag thread. I'll come along without a fuss."

Daemon hesitated, but ultimately nodded. He really didn't have much of a choice since their jurisdiction ended at the forest line. "Thank you, Dr. Brownhide. We appreciate your cooperation."

"Thank Wynona," Dr. Rayn declared. "I'm doing this for her."

Now the questions were choking Wynona. Why was this about her? What did Dr. Rayn know? And how was she supposed to follow the magic? The entire city of Hex Haven was magic. What magic was the dragon talking about? The rainbow? Or the green slimy stuff Mr. Thathion had?

"Wynona?"

Wynona's head snapped to her left. She'd been watching Dr. Rayn walk with her head high straight down the road that led out of the grove and had completely forgotten about the dragon's assistant. "Quinin," Wynona breathed. "Thank you so much for your help." She stopped talking when she saw the tears in the owl's eyes. "What is it?"

Quinin sniffled and wiped at her nose with her sleeve. "I found out some information I think you should know," she whispered, her eyes darting to the officers several times.

"Would you like to go to the precinct?" Wynona asked. "You can stay close to the doctor and you can tell me all about it."

Quinin chewed her bottom lip. "I'm afraid to tell them," she said, tilting her head toward the visitors.

Dread began to simmer in Wynona's stomach. *What now?* "Why?"

The tears grew heavy enough to trickle down the owl's cheeks. "Because it won't look good," Quinin said, then quickly pushed on. "I'm not sure it really means anything, but after our...last conversation, I felt like it might be significant."

"About Dr. Rayn?"

Quinin nodded jerkily.

Wynona sighed. At this rate, her ability to refute all the evidence aimed at the doctor would be impossible. "If you think I need to hear it, then you can talk to me, but I'll have to tell the police if it proves to be relevant."

Quinin closed her eyes, sorrow written in every line of her face. "I know."

Wynona wrapped an arm around the young woman and began to follow the officers. "Let's get it over with. Then you can rest."

It took them nearly an hour to get to the station and Wynona was already exhausted, but she forced herself to hold it together. There were more important things than sleep.

Rascal raised his eyebrows at Wynona when she walked into the precinct, but Wynona just gave him a small shake of her head and he moved on. She was sure they would talk about it later.

"I need one of the interrogation rooms," she said to him when Dr. Rayn had been taken away.

Rascal glanced at Quinin and gave her a quick nod of acknowledgement. "Number three is open."

"Thank you."

Do you need me to join you?

She specifically asked to speak to me, Wynona sent back. *But I'll keep my mind open.*

Rascal nodded again.

"This way," Wynona said to Quinin, then waited for the shifter to catch up. The owl looked terrified, as if something were going to jump out and eat her for daring to come to the station. It made Wynona all the more wary about whatever information Dr. Rayn's assistant had to share. "Please have a seat."

Quinin sat down on the edge of the chair, her leg bouncing like she was struggling to sit still.

"Tissue?" Wynona held out a box toward the owl, who took several.

"Thank you," Quinin whispered, dabbing at her eyes and blowing her nose.

Rather than sitting across the table, Wynona sat down in the closest chair to the shifter. "What did you want to tell me?" she asked softly.

Quinin opened and shut her mouth several times before finally managing to speak. "You were right," she blurted out in a rush of words. "Rayn's in trouble."

Wynona frowned. Of course the dragon was in trouble. She was being accused of murder.

"Financial trouble."

Wynona jerked back. "What?"

"After our last chat, I did a little digging." Quinin's eyes filled again and her voice dropped to barely above a whisper. "I looked through her books and paid more attention to the bills and credit receipts that came through." Quinin opened her mouth, but her face crumpled and she broke into a sob.

Unable to help herself, Wynona reached over and began rubbing the young woman's back, ignoring the sensation of the owl's damp T-shirt. The walk through the forest had left all of them a little sweaty. "Easy," she soothed. "Just take a minute to breathe." It was difficult to wait for Quinin to get a hold of herself, but Wynona forced her own impatience back. This had to be very difficult for the inventor's assistant. It was akin to finding out her entire life had been a lie.

"Thank you," Quinin murmured, blowing her nose again. "I...I just had always assumed that the credits were taken care of because the groceries were always there. I mean, we have power, we have running water." She sniffed again. "So I never thought about whether we had enough."

"But you said that Dr. Rayn didn't always pay you," Wynona pressed. She still didn't believe Rayn was guilty of murder, but if there was some kind of financial angle, it might be a clue as to why Rayn was being targeted.

Quinin shrugged. "She's absent-minded. Gets caught up in her inventions. But I never went without. I eat and sleep at her house. The only thing my bank account gets used for is clothes and maybe a night out once in a while."

Wynona nodded. "So how did you discover there was a problem?"

Quinin pressed her lips together, then leaned in. "I found a stack of bills," she whispered, as if afraid their conversation would be overhead. "They were all, and I mean *all*, overdue. Every single one of them."

"Could Dr. Rayn have simply forgotten to pay them?"

Quinin shook her head. "No. She could have easily passed them onto me. I often write checks for her. But this time, she had held onto them. The stack was large, maybe a dozen or more. They were all dated within the last few months. No…" Quinin's shoulders drooped. "She was keeping this from me."

Wynona felt like the little bit of hope she had been holding onto was slowly slipping from her. What was she supposed to do with this? Could Prim's rumor be true? She'd need to find out if her friend had managed to figure out where the rumor was coming from. Maybe finding its origin would help ascertain its truthfulness.

Wynona patted Quinin's arm. "Thank you for telling me."

"Please don't let her know I told you," Quinin said, panic suddenly in her eyes. "Dr. Rayn can be such a private person and if she knew I was spilling her personal life for all and sundry, she'd fire me for sure."

Wynona bit back a sarcastic response that if they couldn't clear the doctor's name, Quinin would be out of a job anyway, but Wynona knew it wouldn't be helpful. "It's fine for this to be an anonymous tip. Thank you." She stood. "Unless you have something else you'd like to share, I'll walk you out."

"That would be nice, thank you." Quinin stood and took a couple of steps. "We won't pass her, will we?"

Wynona shook her head. "No. They'll have her in a different area of the precinct." *Probably getting a mugshot,* Wynona thought sadly. She needed to get a move on this. Her efforts to sneak through the lab had been interrupted, but Wynona still felt like it would be a good thing to do.

But how? Quinin was probably going to go back and that meant the castle wouldn't be empty and would be all the more difficult for Wynona to manage. Plus, Rayn had known Wynona and Rascal were coming the first time. They probably had spells on the property to announce visitors.

"So…are you going back to the grove?" Wynona asked casually while they walked down the hall.

Quinin shrugged. "Where else do I have to go?"

"Do you feel safe being out there by yourself? Do you have a good alarm system or anything?" *Ha! I'm getting better at this!* She heard Rascal chuckle in the back of her mind and Wynona smiled, but quickly schooled it when she remembered Quinin was beside her.

"Sort of," Quinin offered by way of response, which wasn't nearly as clear as Wynona would have hoped. "I'll be safe enough, but…" Her bottom lip began to tremble again. "I don't know that I want to be there by myself. Everything will remind me of *her*."

Wynona nodded and rubbed Quinin's back. "Do you have family or friends you can stay with in town? It might be good to take a break for a few days."

Quinin paused at the door. "That might be a good idea. I have a friend who would probably let me crash on their couch for a few nights." She grinned. "Although, I suppose I would always sleep in a tree, as well. The summer is the best time to do it." She shivered. "I hate sleeping outside in the winter."

"Totally understandable," Wynona agreed. "How about you take that little break and I'll contact you soon to check up on you?"

Quinin gave Wynona a grateful smile. "You're so much nicer than the rest of your family. Thank you."

Wynona kept her smile in place. "I hear that a lot," she said. "And thank you." She pushed open the door and waited while Quinin walked through. "Take care and we'll chat soon."

Quinin waved, then headed to the street and flagged down a taxi.

Wynona watched through the glass door, contemplating the situation. She would give it a bit, but she needed to try again to get into that lab. And she had a feeling that if she didn't succeed and find something soon…it would be too late.

CHAPTER 23

Wynona was about to leave the office when Rascal interrupted her movements.

Did you want to see Dr. Rayn?

Wynona hesitated, then spun on her heel, nodded at Amaris and walked back to the interrogation rooms again. *Are you still interrogating her?*

Sort of. But I don't think Chief will mind if you come in. It sounded like you were done with Quinin.

I am.

Anything we should know?

Yes. But I'll have to share them when you're not with the doctor, she replied. *I think...* After a moment's thought, Wynona wondered if it would be wise to bring up the finances with Dr. Rayn. Maybe she could clear up some of the issues. *Or maybe not. Quinin told me some things about Dr. Rayn's financial situation that might be personal but could also be a motive.*

Rascal sighed through their connection. *Thanks for admitting that. I'm sure that was hard for you.*

Wynona nodded even though Rascal couldn't see her. It *was* hard to admit, but she wanted to get to the truth and that might require digging through some junk that Wynona didn't want to admit existed. *How is she doing?*

Still agitated. I'm actually a little concerned about bringing you in, but Dr. Rayn likes you, so maybe it would be helpful.

Wynona's mind came to a screeching halt. *Give me ten minutes. I have someone else I think might be an even bigger help.* She heard Rascal groan.

Are you sure that's wise? I don't know how I'm going to get this past Chief.

Tell him that it will help her cooperate. At least I think it will.

Right, he said. *I'll see what I can do. You go get him.*

"On it," Wynona muttered out loud before catching herself.

Rascal chuckled. *I heard you. See you in a few.*

Wynona turned once again and went back to the front. She gave the now confused Amaris a quick wave, then headed outside. The quickest way was to port and Wynona didn't need a bunch of witnesses to her work. She'd already landed herself in hot water a few times in the last few days.

Walking around the side of the building, she closed her eyes and tried to make the process a little quicker than before. A short, hard burst of magic had her stumbling and catching her breath, but it was her own dining room table that kept her from falling, so she was grateful that it had at least worked, even if it had taken a harsh toll.

Once again, she pulled on a mental connection. *Violet?*

It took a moment, but finally the mouse responded. *Yeah?*

I need you to bring Lusgu out here. It's important, Wynona added.

Okay...hang on a sec.

Wynona wrapped her arms around her chest and tapped her fingers against her upper arm. It was only a minute until Lusgu and Violet came through the portal, but it felt like an eternity, since Wynona's sense of urgency was eating at her.

"You called?" Lusgu said wryly.

"Dr. Rayn's been arrested," Wynona blurted out, feeling like she didn't have time to ease him into it. She hesitated, however, when his muscles tensed. "Plans for the weather device were found in a safety deposit box in her name in Shade Banking and Loan. Chief Ligurio thought that was enough to pull her in and arrest her for the murders."

Lusgu spat on the floor, but it dissipated quickly. Even in his anger, he couldn't let a mess sit unattended.

It almost made Wynona smile…almost. "I'd like to take you to see her," she said more softly, trying to gauge his reaction. "I think you can help her cooperate and together we can get an alibi that will free her."

"Why doesn't she already have an alibi?"

Wynona gave him a sad smile. "She's about as forthcoming about her movements as you are."

"Stubborn woman," he muttered. His eyes dropped to the floor and were distant for a few moments.

Wynona had seen the look before, but she was confused at seeing it on Lusgu. She and Rascal both got that look when they were talking to each other, but who in the world could Lusgu be talking to? He didn't have that ability as far as Wynona knew.

Not like I know a lot though.

His mouth pinched and he squeezed his eyes shut, shaking his head in what appeared to be disgust. "Okay. Take me to her."

Wynona blew out a breath she hadn't realized she was holding. "Great." She held out her hand. "We're porting."

Lusgu grumbled again under her breath, but Wynona didn't even try to figure out what he was saying. There was no way it was complimentary.

Hang on, Violet said. She scrambled from Lusgu's shoulder down to the floor and then up Wynona's side. Once she was settled on Wynona's shoulder, the tiny mouse sighed and curled her tail around Wynona's neck.

A sense of rightness filled Wynona to the point that she closed her eyes to enjoy the feeling. It had been too long since her familiar had been where she belonged.

Soon, Violet reassured her. *This will be over soon and then I can come back.*

I'll be ready for it, Wynona responded. She missed Violet, yes, but she was grateful that Lusgu wasn't alone.

Closing her eyes, Wynona concentrated and tried to take them back in a slightly easier manner than she had arrived. The squeezing and popping sensation wasn't any better, but at least this time Wynona's knees didn't buckle like they normally did. *Progress.*

Violet snorted.

Lusgu ripped his hand away from Wynona's and scrubbed his long fingers over his face. "You need lessons."

"I'd love some," Wynona replied, trying not to feel the sting of his words. "But I've been a bit busy."

To his credit, Lusgu took the scolding to heart and gave her a grateful look. "You name the day," he said in his gruff voice.

Wynona smiled. "Let's go save a dragon. Then we'll start scheduling class."

Lusgu nodded, straightened his small body to as tall as it would go and together they went inside.

Amaris's eyes nearly bugged out of her head and her mouth gaped, but she didn't say a word as Wynona and Lusgu walked by.

Not feeling like she wanted to explain anything, Wynona simply nodded and took Lusgu straight back.

They reached the interrogation room quickly and Wynona glanced down at Lusgu, noting that he was standing stiffly, but there was sweat beading at his forehead. The brownie was nervous. That was absolutely a first.

Like a Band-Aid, Violet suggested.

Wynona nodded in return, knocked and took them inside. The first thing she saw was Chief Ligurio scowling deeply enough to give himself permanent wrinkles. If vampires could have wrinkles anyway.

She studiously ignored the chief and put her focus on Dr. Rayn, then Lusgu, then back again. Dr. Rayn looked completely shell shocked and Lusgu had such a look of hope on his face that it nearly broke Wynona's heart.

"Lusgu..." Dr. Rayn breathed.

There was no second guessing the sound of longing. A creature would have had to be deaf, dumb, and blind to not see what was going on between the two.

A brownie and a dragon. Who'd have thought? Rascal said in awe.

Wynona gave him a look. It was true. The pairing was odd, but who were they to make that decision for them? The real question was, what had torn them apart? Why hadn't Lusgu followed Rayn when she'd gone to live in the grove? It was clear they still had feelings for each other.

Lusgu opened his mouth a couple of times, but nothing came out and he finally cleared his throat. "Tell them what they need to know," he croaked. "Tell it to them and get yourself out of here."

Dr. Rayn's shoulders dropped. "Oh, Lu…"

Rascal choked on a laugh. Nobody called Lusgu "Lu" except for him. Now it was a term of endearment. No wonder it had made Lusgu so mad when Rascal used it.

Lusgu didn't even bother glaring at the shifter. "You can't do anything from the inside of a jail cell," he argued.

Rayn nodded slowly. "I know. But we promised."

"This has nothing to do with that promise."

Dr. Rayn's eyes shot to Wynona, then back to Lusgu. By the shifting of everyone's weight, nobody missed the exchange. "It's not that simple," Rayn murmured.

"It's not that hard either."

Rayn sighed and looked away.

"Chief…" Wynona said softly. "Do we all need to be in here?"

The chief's shrewd look said he knew exactly what she was trying to do, but he didn't argue with her…thank goodness. "I suppose two less bodies would be fine." He gave Rascal a look, but the shifter balked.

"You can't be serious." Rascal turned to Wynona. "Do you really think I need to go?"

Wynona turned to Lusgu, leaving the question to him.

Lusgu rubbed his forehead. "If you don't mind, Hugo. You'll know what happens anyway."

Rascal growled low, but Wynona wasn't sure if it was because

Lusgu used his real name, or because of the request. "Don't call me that, and I don't trust you with her," he ground out.

Lusgu nodded, looking utterly defeated. "And I deserve that. But I give you my word she's safe." His black eyes met Rascal's. "Never again will I harm her in any way, shape, or form, unintentional or not. This I promise you."

A tremor went through the room, unmistakable, yet something Wynona had never experienced before.

"Lusgu!" Rayn gasped. "Was that necessary?"

Lusgu didn't look away from Rascal as he nodded. "It was."

"What did you do?" she asked, sounding slightly afraid of the answer.

Lusgu didn't respond, but held eye contact until Rascal nodded.

When the shifter stood, Chief Ligurio followed and gave Wynona a look. "We'll talk later?" the vampire said. It wasn't really a question.

Wynona murmured her agreement.

The room held its breath until the two men were gone, but as soon as the door closed, Lusgu bolted to Rayn's side. He cupped her cheeks tenderly, his eyes tracing her face lines. "How are you?" he croaked.

Rayn wasn't even trying to stop the tears streaming down her face. "Surviving," she said with a sad smile. She brushed her fingertips across his cheek. "Better than you, I think."

Wynona felt like a voyeur, intruding on a private moment, but she also couldn't get herself to look away. Yes...these two loved each other, but there was still something Wynona was missing. She could feel it. There was more to this than the obvious and Wynona had a sneaking suspicion it revolved around her, but she couldn't figure out why.

Saffron, Violet offered. *You'll learn in time.*

Wynona huffed. She hated all this, but there were other priorities at the moment. "So...Rayn, Lusgu, I hate to interrupt, but I really need us to talk about your alibi." Wynona pulled up a chair. "I need something more concrete than you were at home during the murders," she pressed.

Rayn sighed. "I don't know what to offer you. I *was* home."

"And where was Quinin?"

Rayn shrugged. "I don't know. She has her own wing of the house. I don't run her life unless we're in the lab together. Any spare time is hers to do with what she will. I know she has a few friends she spends time with. She could have been in her rooms or in town. I have no way of knowing."

Wynona squished her lips to the side. "And the papers?"

Rayn gave a disgusted huff. "They're mine," she admitted. "But I didn't take out that safety deposit box."

Wynona stiffened. "You didn't?"

"No," Rayn ground out. "Why would I? Anything of mine is safest in my own possession." She smiled sarcastically. "I'm a dragon, Ms. Le Doux. Or have you forgotten?" A puff of smoke came out of Rayn's nostrils.

"Rayn…" Lusgu warned.

She gave the brownie a look. "I'm not threatening her. I'm helping her understand. No one can protect treasure like a dragon can."

Lusgu shook his head. "My promise is buzzing. You were going too far."

Rayn huffed, but nodded. "Fine."

Wynona almost smiled. To have the doctor sound like a petulant child was a little amusing, and if they weren't speaking of something so serious, she might have allowed herself the indulgence. "You're sure about the box?" Wynona asked. "They said the box had been there a few years."

Rayn shook her head. "Nope. Didn't do it."

Wynona took in a long breath. "So someone impersonated you? How would that be possible?"

Rayn shrugged. "Not a clue. Maybe you could show the Shade Banking president my photo? See if that's who they spoke to?"

"We could try," Wynona said with a nod. "But they said their system showed you hadn't been there in a while. It's possible no one remembers what you look like." She tapped her fingers on the arm of the chair. "Is there nothing else you can give me? Nothing that would help me clear your name?"

Lusgu grumbled, but his hold on Rayn's hand never faltered. "Let her in."

Rayn's eyebrows shot up. "You think so?"

He nodded gravely. "She has the sight."

Rayn's head whipped toward Wynona and she narrowed her eyes. "You can see magic?"

Wynona felt like a bug under a microscope. "Yes…"

Rayn's lips thinned, then she nodded. "Have you examined the weather boxes?"

Wynona nodded.

"Then you have permission to go through my lab," Rayn said as if making a decision. "You'll see that they're not mine."

"The magic in the boxes is rainbow. It could be anyone's."

Rayn's smile was completely mercenary. "You'll see. I can't share it all…at least right now…but you're on the right track. I told you to follow the magic, but this will make it much easier."

Those words. Rayn had spoken them before. But Wynona was still lost as to why Rayn couldn't just explain it all. "You're willing to risk incarceration on that?"

Rayn nodded and smiled fondly at Lusgu. "We are."

"We?"

Lusgu gave Wynona a look. "Free her. And more of it will become clear."

Wynona sighed and stood. "That would be a lot easier if you would just tell me what was going on."

"Some secrets are held back for a reason," Rayn said. She smiled again when Wynona glared. "Follow the magic."

Wynona nodded. "I'm sorry, Lusgu. But you'll have to come with me. And Rayn, I'll be taking you up on that visit to your lab."

"Wynona?"

Wynona turned back to the couple, her eyebrows raised.

"Quinin won't understand," Rayn said, her smile softer. "Go at night and use your shield. My alarms won't see you."

Lusgu growled and leaned up to kiss Rayn's cheek before walking toward Wynona. "Careful," he snapped.

"She'll know soon enough."

Lusgu paused at Wynona's side and looked back. "We can only hope."

"We'll fix it," Rayn assured him. "We have to."

Lusgu's head fell and he shook it. "I don't know if I have hope anymore."

Rayn's face hardened. "I refuse to give up."

"And I refuse to hurt you."

Rayn put a hand on her chest as Wynona's head whipped back and forth between the two. "I'll hope for both of us."

Lusgu groaned in pain and nodded. "Soon." Then he turned and led the way out of the room.

Wynona was more confused than ever. She didn't even know what to report to the chief.

Best to do the lab visit. It's probably the only place to start, Violet offered.

Wynona ground her teeth. *I shouldn't just be starting. I should be solving.*

All in good time, Violet responded. *I know it's horrible. But it really is best to get the murder solved first. The rest will inevitably come out after.*

I'll hold you to that, Wynona argued.

Violet purred and wrapped herself tighter around her witch. *I'll see that you do.*

CHAPTER 24

The last of the dishes floated to the table and Wynona tried to push down the worry in the back of her mind that she should be snooping right now. It was dinner time and she had a houseful of guests, including Prim and Daemon, who had been digging for the financial rumor origins, so though it was information Wynona was interested in, she was growing restless with the desire to be in Rayn's lab…especially since she had permission.

"Wy."

Wynona turned around at Rascal's call and raised her eyebrows.

He gave her a soft smile. "Come sit down and eat."

Wynona blew out a short breath. "Yeah. You're right." She forced herself to walk to the table and sit down, but her knee wouldn't stop bouncing.

You'll give yourself away, Violet said wryly.

Rascal's eyebrows went up.

Wynona gave her familiar a quick glare, but Violet only giggled.

"What's going on?" Prim asked, a smirk on her face.

"Nothing," Wynona muttered. "Just annoying familiars who won't mind their own business."

Violet laughed harder and the entire room looked at her as she sat on the edge of the table.

Lusgu grunted and shook his head, Prim and Daemon both appeared amused and surprised and Rascal was immediately suspicious.

Care to share? he asked.

"Nope," Wynona answered out loud. She cleared her throat as she realized her mistake. *The less you know, the better, remember?*

Rascal's grunt sounded an awful lot like Lusgu's, but Wynona didn't point that out. She was pretty sure he wouldn't appreciate the comparison.

"So…Prim," Wynona began. "Would you like to tell us about your adventures?"

Prim pursed her lips as she finished chewing, then rolled her eyes. "It was far from an adventure," she pouted. "The whole thing was rather…boring."

Wynona waited her friend out. She knew Prim liked to have everyone's full attention.

Prim preened a little under the attention, then leaned over the table. "I asked Sulanara who she'd heard the story from, but she couldn't quite remember."

Daemon rolled his eyes behind Prim's back and Wynona bit her lip. It didn't surprise her that the black hole had no patience for the women at the Curl and Die. They were a gossipy, excitable bunch, but Prim loved them and that was good enough for Wynona.

"So she poked around for a few days," Prim continued. "Asking patrons as they came through, testing to see who had heard the rumor and who might have spread it."

Wynona waited…and waited…"And?" she finally pressed, figuring Prim was waiting for some sign of interest.

"And she never found them!" Prim finished in a flourish. She narrowed her eyes. "But don't worry. I didn't let that get me down."

"Prim," Daemon warned. "We need to tell her what happened."

Prim waved him off. "I'm getting to it."

His groan might have been to tell the table how annoyed he was, but Wynona could see a hint of a smile on his face. The black hole was amused...whether he wanted to admit it or not.

Lusgu, however, was not. "Just get to it, girl!"

Prim frowned, but ultimately ignored the brownie. "One of the biggest gossips in town is Melalanth, one of the waitresses from the Sultry Spirits," Prim explained. "And she's a regular at the Curl and Die."

Wynona leaned back in her seat. "The witch?"

Prim nodded. "Her witch magic is pretty weak, but she..." Prim made a face. "Compensates for it in other ways."

Wynona huffed. The Sultry Spirits was the most popular bar in town, known for having your drink ready before you ever arrived. But the patrons were largely men...and for good reason. It seemed the workers at the Sultry Spirits were in a constant contest to see who could garner the most attention from their customers and they were covered in more magic illusions than a poisoned apple.

Rascal chuckled, but stopped short when Wynona glared at him. "What? I don't go there," he said in defense.

Wynona shook her head. "What did you find out, Prim?"

"I knew Melalanth would never tell me anything." Prim fluffed her hair. "We've never gotten along. But just outside the pub is a long hedge of hydrangeas." Prim grinned. "Hydrangeas never miss a thing."

Rascal choked. "You were talking to the flowers?"

Wynona whacked his arm. "She's done that before, don't you remember? It was how we knew Mr. Pearlily was abusing his wife."

Rascal scratched behind his ear. "True enough. It just seems..." He hesitated, obviously thinking better of his words.

"We all have different gifts," Prim said with a sniff. "Understanding plants is rare." She straightened. "But so is a wingless fairy."

"And I'm grateful you're both," Wynona said firmly. "Otherwise, we probably never would have met."

Prim made a face. "I hate to admit you're right, but...you're right. If I had wings, my parents wouldn't have hated me and I never would have run away from home."

"So what did the hydrangeas tell you?" It was time to get off that subject. Poor Prim had dealt with almost as much as Wynona had. It was one of the things that drew the two women together, but also made Wynona protective of her friend. Neither of them spoke of their pasts unless they had to.

Prim waited, the pause as dramatic as she could make it. "Certain groups of men have been visiting the pub lately," she whispered. "Men who rarely show their faces above ground."

Wynona frowned. "I'm lost."

"She's talking about the mafia," Rascal clarified, his jaw tight. "We usually have eyes on the Sultry Spirits, but it looks like whoever's on duty must be missing something."

Prim shrugged. "That I can't help you with, but with this group of men, there has also been a slightly large influx of women."

Wynona could only guess why. What was it about powerful, dangerous men that seemed to draw in women? It made no sense. Breaking the law and breaking creatures were not something Wynona found attractive.

And yet you're marrying a predator, Rascal teased.

A predator who UPHOLDS the law, she shot back. *Much more my style.*

He winked at her, then turned back to Prim. "Anything else?"

"It would appear that no one is sure who the women are," Daemon added, earning a glare from Prim for bursting in. "They haven't been seen in the area before, or at least not enough for them to be well-known."

"So the hydrangeas don't know?" Wynona asked. "Or the regulars at the bar don't know?"

"Both," Prim said quickly, stealing back the limelight. "The group comes about once a week, the women arrive shortly thereafter, and they all meet in a private space in the back. They don't hang around with the regulars, so no one has been able to catch any names."

"However," Daemon said, stepping in again, "a limousine has been seen a couple of times, coming up to the back and going through a door that leads directly to the private spaces."

Wynona stiffened. Very few people used limousines in Hex Haven.

Between magic and the abilities of many creatures to transport themselves in creative ways, there weren't a lot of individuals that preferred to be chauffeured around. A limousine could only mean one thing...

"It's either your dad or one of his lackeys," Rascal said softly.

Wynona nodded. "Yep." She stuffed a bit of pasta in her mouth. How she hated talking about her dad. His finger was in one too many pies and every time she thought of her parent, Wynona was reminded of how Granny Saffron wanted Wynona to usurp the man for the presidency.

President Le Doux had been in power for over a hundred years and showed no signs of slowing down. They might use the term "president" in their city, but truly it was a monarchy. Until someone had more power, Wynona's father would stay where he was.

Problem was...she was the only creature they knew who might possibly be able to fight for that position, and Wynona wanted no part of it.

A popping sound came from the front room and half of the table was on their feet before Wynona could turn her head.

Celia walked into the kitchen, her hands up. "Peace, fellow creatures." She smirked and tossed her dark hair over her shoulder. "Looks like I arrived just in time."

Wynona slumped. "Celia. You can't just pop in like that."

Celia's eyebrows shot up. "Why not? I used to live here."

Wynona closed her eyes, begging herself to be patient, even though she was at her wit's end. "Because this is my house and I have a right to privacy. I'm happy to have you visit, but you need to use the front door just like everyone else."

Celia huffed and snapped a chair up to the table, along with a plate, glass and utensils. While everyone else watched, she filled her plate and began to eat. "What?" she finally demanded. "Haven't you ever seen a hungry witch before?"

Wynona sighed. "Celia, have you ever known Dad to frequent the Sultry Spirits?"

Celia paused and leaned back in her seat. "The Sultry Spirits? I don't know. Why?"

Wynona glanced at the rest of the table, but they were silent. She was pretty sure they were all terrified of her sister, but no one wanted to admit it.

"We're in the middle of an investigation," Rascal began. "If you have anything you think might help us, tell us now."

Celia threw up her hands. "I don't even know what this is about."

Lusgu grunted. "Tell us about your father, girl!"

Celia glared at the brownie, but even she wasn't going to cross the small creature. Wynona knew that Celia had seen Lusgu's power a couple of times. It was stronger than it should be for a creature of his background. There were times Wynona thought he might even be stronger than her.

She shuddered as a reminder of her brush with Cold, Silent Killer Wynona came to her mind.

He's strong, but not stronger than you, Rascal sent her way.

Wynona reached under the table to hold his hand. *I wish he was.*

Rascal huffed, but didn't reply.

"I don't know what all my dad was into," Celia said in a dark tone. "If I did, I'd turn him over to the police without losing a moment's sleep. All I know is that he's got something up his sleeve and he was using me to do his dirty work until I came here." Celia paused and turned to Wynona. "Speaking of, what did you do with those grimoires?"

Wynona hesitated. She didn't really want her sister to know where they were. "They're in a safe place," she stated carefully.

Celia snorted. "I don't want them. I just was curious if you found what you were looking for."

Wynona played with the food on her plate. "Not yet. I haven't had as much time to look through them as I would have hoped."

Celia nodded again. "I suppose losing your business would keep you a little busy. Are we going over plans this week? The building should be just about done."

"I can't until the case is solved," Wynona said, pushing her hands into her hair. Her stomach suddenly didn't want anything more to eat. She had so many things on her shoulders at the moment. The murder, Dr. Rayn, the secrets about Wynona herself, the grimoires, getting the tea shop back up and running… When would it end?

It seemed that every time she felt like things were going well, something exploded…right in her face.

"What about wedding plans?" Celia smirked. "Where's that headed?"

Rascal rubbed Wynona's neck, massaging slightly, and she wanted to groan at how good it felt. "We're working on it."

Celia laughed. "In other words, you've done nothing."

"Not true," Prim defended. "We've got the flowers figured out."

"Right," Celia said.

Wynona held up her hands. "Okay…enough. Please…I'm not going to sit here and referee a fight. Either get along, or get out."

The room was silent. Wynona often broke up the bickering of the group, but she wasn't usually quite so forceful about it.

"Way to go, sis," Celia said, with a slow, deliberate clapping of hands. "Maybe all this stress is good for you."

Rascal growled.

"Celia, have you ever heard of Dad meeting with the mafia?"

Celia choked. "Excuse me?"

"Do you know if he's got ties to the underworld?"

Celia pursed her lips, giving the question honest thought. "While I wouldn't be surprised, I actually can't give you a definitive answer."

"Do you think anything you did for him would tie into Eve Guanaco or Arave Smouldon's deaths?"

Celia's eyes became distant for several seconds. "Again, not that I know of, but I don't really understand his bigger picture. I never delivered messages to them, if that's what you're getting at. Not like the other ones we spoke about."

Wynona nodded. "Good enough." She turned to the rest of the table. "At this point, I'm going to assume the mafia bears watching, but isn't necessarily involved in our current case. Unless we can find some kind of tie between Dr. Rayn and them, or my father, there doesn't seem to be any kind of link."

"What about the selling of the machines?" Rascal asked. "You told us that Quinin admitted they were in financial trouble."

"Right." Wynona took a deep breath. "Prim, would you and Daemon do one more thing for us?"

"Anything," Prim said happily, bouncing in her seat.

"Can you take a picture of Dr. Rayn to the hydrangeas? See if they recognize her?" Wynona hoped she wasn't setting the trap to put Dr. Rayn behind bars for good. "If she's been seen lately at the Sultry Spirits, then we just might have found our connection to the financial troubles and the weather boxes being found on the black market. If not…" Wynona shrugged. "Then I think we're headed the wrong direction."

"You realize that won't prove her innocence?" Rascal asked softly.

"I know," Wynona responded wearily. "But maybe it'll turn up something else instead." It was the only hope she had at the moment. That and getting into the dragon's lab. That had to become priority number one at this point.

Follow the magic.

It wasn't much, but it was more than nothing.

CHAPTER 25

It seemed to take forever for everyone to go home and Rascal had been particularly slow.

Not that Wynona minded an hour spent in his arms or his sweet and fiery kisses, but tonight…she was on a mission. She needed to get to Rayn's lab and she needed to do it now. Time was of the essence and with the mix of clues, half of which led nowhere and the other half which only led to Rayn, Wynona knew that if she didn't find something else soon…the good doctor would be put before a court and it might be too late.

Taking a cue from the last time she'd tried some sneaky sleuthing, Wynona dressed all in black, downed a cup of green tea to keep herself awake and stood in her dark sitting room. She squeezed her eyes shut and imagined herself at the entrance to the Grove of Secrets.

She was obviously getting better, since it only took a few seconds for Wynona to feel her feet hit the ground. She sucked in a deep breath and steadied herself, then looked at the dark forest. It was much more forbidding at night. It would definitely have been easier to simply port to Rayn's house, but Rayn had told Wynona to use her shield, and Wynona had no idea how to port with the shield on.

So she'd ported to the entrance of the forest and would wear her shield as she walked the path. It seemed the safest way to steer clear of Rayn's alarms and to make sure Quinin didn't get in the way.

"Provided Rayn was telling the truth," Wynona muttered. Her heart was pounding in her throat, but she swallowed down the fear. It wouldn't serve her right now.

Calling on her magic, Wynona spun a finger and pulled her shield up, keeping it as close to her person as possible. She didn't want it brushing up against anything without her knowing it.

Instead of a large bubble, the purple outline followed the lines of Wynona's body, looking more like armor. She held out her arms and studied it. She was almost of a mind to truly let Rayn have at it. Wynona wasn't quite sure what kind of magic it was, but it had been helpful over the past couple of years. It was one of the first things she'd conjured, even before she knew she could do it.

The sound of a hooting owl had Wynona's head jerking up and her stomach turning flips. Time to go.

Stepping forward carefully, Wynona flipped on her magic vision and began to carefully work her way down the trail. She wanted to take the time to study everything around her, as the forest was such a mystery, but now wasn't the time. The weight of the forest's magic was as prevalent as ever, but Wynona's shield helped her feel slightly safer.

At least until the wolf howl came. Every few minutes the creature announced its presence, sounding closer each time, and Wynona wished she'd brought Rascal with her. Surely, he would know how to handle a wild animal. A shiver ran down Wynona's back. *Too close.*

She picked up her pace, unable to stop from nearly running to get away from the sounds. Footsteps in the woods followed. She could sense them keeping pace, but the howling stopped.

Sweat trickled down Wynona's spine as she realized she had, in that moment, become prey. She stumbled, nearly hitting the ground as she ran toward Rayn's house. Maybe coming at night hadn't been such a good idea. The idea of porting home was becoming more and more appealing.

You NEED this! Follow the magic! Wynona shouted to herself.

She would never be able to move on if she didn't get this taken care of. And she needed to move on. She needed to know about her magic. She needed to know about Granny Saffron. She needed to know why Rayn and Lusgu had broken up and why they were keeping secrets. She needed to open her shop and marry Rascal and figure out her relationship with Celia, not to mention figure out what her dad was up to and how to stop it without causing an outright war.

In other words, she needed her life back.

She needed peace.

Her determination rising, Wynona ducked her head, picked up her speed, doubled the thickness of her shield and ran on. Footsteps kept pace, but she ignored them. She especially ignored them when they doubled, then tripled.

No creatures were going to stop her from arriving at Rayn's house.

She almost didn't realize when she'd reached the meadow and came to a stumbling stop. The moon shone down on the castle, making it appear nearly medieval, minus the gargoyles.

Breathing heavily and keeping her eye out for charms or spells, Wynona kept her footsteps careful. It took a moment to realize that the footsteps that had been following her had stopped and Wynona spun, gasping when she saw dozens of eyes glowing yellow in the light.

She and the creatures stared at each other for a moment before one set of eyes blinked and the creatures slowly disappeared.

Wynona's heart didn't slow down even when she was finally alone. Or at least when it felt like she was alone. She had no idea if it was a group of wolves, or if there were different creatures in the group together, but there was something not…threatening about them.

And that worried Wynona the most.

If she couldn't feel the danger around her, how was she supposed to protect herself?

Shaking her head, grateful none had followed her into the meadow, Wynona began her tiptoe to the house. Walking away from the forest did nothing to help her calm down. Wynona felt like her head was being jerked on a string as she tried to take in every corner and shadow, looking for the spells Rayn said would be around.

Other than a general red shimmer around the home itself, Wynona saw nothing. Carefully, she walked around the side of the mansion until she reached a door she was certain was close to the lab. At least she hoped so.

The door was locked, which was to be expected. Wracking her brain, Wynona stepped close enough that she was able to bring the doorknob into the cover of her shield, then she closed her eyes just as she had when opening the safe at Killoran's mansion several months back, and spent the next couple of minutes reworking the lock.

When it finally clicked open, Wynona had to wipe the sweat from her forehead. She would be lucky if she had the energy to get home after all was said and done. Though, it wasn't as if Rayn would press charges if Wynona were caught, but still, Quinin might not handle the interruption so well and Chief Ligurio would certainly be upset.

A dark broom closet met Wynona's view when she finally slipped inside. She paused, waiting to listen for alarms, but nothing happened. Hopefully, Rayn's promise that Wynona's bubble would keep her safe was coming true.

Carefully closing the outside door, Wynona fumbled her way to the door leading to the house. A few lights were on in the hallway, but there was no movement to indicate signs of life, so Wynona stepped fully into the space.

She walked, tracking herself and trying to remember just where she'd been when visiting only a few days earlier. When she came up on the entrance to the kitchen, she knew she'd gone the wrong way, though Wynona paused anyway.

There was magic in the kitchen.

Tilting her head, Wynona wandered in, watching the dancing lights. They were all over the place. Several of the appliances had a distinctive red hue, the color of Rayn's magic. But every once in a while, Wynona found another color. Yellow, green or blue seemed to be the most prominent ones.

The toaster in the corner had the strongest colors and Wynona stopped near it. If she hadn't been so afraid of taking down her shield, she would have tried to touch it. Unlike some of the other magic she'd seen, this one didn't have the holes in it. The rainbow was in perfect shape.

But what was causing it?

How did magic have more than one color? It was mind wracking.

Shaking her head, Wynona decided she needed to continue to the lab. That's where Rayn had told her to go, after all. Now that she was in the kitchen, she had a better idea of how to get to where she wanted to get to.

Heading back down the hallway and past the broom closet, she made her way with only a couple of mistakes to the large double doors marked as the laboratory. Wynona could feel the pulse of magic inside, it tugged at her core and made her shield shake slightly.

Taking a moment to reinforce it, she reached for the handle, but hesitated. A gurgle of fear rose in her throat. What would she find inside? Why was Rayn so positive that the answer lay in there, but couldn't tell Wynona what it was?

Far too much seemed to be riding on this little mission, but Wynona felt as clueless as ever. None of the clues made sense, unless Dr. Rayn and Lusgu had been lying the whole time, and Wynona was positive they weren't.

In her mind, the only liar was Mr. Thathion, but everything for him seemed to come up roses, except for the loss of his fiancee. Though, Mr. Thathion had been less than broken-hearted.

Quit stalling.

She took a deep breath, forcing herself to swallow her anxiety. She hadn't come this far to only come this far. It was time for more action and to move on with her life.

Though her fingers trembled slightly, Wynona reached out, gripped the handle and twisted.

CHAPTER 26

The whirring and clicking of machines and the smell of unknown substances hit Wynona in the face as soon as she got in the door. Her eyes, however, were hit with colors. All. Sorts. Of. Colors.

The dominant color was definitely red. Wynona could see where Rayn had been working. There were entire tables full of red. It swirled and floated around toasters, teapots similar to what Wynona had purchased, forks, spoons, pots… Almost every small appliance that existed was sitting around the space.

There was even a dishwasher in a half state of disrepair. Gears, bolts and wires lay scattered on the floor, all covered in a haze of red.

Wynona crouched down, touching a couple of the pieces. The magic felt…warm, similar to the magic of her teapot. But what were noticeably missing were the holes that Wynona had in her own appliance.

Pushing out a breath, Wynona frowned and considered what she was seeing. Lusgu, Quinin and Mr. Thathion had all said that Rayn's biggest goal was to bring magic to those who had none. Was she spending her days trying to enchant everyday objects in order to do that?

"But what can you do with a dishwasher?" Wynona murmured softly. She didn't dare turn anything on, unless Quinin's sharp owl ears heard something and came to investigate.

Standing, Wynona stared a moment longer, then moved around. She stopped at a beaker full of red liquid. It was being held in the air by its neck and Wynona guessed that a flame could be inserted underneath if Rayn wanted it heated. *Or she could just use her own flame,* Wynona reminded herself.

She kept walking. She wasn't even sure what she was looking for, but she hoped something would eventually catch her attention.

A flash of yellow finally did just that and Wynona paused. This beaker was empty, but along with the red magic, there was a small trickle of yellow. Wynona leaned in closer. *It's not the same.* She pressed her lips together. The magic was different. The red floated, light as a breeze. The yellow looked heavier and oozed like liquid peanut butter. It seemed to come from the beaker itself, rather than enveloping it in a soft hug like the red.

Wynona poked at it with one finger and was shocked to watch the yellow dance away from her purple covered finger. She reached out, trying to catch it, but the magic kept just out of reach, about a half inch away from her finger.

What was that? Why could she touch the rainbow earlier on the weather box, but not this? Wynona squished her lips to the side, contemplating the issue, but nothing was coming to mind.

Setting it aside for the moment, she pushed on. Red, red and more red, but then she found a small box covered in solid rainbow. Wynona paused and picked it up. The magic felt oily and had that same viscous quality of the yellow, but it didn't run away.

Ignoring how gross it felt against her hand, Wynona turned it over, trying to figure out what the box was used for, but it seemed to simply be a cube. There was no opening, no obvious usage.

Running her finger along the silver edging, Wynona stopped. Something was tickling her brain. Her eyes darted around, looking for anything that would help trigger the memory. When they landed on the red beaker, Wynona froze.

The silver. It wasn't warm.

Quickly walking back to the dishwasher, Wynona ran her finger along the silver detailing. Yep. Warm. But the silver on the rainbow box wasn't.

But what does that mean?

She growled under her breath. Clues, but no answers. It was enough to make her want to scream.

Going back to the counter where she'd found the box, Wynona tested her discovery on every object that emanated magic. Anything with red magic had the warm trim, anything with rainbow, or other colors, did not.

So Rayn's magic was warm…but where was the rainbow coming from? The only other creature in the lab, according to Rayn, was Quinin, who was a shifter. Like Rascal, shifters didn't have extra magic. So none of this would be the owl's.

Had Rayn been lying? Or was someone breaking into the lab and messing with things? Was Rayn responsible for the weird magic, but how was she creating it? Did it have to do with giving magic-less creatures magic of their own?

Wynona wanted to throw something. She was so confused and so frustrated. All of this could be answered in two minutes if someone…anyone…would actually answer some stupid questions!

If given the chance, Wynona was definitely in the mood to strangle both a dragon and a brownie, so it was probably good that they weren't all in the same room. She hated to admit it, but Wynona knew she might have a hard time containing Crazy-Wynona if she confronted the two secret-keepers right now.

She flexed her hands and tried to calm down, though it was difficult. Her magic was responding to her emotions and the whole room was becoming purple, which made it difficult to distinguish what else was in there.

Closing her eyes, Wynona took slow, deliberate breaths until she felt her heartbeat slow down to something that was near to normal. Opening her eyes, Wynona glanced at the clock and told herself it was time to hurry. She'd been there too long already, and all she had to show for it were more questions.

Standing in the middle of the room, Wynona put her hands on her hips and huffed. There had to be something she was missing. *Follow the magic.* Well, here she was. She was looking right at the magic, but was seeing no answers.

Wynona hesitated. "I'm looking at the magic," she murmured. What if she *didn't* look at the magic? What if she looked at the objects?

Wynona blinked a couple of times, letting her magic vision dissipate. The color in the room disappeared and the appliances suddenly looked very ordinary.

Slowly, Wynona let her eyes scan from table to table. Everything seemed fine. Nothing...wait. She squinted. Maybe it was the darkness playing tricks on her? Slowly, Wynona walked forward. She could practically feel her eyes dilating as they tried to adjust to the darkness in order to see better.

Maybe it was a different beaker?

Wynona stopped in front of the table and blinked her magic vision back into play. The beaker with the mix of red and yellow magic was in front of her. Wynona reached out, giving one last test and true to form, the yellow darted away from her touch.

Letting her magic go, Wynona watched as the beaker began to flash back and forth between an actual beaker, and a wine glass. It was as if the object couldn't make up its mind as to what it truly wanted to be.

But how? And why?

She put her vision on again and leaned in closer. She needed a better look at that yellow magic. The red looked just like all the other red. It was the yellow that was different.

Unable to see anything due to the magic constantly running away, Wynona looked around, finally spotting a magnifying glass on the wall of tools. She ran over and grabbed it, coming back and positioning herself to get a really good look at the escaping power. If she kept just a bit of space, she could see it quite clearly.

The yellow had holes in it. They were tiny, almost indiscernible, but like the magic on the teapot and the rainbow on the weather box...it had holes in it.

Wynona leaned back. Some ideas were beginning to churn, but she needed to sit down and lay it all out to get a better look. Right now, her mind was too full to piece the puzzle together, but she could fix that.

After putting the magnifying glass away, she left the lab, making her way back to the broom closet and eventually slipping out into the night. She chewed her lip, debating the merits of simply porting from where she was, but ultimately decided it was too dangerous.

The idea of running back down the small trail in the forest was utterly unappealing, but Wynona felt as if she had no choice.

"At least they left you alone," she murmured, trying to bolster her courage. "No one actually came out of the forest line."

Throwing back her shoulders, Wynona double checked her shield and headed out. The trail was easy enough to find once she had her magic vision running, but the creepy vibes of the forest, and the feeling that the creatures were gathering again, couldn't be ignored.

Unable to keep her panic at bay, Wynona finally stopped a little way into the trail, closed her eyes and ported herself to the back of her house.

Her landing was anything but graceful, as she fell onto her backside. But she was in one piece and she had landed where she wanted to be. That was enough for now.

Rascal?

Hmm? He sounded sleepy, and Wynona felt bad about waking him up.

First thing in the morning, we need to talk. She could feel his mind waking up and knew he was trying to dig around in her thoughts. She let down the wall she'd been holding up and waited for his frustration.

Rascal sighed. *I suppose I kind of gave you permission, didn't I?*

You did.

I don't like what I'm seeing, but I understand. He growled. *Be there in five.*

"You don't have to—" Wynona cut off her own words when she

realized he wasn't paying attention. She pulled her hair out of the bun on top of her head and shook it out, then headed inside. A pot of matcha was in order. It was going to be a long night.

CHAPTER 27

Wynona heated water and began to set the table with a couple of cups. She rummaged through the fridge, knowing that Rascal would want to eat. She was low on treats since she'd stopped her orders from Gyoz and Knuq while the shop was closed.

"Have to pick up a box of something if I'm gonna keep having these meetings," she murmured.

We're here.

Wynona blinked as she watched Lusgu and Violet come through the portal. "Hello."

Violet grinned. *Got any cookies?*

Shaking herself out of her surprise, Wynona snapped her fingers and began pulling more things out of the cupboard. "No cookies," she replied. "But I've got some crackers."

Violet sighed. *That'll do. This guy has no snacks at all. It's pathetic.*

Lusgu grunted, as if he'd heard the conversation and began shuffling through the kitchen, heating more water and bringing out half a dozen cups.

"Uh…" Wynona wasn't sure if she should address the fact that the brownie understood Violet, or if she should let him know that they were only expecting one other person.

There was a knock on the front door, taking the momentary decision from her. Wynona raced over and opened the door, then snorted. "Did you call the calvary too? Should I expect a lawn full of soldiers within the next ten minutes?"

Rascal gave her a look. "Funny, Wy. Very funny."

Wynona shook her head, stepped back and waved everyone inside. "I'm sorry he woke you all up," she said as Prim, Daemon, Chief Ligurio and Rascal walked in.

One last person waited on the front stoop and Wynona waited her sister out.

"Are you sure you want me here?" Celia asked. "I'm not officially part of the pep squad."

There was a bite in her tone, but something whispered to Wynona that Celia *wanted* to come inside. "You're always welcome," Wynona reminded her sister. She smiled. "Thank you for using the front door this time."

Celia tossed her hair over her shoulder and huffed. "I didn't have much of a choice," she muttered while walking past Wynona.

Wynona smiled slightly. Celia was softening. It made Wynona wonder what this would mean for her sister and Chief Ligurio. Maybe past hurts would finally be put to rest.

Wynona closed the door and went to the kitchen, pausing in the doorway to watch the chaos for a moment. If they hadn't been there to discuss a murder, this would actually have been her very favorite thing.

Light bickering, teasing, smiles and yawns...all of it was exactly what she had never had growing up and what she loved about her new life.

Rascal's golden eyes came up from the table and landed on hers and Wynona felt a giddy blush climb her throat and face. He smirked at her, waggled his eyebrows and waved her over.

We're waiting on you, beautiful.

Wynona nodded, pushed her shoulder off the doorframe and came to his side. She was grateful that Lusgu had obviously had the foresight to set out tea for everyone and after waiting a few more minutes for the group to raid her cupboards and fridge, Wynona called the meeting to order.

"Thank you for coming," Wynona said a little louder than normal. When the group quieted down, she brought down her volume as well. "I realize we're all losing sleep over this, but I have a few things I think we need to discuss."

"It had to be at night?" Chief Ligurio snapped.

Celia whacked the vampire's arm. "Apparently it did, or she wouldn't have called us here."

Chief Ligurio narrowed his red eyes. "Thank you for that astute observation," he ground out.

Celia smiled a little too sweetly. "Always glad to help those who struggle to grasp basic concepts."

"Children," Wynona warned. She knew they both egged each other on on purpose, but their odd form of flirting would have to wait. Despite how much she loved these creatures, she was surrounded by frustrated couples who often took out their bitter emotions by snarking at each other. "You can argue on your own time."

Chief Ligurio shot one more warning glare at Celia before turning to Wynona. "I hear you took an unauthorized search."

Wynona smiled. "Actually...I had permission."

The chief's black eyebrows slanted down. "Excuse me?"

Wynona stood a little straighter. "Dr. Rayn herself told me to search her lab. She told me the best thing I could do was follow the magic."

The entire room stirred in interest and Chief Ligurio folded his arms over his chest, leaning back in his chair. "Will she testify to that? Otherwise any evidence you found won't be applicable."

Wynona nodded. "I believe she will."

He nodded back. "Then by all means..."

"What did you find?" Prim asked, bouncing in her seat. Her pink hair was up in an extra high ponytail and flipped back and forth at her excitement.

Wynona glanced at Lusgu, but he was sitting calmly, watching her. She couldn't read his expression, but since he wasn't making a fuss, Wynona let it go. "After getting inside, I used my magic vision to look around."

Celia frowned. "Magic vision?"

"I can see magic," Wynona explained. Her sister's jaw dropped.

"But...how is that even possible?"

Wynona shrugged and decided to keep Daemon's ability a secret. Not that she wasn't starting to trust Celia, but perhaps it was best to not let the whole world know of all the skills this group had. "I'm not sure, but I can do it." She blinked, turning her eyes purple, and Celia gasped. Blinking again, Wynona watched Celia shake her head.

Finally, the witch snorted. "Tell us what you found."

Wynona put her palms on the table. "Okay...what I've got are a bunch of random pieces, but I'm hoping by laying them all out, we can put a few together." No one said anything, so she plowed on. "Most of the magic was red, which is Rayn's magic. I've seen it in action and recognize it."

Chief Ligurio grunted and Lusgu shot him a glare that was completely ignored.

Wynona turned to the brownie. "Lusgu, you said Rayn's specialty was trying to develop magic for magic-less creatures to use. How exactly did she do that?"

Lusgu cleared his throat. "She would use everyday objects and try to imbue them with powers so that the user could do more than simply the original intent of the object."

"So...like a dishwasher that would allow the user to do what?" Wynona pressed, grasping at straws.

Lusgu shrugged. "I don't know. Could have been anything from allowing the user to magically put the dishes away, to magically put them in the dishwasher themselves."

Wynona nodded. "Okay...and how did she create magic to allow that to happen? I've noticed that all her inventions have silver on them." Wynona took a wild guess. "Does silver enhance dragon magic?"

Lusgu's small eyes flared. "Yes…" he said carefully. "Many precious metals do. Dragons don't only have hoards because they need money."

"Ah." Wynona nodded and pursed her lips. "I gathered as much."

Prim raised her hand. "I'm lost. What does this have to do with anything? How do these inventions either make her the murderer or clear her name?"

Wynona shook her head. "I'm not sure yet, but I suspect that Rayn was trying to create…" She made a face. "For lack of a better word… man-made magic." Wynona should have suspected the gasps that echoed through the room, but since she'd already been chewing on the idea for a bit, she found herself a little caught off guard.

"That's not right," Daemon said in a low, dark tone. "Messing with the magical equilibrium could have lasting cosmic consequences."

Wynona frowned. "How do you know that?" she asked, then held up a hand. "I'm not saying you're wrong, I'm simply trying to understand."

Daemon looked around, but no one else offered an explanation, so he shrugged. "I'm not sure. But humans, I think, would say it was like playing God."

Wynona nodded. "While I see your point, I don't exactly agree. Playing God, as far as I understand it, would mean that someone believes they have the rights over life and death."

"Exactly."

"But I don't think that's what Rayn was trying to accomplish," Wynona argued. "To me, it's more like she was creating robots. Knockoffs of real live magical creatures."

Lusgu huffed. "All she wanted was to make life easier for those with no powers. There's nothing wrong with that and she never thought it made her above others."

Daemon scowled. "Magic isn't a toy."

Lusgu slapped the table. "Do you really think she doesn't know that? You're nothing but a child!" he shouted. "What makes you think—"

"Lusgu," Wynona said, resting her hand on his arm. She jerked it back when the touch stung.

Rascal growled, but Wynona shook her head, then rubbed her fingertips together.

Lusgu folded his arms around himself and leaned as far back in his seat as he could, as if trying to make himself smaller.

Let it go, Violet warned. *It's one of the pieces that will come soon, but not today.*

Wynona felt that flash of anger again, but set it aside. No one needed to die tonight, thank you very much. "I'd like to research further, to make sure what I'm seeing is correct, but I'm not actually sure where to find anything like that."

There was a moment's pause before Celia piped up. "The grimoires."

The truth of the suggestion slammed into Wynona like a cast iron cauldron and she looked at Rascal, who was shaking his head.

"Not safe," he growled.

"Of course not," Lusgu grumbled. "Why would the ramblings and spells of black witches be safe?"

"Where else would I find it?" Wynona asked softly.

"What grimoires?" Chief Ligurio demanded. "Where did you get them?"

Wynona turned to the man who was a sort-of friend, but trusted nonetheless. "They're my family grimoires. I…" She changed what she was going to say to protect Celia. "They were retrieved for me so I could try to learn how to control my magic through Granny's journal."

The vampire's eyes narrowed. "And?"

"And some of them are definitely from very dark witches and I've had a bad reaction to them."

"I can help."

Wynona turned to the black hole. "They're strong."

Daemon nodded. "I can do it. Bring them out."

Feeling anxious, but slightly hopeful, Wynona went to her bedroom, Rascal dogging her heels.

"I don't think this is a good idea," he grumbled.

"What choice do we have?" Wynona asked, throwing open her

closet door. She took a deep breath and undid the spell she had, hiding the box of books. Instantly, the foul stench of black magic permeated the air and Wynona stepped back into Rascal's chest.

Rascal growled and pulled her behind him.

"I got it." Daemon came into the room and Wynona felt a swift change as the magic stopped abruptly.

She took a deep breath, grateful for her friend's power.

Daemon, however, stumbled slightly and his forehead was slick with sweat by the time he reached the closet.

"What can I do to help?" Wynona asked anxiously.

Daemon shook his head, his jaw clenched as if speaking would break his concentration. Grunting, he picked up the box and walked out.

Wynona and Rascal followed, but Wynona felt helpless.

The box landed on the table with a thud and the whole room jumped, including Lusgu.

Landing hard in his chair, Daemon put his face in his hands. "Better do it quick," he ground out.

Prim rubbed Daemon's back, her pink brows pulled tightly together. "Nona?" she whispered.

Wynona nodded and began pulling out books. "Everyone grab one and see what you can find."

"Can you use your magic to find it?" Rascal asked.

Wynona shook her head. "No. He's taken away the magic."

Rascal huffed. "Forgot."

Everyone grabbed a book and the reading began. Daemon's pallor grew worse and Wynona began to suspect he was going to be ill if they didn't find something soon.

"I think I got it," Chief Ligurio said, handing the book to Wynona. "You'll probably understand it best."

Wynona groaned inside when she realized the book was one of the worst ones. Daemon couldn't let go just yet. She began to read what the chief had discovered and her hope began to rise. "He's right," she said excitedly. "This says that created magic comes in all colors and can be manipulated to perform even by those who have no magic of their own." She continued to skim and her happiness faded. "It also says it's highly volatile," Wynona continued, her voice softer. "That it lacks foundation and cannot be controlled in a way to keep anyone, including the user, safe. And that normally a user will manifest a specific power that becomes their specialty, when the magic works."

Wynona shut the book, swallowing back bile. The book had continued to say how to use such a device to gain power over others, but Wynona wanted nothing to do with that. She had her answer.

Rascal snatched the book from her hand and began stuffing them all back in the box and raced it to the room. "Wy!" he shouted.

Wynona started to follow, but stopped. Something wasn't quite right. She turned. "Lusgu!" she cried, just as the brownie tried to slip into his portal. Without thought, Wynona reached out her hand and shot a wall of purple to stop the creature from disappearing.

With a cry, Daemon fell from his seat and landed on the floor, unconscious.

"NONA!" Prim screamed, dropping to the floor beside Daemon.

Instant guilt landed in Wynona's stomach, but she waited. The blackness of the grimoires was floating out of her room and down the hall, but she had to finish this first. "Give me the book," she demanded.

Lusgu hesitated, but some angry chittering from Violet had him turning around, his chin on his chest. He held out the grimoire and Wynona used her magic to bring it to her hands. She didn't need to glance down to see who it had belonged to. She knew Lusgu wanted Saffron's journal. She'd known it for a while, and had no problem sharing, but it was to be under a controlled situation, not him simply stealing the book right out from under her nose. "I trusted you," Wynona said, her vision blurry.

"Nona," Prim whispered thickly.

Biting back the other words she wanted to say, Wynona spun, ran into the bedroom, viciously throwing up the wall in the closet and rushed back to Daemon's side. She put a hand on his forehead, closed her eyes and sent soothing, healing vibes throughout his body. As best she could tell, he was burned out. Her blast of magic had been too much for him and had short-circuited his brain.

Wynona spent an extra few seconds making sure there was no permanent damage before she leaned back and waited.

Daemon blinked almost immediately and his eyes only stayed on hers for a second before landing on Prim.

Prim gave him a teary smile and continued to brush his hair away from his forehead. "Don't ever scare me like that again," she scolded in a whisper.

"You *do* care," he said in awe.

Prim huffed. "Stupid creature. Of course I care!" She held onto his arm as Daemon got to his feet, his legs slightly shaky, but he stood tall.

His eyes, however, never left Prim's. "I think I'm done for the night," he said without looking up. "I'll meet you all in the morning."

No one spoke as Daemon and Prim walked out, never turning from each other.

Celia snorted. "Well, that's one way to go about it," she muttered.

Chief Ligurio stood. "I think that's our cue." He paused before leaving. "So the weather box is run by created magic," he affirmed.

Wynona nodded. "Yes."

"Which means anyone with access to Dr. Brownhide's inventions could have committed the murders." His brows pulled together. "Which is anyone on the black market…except we still have the issue with the bank. What about the plans? And the anonymous call?" he grumbled. "This actually doesn't help as much as I thought."

"Actually…" Wynona began. "I think it does." She straightened her shoulders. "How soon do hospital visiting hours start?"

CHAPTER 28

Wynona never managed to get any sleep, though visiting hours didn't start until later in the morning. Rascal slept on her couch and Wynona tossed and turned in her room, until she finally stood and finished the night away by pacing.

Ideas wouldn't stop moving through her head. She felt like she was on the right track, but maybe she was wrong? This was new territory for her. Wynona had never dealt with created magic before. Was she giving it too much credit? Was she completely off base? Were her own personal biases coloring her judgment?

She paused and rubbed her forehead. Today's migraine was on its way to being legendary.

Magic, Rascal muttered through their mental connection.

Wynona growled lightly, then fixed her head. The pain relief was wonderful, but her mood didn't budge. This whole situation was driving her crazy.

Her door squeaked and Rascal stood at the threshold, his hair standing straight up and his jaw cracking with his yawn. "Come on. We'll see if I can get special privileges since I'm a cop."

Wynona shook her head. "Sorry. I didn't mean to be thinking so loud."

He shook his head. "It's fine. I've gotten used to trying to sleep when stressed." His smile was lazy. "Let's hope you don't ever have to learn the same skills."

"If people keep holding back secrets from me, I just might," Wynona muttered. She took a deep breath. "I'll be out front in five."

Rascal nodded and walked away, scratching behind his ear as he went.

Wynona couldn't help but smile a little. She couldn't wait until they were married. Waking up next to that handsome creature was going to be wonderful.

Name the day. And eloping will always be an option.

"Get out of my head!" she called.

Never.

She snorted and headed to the bathroom, and forced herself through her normal get-ready routine. She wanted this over and done with, but she was going to do it feeling good about herself, not looking like a hag. It was time to bring Mr. Thathion to justice and get the rest of Wynona's life back on track.

Marching down the hall, Wynona waited while Rascal scrubbed some cold water over his face at the kitchen sink.

He turned and grinned at her. "Morning, beautiful."

Wynona rolled her eyes. "I'm ready when you are."

He whistled low as he looked her over. "Someday, I won't have to keep sharing you with criminals."

Wynona smiled back. "Someday, you won't have to share me at all."

Rascal's eyes glowed as he walked across the room and gave her a lingering kiss. "I can't wait."

Wynona could have melted into the floor. "Me either." Moments like this were exactly why she kept fighting. She wanted her time with Rascal. She wanted justice for those who deserved it. She wanted the freedom to pursue her business and relationships and figure out her magic and she *didn't* want unsolved murders and secrets ruining it all.

Rascal put his phone to his ear, took Wynona's hand and headed out to his truck. "We're going now," he said into the phone. "Uh-huh." Rascal nodded. "See you in ten." The phone went into Rascal's back pocket as he opened the passenger door and helped Wynona inside. "Chief will meet us there."

"I think we should bring Daemon," Wynona said, pursing her lips. "If he's up to it anyway."

Rascal chuckled. "He already checked in. Apparently, Prim pulled some magic of her own last night because he's feeling *much* better."

Wynona's eyes widened. "Are you kidding?'

Rascal shook his head. "I think his little stunt yesterday just might have finally broken through her barriers."

Wynona gave her fiance a look. "It wasn't a stunt, Rascal. We owe him a great deal for taking on that nasty magic."

"True enough." Rascal stole another kiss, then headed around to the driver's side. "But don't thank him too much," he said while getting the engine roaring. "It'll only go to his head."

"I think it's your head we should be worried about," Wynona responded wryly.

Rascal's dark chuckle wasn't the least bit repentant.

The ride to the hospital was blessedly short. The closer they got, the more Wynona worried she was jumping to conclusions. Mr. Thathion was a powerful creature. If she messed this up, he had the ability to ruin her and her friends.

"Don't do it," Rascal said as he got out. "Don't give that guy any more of your head space than he deserves."

Wynona nodded and waited for Rascal to come to her door. She enjoyed the feel of his hands on her waist as he helped her down and his nearness kept her stronger than when she was by herself.

The walk inside was unremarkable, and Wynona began to think they would get into the room without anyone giving them any trouble, but on the level where Mr. Thathion was being kept, the nurses finally took notice.

"I'm sorry," one said, coming to step in front of Rascal and Wynona. "But visiting hours don't start for a while yet."

Rascal flashed his badge. "We're here in an official capacity."

The nurse didn't look completely convinced, but she nodded. "And your name?"

"Deputy Chief Strongclaw," Rascal stated in the same tone he used with his officers at work. It was deep and strong and had a slight bite to it, making it clear why he held the position he did.

The nurse backed down even further. "Of course. Who are you wishing to see today?"

"Mr. Thathion," Wynona supplied.

The nurse frowned. "You really shouldn't continue to bother him. We'll never be able to figure out what's going on if you and the media don't stop harassing him."

Wynona paused. "Wait…what do you mean, you won't be able to figure out what's going on? I thought he was hurt from the lightning strike."

"He was," the nurse said defensively. "But that was healed several days ago."

"Then why is he still here?" Rascal pressed.

The nurse took a step back, obviously a little unsettled at his aggressive stance. "W-we're not sure," she stammered. "He says he still has pain in his legs and abdomen. We've been running tests to figure out why, but everything has come up clean and further treatments have proven unsuccessful."

Wynona's anxiety began to clear. "Bingo," she murmured, giving Rascal a wide smile.

"You got it?" he asked.

Wynona nodded. "I think so. At least I'm more sure than I was when we first arrived."

"Great." Rascal waved an arm past the nurse. "Lead the way."

The nurse huffed and puffed for a moment, but didn't stop them as Wynona and Rascal walked to the guarded door. They greeted the officer, both of which Wynona barely knew, then knocked and went inside.

Mr. Thathion lifted his head, blinking heavily as if he had been asleep. "Ms. Le Doux? Deputy Chief Strongclaw?" He cleared his throat. "What brings you two by so early?"

Wynona smiled, though there was no warmth in it. "I have a few questions."

Mr. Thathion's eyes darted from her to Rascal and back and his demeanor shifted. Wynona could see his mind calculating their presence, the looks on their faces and the possibility of why they had come. When his face became stoic and all emotion disappeared, she knew he was onto them. "I think perhaps the next time we speak we should do it through my lawyer," he said smoothly.

Wynona nodded. "If that's what you want. But I think maybe we can do without those formalities."

Mr. Thathion's nostrils flared. "What do you want, Ms. Le Doux? I daresay your father won't be happy to hear that you're harassing me."

"I realize at your age that you might be struggling with your memory," Wynona shot back, "but believe when I say…*again*… that my father has nothing to do with my life or my choices."

There was a muscle tic under Mr. Thathion's jaw. "Say your piece," he ground out.

Wynona's smile grew and she leaned in closer. "I can see your magic," she said softly.

HIs eyes widened and for the first time ever, Wynona could see fear in the creature's eyes.

"I know that one of the inventions you stole from Dr. Rayn was a way to give magic-less creatures their own powers. It's how you've lived so long, and it's how you've been manipulating the world around you."

Mr. Thathion snorted. "You know nothing of the sort."

Wynona knew her face was smug, but she didn't care. "You're not really hurt," she pressed. "Yes, you were originally burnt by the lightning, but it was quite convenient how it killed your fiancee and not you, don't you think?"

Mr. Thathion must have decided to go on the defensive because he raised a single eyebrow and the look he gave her made Wynona want to buckle. She felt fairly certain it was the look he used in the boardroom. "Are you saying I had my fiancee killed? To what purpose? If I didn't want to marry her, I could have easily broken off the engagement."

"You needed her to die," Wynona continued. "Because you needed a way to have an alibi for Eve Guanaco's death."

Mr. Thathion looked bored and leaned back against his pillow. "Finish your fishing, Ms. Le Doux. My sleep has been interrupted and I would like to continue recovering." He sneered. "As you say, I'm rather old. I don't recuperate quite the way I used to."

"You needed to be in the hospital in order to have an ironclad alibi for Eve's death," Wynona responded.

"And why would I want to kill Eve?" Mr. Thathion asked sarcastically.

"Because you were trying to pull Rayn out of hiding."

Mr. Thathion snorted. "Why would I want to do that? I assure you, Ms. Le Doux, if I wanted to find Ms. Brownhide, I could have done so without bringing the entire paranormal world into it."

"Maybe so," Wynona said. "But you didn't just need her out of hiding, you needed her back in the public eye."

"But again, I ask…why?" Mr. Thathion asked. "Why would someone of my stature and power have been so desperate that he would kill…twice, mind you…in order to pull out a disgraced, washed up inventor, from her solitude?"

"You wanted her inventions."

Mr. Thathion snorted. "Did I?"

"Let me put it another way," Wynona clarified. "You *needed* her inventions. Or at least you needed her latest model for created magic." She clasped her hands at her waist. "You see…your magic is…broken, for lack of a better word." Wynona gave him a humorless smile. "It's thick and oily, and has holes in it. Odds are, it doesn't always work properly because its problems make it unstable. Over time, those instabilities became stronger and you reached a point where you were either going to lose it, which in your case, meant you were going to die, or you needed the upgraded version." Wynona took a couple of steps toward the bed. "But the problem was, you'd already exiled the one creature you knew who could fix your stolen abilities."

Mr. Thathion looked far from impressed. "I already told you, I didn't kick her out the same way my colleagues did. She's the forgiving sort. I'm sure if that inane story were true, all I would have had to do was find her and speak to her."

Rascal laughed. "Dr. Brownhide? The forgiving sort? I think you must be thinking of another dragon."

Mr. Thathion's face tightened. "You're forgetting one important part of the story, Ms. Le Doux."

Wynoan raised her eyebrows.

"How did I kill Eve from the hospital?"

Wynona hated to admit that that was something she hadn't worked out yet. She knew the box worked on created magic and she knew that Mr. Thathion had a green colored magic, but how to tie the two together was still a mystery.

Mr. Thathion chortled. "You don't know. You don't have any answers." He sighed and relaxed. "They call that grasping at straws, Ms. Le Doux. And it's never good form for a detective to do so."

"I'm not a detective."

"Yet here you are, accusing me of murder."

Rascal growled, but Wynona put her hand on his arm. "I'm simply an attentive, concerned citizen," she said. "Doing her best to keep innocent creatures out of jail."

"And put not innocent ones in?" Mr. Thathion teased.

"That's one way of putting it."

"Well, go about doing your duty, then," Mr. Thathion said. "Because while I'm far from innocent, I'm not the creature you're looking for."

Wynona stiffened. *He had an accomplice.*

Rascal glanced her way. *Are you sure?*

Wynona held back. She didn't want Mr. Thathion to know they were talking and she wasn't always good about keeping a poker face. "Thank you for your time, Mr. Thathion," she said a little too sweetly. "Don't worry, we'll be back."

Mr. Thathion's frown deepened and that same look of worry flashed through his green eyes, but Wynona didn't give him a chance to ask questions. Spinning on her heel, she practically dove through the door.

Once in the hallway, she grabbed her phone, but a voice from down the hall stopped her.

"You didn't wait, did you?" Chief Ligurio growled.

"Chief!" Wynona cried, rushing to meet him. "Where's Daemon?"

"Officer Skymaw should be here any second."

"Okay."

"What's this all about, Wy?" Rascal asked from behind her. "I mean…I agree now that Mr. Thathion is involved, but like you said, he obviously couldn't have done it alone."

Wynona shook her head. "I need Daemon, just to clarify something."

"And then?"

Wynona felt her eyes fill with tears. "And then I think we'll be picking up a killer."

CHAPTER 29

The group walked to the hospital lobby and Wynona waited impatiently for Daemon to arrive. She needed to make sure of something he saw at Eve Guanaco's crime scene.

"Tell me what happened?" Chief Ligurio demanded of Rascal while they were waiting.

Rascal looked to Wynona before answering. "Thathion is full of that created magic that Wynona was talking about last night. But Wynona has noticed it's unstable and she's convinced that he's been trying to get Dr. Brownhide out of hiding so he can access her latest works on keeping his magic alive."

"Without it, he'll die," Wynona said, her eyes continually darting toward the doors. "He's only alive because of the magic and it's getting flighty. He needs to upgrade it in order to live."

"I thought Dr. Brownhide worked on *devices* with that kind of magic. Ones that magic-less creatures could use. Not magic for themselves," Chief LIgurio stated.

Wynona nodded. "True. I believe that was her intent. But I'm positive that if we dig into the court records from when she was kicked out of the company, we'll find the company managed to get their hands on the plans she had for creating that magic."

"And you think they changed its purpose." It wasn't a question.

"Exactly," Wynona said. She looked back at the chief. "On one of the pieces I found in the lab, a beaker that kept flipping back and forth between being a beaker and a wine glass, the holes were so small I had to find a magnifying glass in order to see the inconsistencies."

Chief Ligurio frowned. "I'm not following."

"In other words, the stability issue is getting better," Wynona clarified. "The holes in Mr. Thathion's magic and in the weather box were much bigger. So were the ones in the teapot I bought." She stepped toward the men. "Plus, I realized while I was in the lab that the silver around Dr. Rayn's inventions was always warm. I believe it was because it responded to her dragon magic, just like Lusgu said."

Rascal's eyes lit up. "The silver around the weather box wasn't warm."

Wynona nodded. "Right. Meaning it wasn't her magic that originated the box."

"But they were her plans," Chief Ligurio said.

Wynona nodded again. "They were. But others manipulated them."

Rascal huffed. "That's why Lusgu got so upset. Rayn was never playing God. Others did that for her."

Wynona felt like her head was in a permanent state of nodding at this point, but she responded the same way.

"Chief." Daemon's deep voice came from behind Wynona.

She turned and looked up. "Daemon. Great. I need to ask you a question."

His black eyebrows rose up.

"Do you remember what color you found on the bush around the weather box in the park? You said there was some spillage of the magic."

Daemon frowned. "I believe it was yellow."

"Ms. Le Doux?" Chief Ligurio pressed.

Wynona couldn't stop the tears from affecting her vision. "We need to go get Quinin," she said.

Rascal jerked back a little. "The owl shifter? You think she was the one helping Thathion?"

Wynona nodded. "And I'm sure I can prove it."

"Let's do that first," Chief Ligurio said. "Then we'll pick her up."

"Do you have a picture of her?" Wynona asked.

Chief Ligurio looked to Rascal. He scowled. "I'm not sure."

"Why do we need a picture?" Daemon asked.

"Daemon, would you please go get Prim? We'll go find the picture."

Daemon's jaw dropped. "The hydrangea. You're going to ask the hydrangea at the Sultry Spirits if she was the woman with them."

Wynona nodded. "Yes."

"So we're dealing with the mafia as well as the Original Five?"

Wynona made a face. "Truthfully, I'm not sure. I actually can't quite connect Mr. Thathion to the mafia in my head. What I think is that Quinin has ties to the mafia and that Mr. Thathion used that to blackmail her into helping get Rayn out of her castle, and framed for murder."

Chief Ligurio folded his arms over his chest. "I feel like we're still missing pieces."

"We are," Wynona admitted. "But once we pin down Quinin, I think we'll be able to fill them in."

The vampire dropped his arms. "Fine. I'm going to hit the office and check on the doctor. Strongclaw, you and Ms. Le Doux get the picture. Skymaw, grab your girlfriend and meet them at the bar."

Wynona hid a smile at the blush on Daemon's neck and the fact that he didn't correct the chief. She would be very interested to hear what happened last night after they left.

But later, she reminded herself.

Rascal put his hand on her lower back. "We have our orders," he said with a grin. They all walked together out into the sunshine, only to separate seconds later as they each turned to their cars.

Once again, Wynona found herself hoisted into the passenger seat and they drove quickly to the police station. It only took them fifteen minutes digging through the police database to find a suitable picture of Quinin and after printing it out, they loaded up in the truck once more.

"You're sure this is going to work?" Rascal asked as they navigated the city streets.

"Maybe," Wynona said. "The thing is, I think Quinin might be able to change her looks a little."

"What do you mean?"

"That beaker? The one that kept changing to a wine glass?"

Rascal nodded.

"It had yellow magic."

"Magic, which you think might be Quinin's." Rascal scowled and Wynona could practically see the wheels turning. "Ahh…so she specializes in creating illusions." Rascal snorted. "That would explain a lot."

"Like how someone was able to open an account at Shade Banking and Loan under Rayn's name without actually being Rayn."

Rascal blew out a breath and pushed his hand through his hair. "Then why do you think showing the hydrangeas a picture will help?"

"I'm hoping she didn't change herself so much that the flowers couldn't recognize her," Wynona admitted. "And it's a stretch, I know. But maybe we'll finally catch a break."

Rascal smirked. "I'm always surprised how you manage to have A and B and come up with Z."

She laughed a little. "I think my brain is just weird."

Rascal took her hand and rubbed his thumb over her knuckles. "Lucky me."

It was all she could do to hold in the girly sigh that wanted to escape and Rascal must have noticed the way her thoughts went because he chuckled in a dark and delicious tone.

"I've already said…name the day."

Wynona gave him a fake scowl. "Murder first."

"Feisty," he teased.

She rolled her eyes. "Soon, handsome. Soon."

Rascal pulled into the bar's parking lot, parked, then tugged her hand to his mouth and left a soft kiss on her palm. "I'll hold you to that. But it looks like Skymaw and Prim are waiting."

Wynona didn't wait for Rascal this time, she was too eager to finally be close to a conclusion. Jumping down from the massive truck, she raced over and handed the photo to Prim. "I need to know if the plants recognize her," she said, out of breath.

Prim looked skeptical. "Kind of an odd request, but okay." They all walked over, following in the fairy's dainty footsteps.

Wynona waited a few feet back, Rascal at her side, but Daemon stayed close to Prim. A little closer than was absolutely necessary.

Rascal snorted quietly. "Closer than is necessary?" He stepped up, brushing against her. "It's always necessary to get closer."

"Would you stop flirting and focus?" Wynona asked, though she couldn't stop from smiling.

"Never."

Wynona closed her eyes and shook her head.

"Nona?"

She jerked her attention to Prim, who was waving at them. "Yeah?"

Prim was studying the photograph. "They're saying she's familiar, but there's something wrong with her hair. Do you have any other photos?"

"What about the hair?" Wynona asked. "What's different?"

Prim rested her fingertips on the plant. "The woman they saw had the same big glasses, but her hair was long and stylish and she wore a mini skirt that showed off more than it hid."

Wynona nodded. "Okay. But her facial features were the same?"

Prim paused again. "Mostly. They said she came several times and looked a bit different at each one."

Wynona turned to Rascal. "That's it. It's her."

"Now we need to find out what her connection to the mafia is," Rascal mused.

Daemon grunted. "And what Thathion's connection to her is."

Wynona put her hands on her hips. "Tell them 'thank you,' Prim. I appreciate their help."

Prim murmured to the leaves, then smiled. "They like you. They said, 'come again.'"

The rustling of the foliage was a little disturbing, but Wynona smiled and brushed the petals of one of the flowers. "Thank you," she said. "I like you too."

The leaves rustled even more and Prim laughed. "Careful. Or they'll develop a crush and your house will find itself covered one of these days."

Wynona tilted her head. "How could they possibly get to my house? I don't live anywhere near here."

Prim continued to grin, then shrugged. "Nevermind."

Shaking her head and getting back to topic, Wynona turned to the men. "I think it's time to set a trap."

"You don't want to just bring her in?"

Wynona shook her head. "No. Quinin is brilliant. We need to catch her unawares. I think it'll be the only real chance we have of getting the information we need. If we just arrest her, she's going to clam up and we'll never figure out the last of the details."

Rascal scratched the back of his head. "Better get the chief in on this one."

"Agreed." The group walked back to the cars.

"Don't think you're leaving me out!" Prim hollered as she and Daemon went to his patrol car. "I'll be at the station!"

Wynona waved and climbed up into the truck. "Time to end this," she told Rascal as he buckled up on his own side.

"You have any ideas?"

Wynona shook her head. "Not yet. But we got this far. We'll get it figured out."

"I never doubted it," he told her with a mercenary grin. His predator was showing and Wynona was reminded of just why he was an officer. He loved the thrill of the hunt and there was nothing better than hunting intelligent prey.

The owl shifter had betrayed Dr. Rayn, Wynona, the police and who knew who else… It was time to bring her to justice.

CHAPTER 30

The night air was chilly and Wynona tried to hold back her shivers, but there was nothing for it.

Rascal grumbled and wrapped an arm around her. "It would have been better to do this during the day."

Wynona shrugged. "Maybe so, but we need her off her guard. This is the best time to do that." Wynona twisted around to see if Prim and Daemon were doing alright. They were parked on the other side of the building and looked to be in a deep discussion.

"At least the owners know we're here," Rascal muttered. "We're lucky they're letting us do this. It would hurt their business if the police came to do busts all the time."

"You really think that much illegal activity goes on in there?" Wynona gasped.

Rascal gave her a look. "For someone who has seen some pretty nasty things, I'm shocked that you're still so naive sometimes."

Wynoan scowled. "I'm not naive. I was raised with the president."

Rascal chuckled and kissed her forehead. "Okay. Incessantly optimistic, then."

Wynona huffed. "Is it really that bad to want the world to be a little better? I don't usually go into restaurants and assume half the people in there are clandestinely meeting their partners in crime."

Rascal shrugged. "It depends on the restaurant. And this place? It's boiling over with them."

Wynona sighed. "I'm sure you're right."

His chest shook as he wrapped Wynona up in his arms. "I love hearing you say that."

She gave a half-hearted push on his chest, but followed it up by laying her head against his shoulder. "I hate that we have to do this. I liked Quinin."

"I know."

"She's been with Rayn for years. Why would she do this?"

"Maybe she's in trouble."

Wynona was silent then. She'd discovered over the last couple of years that criminals were often those who felt they had no other choice. Just what had happened in Quinin's life to make her feel like she had no other choice? And why would she deliberately go against her benefactor?

Dr. Rayn had taken Quinin in, given her a place to stay, paid her for her time…most of the time…and the owl shifter got to invent to her heart's content. If she was unhappy, why hadn't she simply walked away? Why frame Rayn? Why lie to the police? Why participate in murder?

A bird call whistled through the air and Wynona perked up. Daemon had demonstrated the sound for them earlier and it meant that Quinin had been spotted. Which was a good thing since it was nearing midnight and Wynona's energy was quickly fading. Two nights of no sleep was starting to affect her.

"Left," Rascal whispered, his eyes glowing softly.

Wynona scrunched her nose. *Dang animal night vision.*

His white teeth gleamed. *You love me for it.*

She huffed and tried to study the part of the parking lot that Rascal indicated. She could tell there was movement, but until Quinin was within range of the lights of the bar, Wynona hadn't been able to distinguish the creature's face.

"You're on."

Wynona nodded, swallowed hard and made a show of stumbling around the bushes. "Oof!" she exclaimed, coming to a stop when she got nearer to Quinin. "Quinin!" she called. "Is that you?"

Quinin looked around, a slightly panicked look on her face. Her hair was long and wavy and her dress tight, just like the hydrangeas had said. The only telltale features were the large glasses and the small pointed chin.

"It is you!" Wynona smiled widely, waved and walked over. "I didn't know you came here. Do you visit often?"

Quinin stared at her. "What do you want, Ms. Le Doux?"

Wynona pouted. "I thought we were friends? Can't you call me Wynona?"

Quinin folded her arms over her chest. "What's going on?"

Wynona threw her arms out to the side. This wasn't working. She apparently was a terrible actress. "I just had a couple drinks inside and was coming back out to my car."

Quinin looked at the parking lot. "I don't see your scooter."

Busted. Wynona put up her hands. "Okay, look. I actually came to see you."

Quinin's eyes widened. "What? Why? And how did you know I'd be here?"

Wynona shrugged. "Lucky guess."

Quinin shook her head. "There was no way you'd guess that. How did you know I was here?"

"The flowers told me?" Wynona ended up phrasing it like a question, knowing just how ridiculous it sounded. Before Prim, Wynona had never known it was possible to talk to plants.

The leaves rustled behind her and Wynona hoped it was a happy sound.

Quinin backed up. Her eyes were darting from Wynona to the bar and back. "I have to go." She spun on her expensive heels, but before Wynona could react, something shoved past her and wrapped the fleeing owl in a mound of greenery.

Wynona's eyes widened as she took in the scene. "What in the paranormal world?"

"Let me go!" Quinin screeched. Her hair went back to its usual messy bun and the make up faded as well. The clothes, however, had apparently not been conjured and they stayed put.

Prim walked from the side, slapping her hands together. "Nicely done," she told the plant.

Wynona still couldn't believe her eyes. The hydrangea had turned from a bush into a vine and had captured their fleeing suspect.

Remind me to stop teasing Prim, Rascal said as he approached.

"You're *all* here?" Quinin cried. Huge tears began to dribble down her face. "How did you find out? How did you know?" She struggled against the bush. "Ouch!" Small cuts began to bleed on her arms. "You can't do this! I have to get inside!"

"About that…" Wynona stepped up. "I'd stop struggling. Hydrangeas don't exactly have soft limbs. You'll only continue to hurt yourself."

Quinin's crying turned to sobs and she slumped inside the plant's hold. "I can't be found like this," she hiccuped. "He'll know."

"Who will know?" Wynona quickly pounded on the words. "Mr. Thathion or the mob?"

Quinin looked up, her huge watery eyes blinking. "I don't understand. It was all planned so perfectly. How did you find out?"

"Quinin," Wynona said softly. "We know that Mr. Thathion has been blackmailing you."

The owl let out a cry.

"We know that you've been meeting the underworld mob leaders. We know that you're the one who set the weather box in the park and that you've been manipulating Dr. Rayn's inventions. We also know that you have extra magic," Wynona continued. She glanced at Daemon, who nodded. Wynona had chosen not to use her sight tonight, she was relying on Daemon, and his nod meant the yellow magic they were looking for was coming from Quinin.

"What we're lacking is the why. Why did you betray Dr. Rayn? What was in it for you? And what's your relationship with the underworld that led to your blackmail with Mr. Thathion?"

Quinin's head hung and her body shook as she cried. "It's such a mess," she managed between sobs. "It was never meant to go this far."

"Why don't you tell us what happened," Wynona said soothingly.

Quinin sniffed. "I…" She shook her head. "They'll kill me."

Wynona shook her head. "Tell us, Quinin. You're smart enough to know that you're headed to jail. A confession and information that gives us Mr. Thathion will only help your case."

Quinin looked at Rascal, who nodded formally. "Okay…" she whispered thickly. "I…have a problem with gambling."

Wynona sighed inside. She had suspected it all had to do with money. It always seemed to come back to two things. Money and power.

"I got in over my head," Quinin continued, "and since my boss isn't very good about paying me, I was struggling to keep up."

"Were you selling her inventions to pay off your debt?"

Quinin nodded. "Yes, but it wasn't enough." Her chin fell to her chest. "And that's when Mr. Thathion approached me. He told me that Dr. Rayn was keeping something that was supposed to be his, the created magic. He claimed the courts had given him the rights to it, but somehow she had managed to hold back the actual blueprints."

"If that was the case, why wouldn't he have appealed to the courts for help?" Prim asked with a derisive snort.

"I asked him that, but he claimed it would take months…years…to get them to follow through."

"Years that he didn't have," Wynona whispered.

Quinin nodded and sniffed again. "Right."

"So you've been planning this betrayal for how long?" Wynona asked. "At least two years, since that's when you planted the weather box plans in the bank."

Quinin tried to shrug, but ended up wincing. "Those were one of the first things we did."

"It must have been exciting," Wynona ventured. "It was probably one of the first times you used the magic that Mr. Thathion helped you develop."

Quinin's eyes widened again. "You don't miss a thing."

"I try not to."

Quinin scowled. "I managed to get into the bank, but only barely. A couple of the shades are older than dirt and seemed a little suspicious, but I managed."

"Then you what? Waited?"

Quinin nodded. "Thathion agreed to pay off my debt if I would work on perfecting the weather box. I spent time doing just that."

"And on making it look like Rayn's inventions. You used your insider knowledge to add details like the silver trim and the dragon language."

Quinin shrugged again and made a face. "Do we have to keep me wrapped up? Aren't there enough of you to keep me under control?"

"In a moment," Rascal said firmly. "Answer the questions, Ms. Greik."

Quinin sighed. Her tears were finally dry, but she remained far from enthusiastic. "I needed the box to work on command and look like something Rayn would make."

"And did you ever figure out why Thathion was really blackmailing you?"

Quinin smirked. "He thought his story was so clever, but it was a pack of lies." She sniffed, this time in disgust. "If I'd been in a position to, I would have blackmailed him in return, but the…" She snapped her jaw shut. "Let's just say there were others that would have frowned on that."

Wynona nodded. "Okay. You can keep that part to yourself. All we want is the reasoning behind Mr. Thathion's work. I know he was trying to get Rayn into town. I know he needed the newest version of the created magic. What I don't know is why he had to murder to get it."

Quinin laughed and the sound sent chills down Wynona's spine. This creature wasn't nearly as helpless as she wanted everyone to believe. "But that's the most important part, Wynona," Quinin said sarcastically. "I'm surprised you hadn't worked that out."

Wynona smiled placidly. "Humor me."

Quinin tilted her head forward slightly. "You should have looked a little deeper into Rayn's work. Or more importantly…her will."

Wynona frowned. "You told us all her inventions will go to Para University at her death." As soon as the words were out, Wynona felt like an idiot. Quinin could have easily lied. Why hadn't they checked out the truthfulness of the owl's claims?

Quinin tilted her head back and forth. "Technically, that's true. But Thathion didn't want her dead."

The puzzle slapped into place so hard Wynona's forehead literally ached. "Oh my word. How did I miss that?"

Quinin giggled. "Looks like you're not quite as observant as you would have us believe."

Rascal growled.

"He didn't want her dead. He wanted her in jail and declared mentally unstable," Wynona said breathlessly as the story came to her. "Then he could argue to the courts that her inventions belonged with the company she had worked for previously."

"It simply wouldn't be safe to send them all to the college," Quinin said cheerfully. "Coming from an insane inventor, the students might not be able to tell what was good and what was junk."

"Unbelievable," Prim spat, folding her arms over her chest. "That Thathion guy is a pig. I'm so glad I didn't end up doing his wedding flowers."

"His fiancee was a sacrifice for his own immortality," Wynona tossed back. "There was never going to be a wedding."

"Skymaw," Rascal snapped.

"Sir?"

"Take her in."

"Yes, sir."

Wynona watched while Prim and Daemon worked together to get the vines off just enough for him to slap a hag's thread on Quinin's wrists. The owl had come down from her confession exuberance and was trying to negotiate a deal while they walked down the sidewalk and into the dark parking lot.

Wynona shivered and rubbed her hands on her upper arms, only relaxing when Rascal came up behind her and wrapped his arms around her. "What a mess," she murmured.

Rascal snorted. "Convoluted, for sure. I'll bet if we took the time to investigate the other side of Ms. Greik's dealing, we'd find just as much illegal activity as we did on Thathion's side."

"I know," Wynona said softly. "And it more than likely would lead back to my dad, if we ever got that far." She sighed. "I have a feeling the underworld side will be a lot harder to break into than scaring an owl shifter into giving up her secrets."

Rascal growled and his hold on her tightened. "There's no way I'll let you be involved in that one when it comes time to take them down."

"Thank heavens," Wynona said on a sigh. "I don't want anything to do with my father and his cronies."

Rascal kissed the top of her head. "Come on. Let's get you to sleep. You have a lot to discuss with Dr. Brownhide and Lusgu tomorrow."

Wynona nodded. Her adrenaline was waning and she was ready to fall asleep on her feet. Really, getting a hold of Quinin had been fairly anticlimactic and the shifter had been much more accommodating than Wynona had suspected. In the end, they hadn't had to trick anything out of her at all.

"It was probably a relief," Rascal said as he opened the truck door and helped Wynona inside. "She'd been holding onto something too big for her for a long time."

"I think you're right," Wynona said with a nod.

Rascal growled. "Next time, we're recording that." He leaned in. "For future generations."

Wynona laughed. "Take me home, wolf. I'll pet your ego later."

Giving a little howl of triumph, Rascal shut her door.

Wynona leaned her head back against the seat and relaxed. Her fiance would see her home and tomorrow, or rather, later today…they would tackle the rest of the mystery that surrounded Lusgu and Rayn.

And it better be good.

CHAPTER 31

The front door slammed open. "It's done!" Rascal shouted as he sauntered inside. He was in his uniform, his hair deliciously messy and a kiss-inducing smirk on his face. "Mr. Meldaeon Thathion has been dragged from the hospital with his dirty hands behind his back and was calling for his lawyer as they stuffed him in the police car."

Wynona smiled and opened her arms as Rascal came to hold her. "Thank you," she whispered against his chest. "I'm so glad to have him off the streets."

"You and me both." Rascal kissed the top of her head. "If he hit on you one more time, he wasn't ever going to make it to the jail cell."

"Which is why I didn't come along when you arrested him," Wynona said. She pulled back. "Now comes the hard part."

Rascal groaned. "Can I just say that your family is a mess? I love you. But whatever happened with your grandma and all her machinations, and your dad and everything…" Rascal shook his head.

"I know," Wynona agreed. There really were no words to figure it all out. The last two years had been one heartache after the other as she unraveled what her grandmother had done before Wynona had ever been born.

From the cursing and loss of her powers, to the mental and emotional abuse Wynona endured at the hands of her parents... Rascal's description was best...it was one big, fat mess.

The door opened again. "Hello in the house!" Prim called out.

Wynona frowned and looked at Rascal.

He widened his eyes and shook his head. "Don't look at me. I assumed this would be a private conversation."

Prim and Daemon wandered into the sitting room.

Daemon made a face. "So...we know we're intruding, but we wanted to be here when you questioned Lusgu. And..." Daemon looked over his shoulder.

Wynona's eyes widened when Rayn came in slowly. "Dr. Rayn?" Wynona stepped away from Rascal and walked over. She hadn't expected to see the dragon for several more days, but really, this made everything perfect.

Rayn looked pale and tired, but she smiled and gave Wynona a hug. "Your black hole was kind enough to see me released quickly so I could be here." She leaned back. "I did promise, after all."

Wynona nodded, her eyes growing slightly misty. Rayn tucked Wynona's hair behind her ear, the movement so motherly it made Wynona's breath catch.

"You've been waiting a long time for answers. We'll do what we can."

Wynona nodded again and stepped back. *Violet. Will you please bring Lusgu out here?*

The room was awkward as they waited for a response, but rather than answering Wynona, Lusgu and Violet simply stepped out of the portal. "Rayn," Lusgu breathed, his face lighting up.

Rayn closed her eyes and smiled, the look of relief on her face palpable in every line of her body. Her red eyes came back up. "Two visits in a few days. What's the world coming to?"

Lusgu walked over and held out his hand. "It appears to be ending."

Rayn laughed softly. "If only that were the case," she whispered.

Wynona shook her head. More mysteries. Would she ever get to the bottom of it all? "Why doesn't everyone have a seat?" she asked.

"I'll grab a tray of tea and snacks and then we can start." She raised her eyebrows and Rayn nodded, though she didn't break eye contact with Lusgu.

The two were so caught up in each other, Wynona wondered how they even knew what conversation was going on around them.

She assumed they'd figure it out. Walking toward the kitchen, Rascal on her heels, Wynona set to work getting snacks and drinks ready for her crew. She knew some of what they spoke about today might be difficult for her to hear, but she was actually grateful that Daemon and Prim were there. They were her friends and their desire to be involved...even in the ugly parts of her life...meant a great deal to her.

Rascal kissed Wynona's cheek. "They're here because of you. Never doubt it." He grinned and took her hand, the tray of food and cups floating behind them as they went into the sitting room.

Wynona came to a screeching halt, her tray almost hitting her back.

Celia gave her a mock salute. "You didn't really think that you could get the lowdown on our family without involving me, did you?"

Wynona blinked as Chief Ligurio cleared his throat and straightened his stance to something a bit more...in charge. "I thought it would be prudent for me to know exactly who I'm working with," he said, tilting his chin up. It was clear that he wasn't sure of his welcome, but he wanted to be involved.

Wynona sighed internally. "You all realize this isn't necessarily going to be a good thing? Your opinion of me might change after what you hear?"

Chief Ligurio snorted, sounding a little more like himself. "Ms. Le Doux. If I was going to have a bad opinion of you, I think I would already have it by now."

Celia tossed her hair and settled herself more comfortably in her seat. She didn't speak out loud, but her actions said she wasn't leaving.

Wynona wasn't sure if she should be worried or flattered.

What are you worried about? Violet asked.

Wynona looked at her familiar. *I don't want to be the latest gossip or* simply a sideshow. I have no idea what we're going to hear today, but past experience has taught me that it's not always what we expect.

Violet scrambled down Lusgu's shoulder and came to Wynona, who bent over and picked up her familiar. *Every single one of these people are here because they want to be part of your life,* Violet said with her nose twitching. *You've treated each of them with respect they don't always deserve and you've given them the benefit of the doubt when no one else would. Now some...ahem...Celia...might not know how to show it in an appropriate way, but do you really think she plans to share her family's deep dark secrets with the whole world?*

Wynona pinched her lips between her teeth. "Probably not," she admitted, forgetting to speak in her mind.

Not to mention, there isn't a single person in this room who doesn't know most of your secrets already. They know you're soulmates with Rascal. They know you have more magic than anyone else. They know that your grandmother cursed you. They know you're struggling to control your magic and that some of your powers are unusual. What else could they possibly learn that would turn them from you now?

I don't know...that's part of the problem.

Violet chittered.

Wynona kissed the top of Violet's head. "But thank you," she whispered. Her familiar wasn't usually quite so sweet and Wynona appreciated the pep talk. Looking up, she realized the whole room was waiting on her. They were quite a crew, but...they were hers.

Putting Violet on her shoulder, Wynona magicked up two more of everything on the tray, set it on the coffee table and sat down in the last available seat. Rascal took his usual stance at her side. Her quiet, constant support.

The room watched her expectantly. "Okay..." Wynona wiped her hands on her pants. "Where do we start?"

"I have a couple questions, if that's alright," Rayn asked.

Wynona nodded. "Of course."

"Quinin." Rayn opened her mouth a couple times, but nothing came out.

"Quinin was recruited by Thathion to help pull you out and frame you for murder," Rascal said succinctly. "Thathion helped give her magic, which allowed her to create illusions, which she used in her dealings with the mob and at the bank to impersonate you."

"And they wanted my blueprints on created magic?"

Wynona nodded as Rascal continued. "They planned on convincing a judge that you were unstable. The hope was they could then take over your inventions, rather than let them go to the university you had planned."

Rayn closed her eyes and hung her head. "When I think of how much trust I gave that owl..."

"Let it go," Lusgu advised, much to Wynona's surprise. He was usually the first to think up revenge. "It's not worth thinking about now. It's been taken care of."

"And her ties to the mob?" Rayn pressed.

Rascal shrugged. "Other than her debt, which Thathion covered in exchange for help with you, we actually don't know what all went on there." He glanced at Wynona, then back. "There's some speculation it goes deep, but because it doesn't relate to the murder of Ms. Smouldons and Ms. Guanaco, we haven't dug into it."

"In other words, you don't have the manpower to handle the fallout," Rayn said.

Chief Ligurio growled. "We're always looking for more help, Dr. Brownhide, if you feel up to the task."

Rayn put her hands in the air. "I apologize. You're right. Not my place."

Rascal huffed and folded his arms over his chest. "Any other questions?"

"How did you know Thathion was involved?" Lusgu asked, his eyes narrowed. "I know you didn't like him...I don't like him either. But how did you figure it out?"

Wynona took a deep breath. "It was the created magic. When I was in Rayn's lab, I realized where Mr. Thathion's magic must have come from. I was about to confront him about it, but it wasn't until the nurse said they didn't know what was wrong with him that I realized his time in the hospital was nothing but a cover up. He *needed* an alibi.

Having Quinin working on the outside gave him the opportunity to hide."

Rayn shook her head. "And all over the idea of immortality." She growled and a bit of smoke came out of her nostrils. "My invention was never meant to be used that way."

Wynona nodded. "I know."

"Now…" Rascal said in a commanding voice. "I believe you owe Wynona some answers."

Rayn's smoke stopped and she glanced at Lusgu before coming back to Wynona. "I knew your grandmother."

Wynona nodded, suddenly feeling slightly anxious.

"Her premonitions of you happened when I was already in exile, but she and I kept in touch."

"Why?" Wynona asked. "Were you that close?"

Rayn shrugged. "I suppose you could say that."

Celia groaned. "Suppose doesn't work, Doctor. Answer the questions."

Rayn gave Celia an unimpressed look. "She always said you were tempestuous. Inherited your mother's temper."

Celia glared, but she didn't say anything else.

"She's right though," Wynona said in a softer tone. "You promised."

Rayn sighed. "Alright. Settle in, children…it's story time."

CHAPTER 32

"Once upon a time..." Rayn grinned as a few groans and chuckles went throughout the room. "There were a bunch of paranormals who thought they owned the world."

Wynona held back a rude retort, but Rascal snorted in disgust.

"Sounds about right," Celia said with a saccharine sweet smile.

Rayn ignored her. "They ran Hex Haven with a powerful hand, but for the most part…all was well."

Wynona stiffened. Rayn wasn't just talking about herself and Granny. This had to include more.

"Until one day, the president was killed."

Wynona gasped and Celia cried out. "What do you mean, killed?" Celia leaned forward and Chief Ligurio put his hand on her shoulder. "Our grandfather died of old age."

Rayn raised an eyebrow. "Did he? Are you sure?"

"What proof do you have otherwise?" Celia growled.

Rayn shrugged. "Whispers. Tidbits. Gossip…intuition."

"But you believe it," Wynona said weakly.

Rayn looked Wynona in the eye and nodded. "We do."

Lusgu shifted next to Rayn, looking uncomfortable.

"Lusgu?" Wynona asked. "Do you believe my grandfather was killed?"

Lusgu hesitated, but nodded. "Yes."

Wynona fell back against her seat. "And what does this have to do with me?"

Rayn cleared her throat and leaned her elbows onto her knees. "Saffron knew something was wrong, but we weren't sure how to handle it."

Celia made more noises.

"Who do you think did it?" Wynona whispered. Her heart was in her throat and she thought she might be sick.

Rayn pinched her lips together and her eyes flared a bright yellow. "We believe someone hired an assassin."

Wynona shook her head. "Who could have the power to do that?" she demanded. "Grandfather was supposed to be even stronger than Grandmother."

Rayn nodded. "True. But black magic can overcome much if administered correctly."

Wynona rubbed her forehead. The room was deathly silent and she wondered if they were all thinking about the grimoires hidden in her closet as well. Some of them were not only powerful, but so dark that Wynona couldn't stand to touch them. Was that the type of power Rayn was talking about?

Rayn was nodding when Wynona looked up. "You've felt it," she said. It wasn't a question.

"The grimoires," Wynona admitted.

Rayn nodded. "Ah...yes. Those would definitely contain it."

"So one of my ancestors killed their own family member?"

Rayn shrugged. "Not every grimoire in that collection is family. Their ties are sometimes...looser than that."

"Can we just get on with this?" Celia snapped.

Wynona didn't blame her. This was worse than she'd thought. Violet wrapped her tail around Wynona's neck and nuzzled under her chin for comfort.

"My apologies," Rayn said. She straightened. "Saffron, myself, and

Lusgu began to make plans to confront the person we thought responsible." At this point, Rayn paused, her hesitation plain.

"You promised," Wynona said forcefully. Now that she'd started, Wynona needed to hear it all.

Rayn waited a second more before nodding in agreement. "So I did. During our quiet investigation, I was having trouble with my company." She reached out and took a cup of tea, sipping it before resting it back in the saucer. "Lusgu and Saffron carried on without me for a while because I was tied up in court. Meanwhile, Wynona and Celia, your father took over the presidency. Between him and your mother, not even Saffron could challenge them."

"Granny was far more powerful than Mother," Wynona argued.

"But she wasn't more powerful than the two of them combined," Rayn argued. "Married couples, and sometimes family members, can combine powers."

Wynona looked at Celia, who was looking back. "You knew that." Celia had combined her powers with Wynona when the shop had been burning.

Celia nodded. "Yes."

"Did you ever see Mom and Dad work together?"

Celia paled and that was all the answer Wynona needed.

Maybe being ignored by them for most of your life wasn't such a bad thing, Violet said tersely.

Wynona nodded her agreement. "I'm sorry," she said to her sister.

Celia shrugged and tried to play it off, but there was pain in her expression. Too much pain.

Chief Ligurio cleared his throat and gave Ryan a pointed look.

Rayn nodded. "Saffron and Lusgu were finally able to confront the witch believed involved, but…" She cut off, choking slightly and grasping her throat.

Wynona leaned forward and reached out, wanting to help heal the dragon, but Rayn put her hand up to hold her off.

Eventually, Rayn caught her breath, but her face was red and her eyes wet. "Sorry," she rasped, wiping at her face. She turned to Lusgu. "I thought with the curse gone, it would be fine."

Lusgu grunted and slumped.

Wynona frowned. "Curse? What curse? The one Granny put on me?"

Rayn shook her head. "I can't say," she replied. "We'll leave it at the fact that the confrontation didn't go well."

"Leave it at that?" Celia cried. "That tells us nothing!"

Rayn looked at Celia, but didn't reply. Everyone had seen only moments before that Rayn had been unable to breathe. Something was stopping her.

"You've been cursed," Wynona breathed.

"After Lusgu and Saffron failed," Rayn said, ignoring Wynona's comment, "I was exiled. Kicked out of my own company, lost my inventions and had to leave Hex Haven." Rayn's eyes filled with tears for a different reason this time as she looked at Lusgu. "Saffron kept in touch, but it was never the same."

Lusgu closed his eyes and hung his head.

Those large red eyes flittered to Wynona. "She told me of your mother's pregnancy and the prophecies surrounding your birth."

"So you knew Granny bound my powers."

Rayn nodded. "I did." She put a hand on Lusgu's knee. "We all did. And we all agreed." She sighed. "There was little I could do from my hideout, so Lusgu and a few other friends were assigned to help you."

"Mama Reyna," Rascal grunted.

Rayn looked up and a smile ghosted across her lips. "She's still alive?" Rascal made a face and Rayn laughed softly. "She must still be as stubborn as ever."

"That's putting it lightly," Wynona muttered.

"Anyway, Saffron knew once your parents found out about her part in your powers, they'd do something drastic, so she made sure she wasn't available for them to deal with."

Wynona swallowed bile. "Are you saying she killed herself in order to save me?"

Rayn made a face. "Not quite. She could feel that she was coming close to her time anyway, so she merely…manipulated the situation a little so it worked in our favor."

Rascal's hand landed on her shoulder. Between Violet's touch and Rascal's warmth, Wynona kept herself grounded, but it was difficult. Even knowing Granny was already close to passing didn't help her feel any better.

Not your fault, Violet snapped. *Don't go down that rabbit hole.*

Agreed, Rascal said. *She made her choices. The only thing you can do now is move forward.*

Wynona didn't…couldn't…respond. Not yet. "And this was all for what? To save my life? Or to put me in a position to take over for my dad?" The air in Wynona's lungs disappeared at the thought and she gasped like a fish for several seconds. "My dad…" Her chest heaved. "Did Granny think my dad was responsible for Grandpa's murder?"

Rayn looked at Lusgu, then they both turned to look at her. Neither said anything.

"I believe it."

All heads snapped to Celia.

Celia's jaw was tight and her face flushed. "I don't know what Dad's up to, but ever since Wynona's curse broke, he's been frantic about some project he'd already been working on." Her black eyes slammed into Wynona's. "Your powers scare him. And you've already proven you can't be controlled."

They could have heard a wand drop as the entire room contemplated what had just been dumped on the table.

Wynona was sure she was going to pass out. In fact, black spots were beginning to flicker in her vision when Rascal leapt in front of her.

"Breathe, Wy. Dang it. Breathe!" He gave her shoulders a hard shake and Wynona sucked in a loud, shaky breath. Rascal knelt down at her feet and pulled her forward, gathering her into his arms. "This doesn't change a thing," he growled into her hair. "Not a thing. You're still mine. We're still going to get married. You're going to reopen your shop and make tea for the world." He leaned back, pressing her hair away from her face and using his thumbs to wipe the tears Wynona hadn't realized were trickling down her cheeks. "Do you hear me? You're still friends with a flower arranging fairy and a purple mouse is your familiar. You still love and care for every misfit this town has to offer and you have the best detective's eye of anyone I've ever met."

Rascal slowly shook his head. "And I love you," he ground out. "I'll always love you and nothing, no past or choices from your stupid ancestors or parents is going to change that." His hands tightened on her head. "You. Make. Your. Own. Future." He brought their foreheads together, softening finally after his little tirade. "You make your own future," he whispered hoarsely.

Wynona leaned into his strength and let herself cry. Her dad was a murderer, even if he'd ordered the hit through another witch. Her grandmother had ended her life early. Her grandfather had been killed. Rayn was cursed to not be able to talk about certain things and Lusgu and Mama Reyna were forced into watching over Wynona when it was probably the last thing they wanted to do. Lusgu, at least, would probably have much rather been with Rayn, even in exile.

Wynona wiped at her face. "I'm so sorry," she said to the room. "I'm so sorry. I didn't know."

Murmurs of assurance and love filtered through the room, but Wynona couldn't hold onto any of them, she was too upset.

"ENOUGH ALREADY!"

Wynona jerked and she stared, wide-eyed, at her sister.

Celia was standing and she was seething. "Quit with the victim thing," she ground out. "So your life has been rough. Boo hoo." She waved her arms in the air. "Wake up, sissy-poo. Everyone's life has been hard! Those choices that brought us here? Yeah…most of them weren't your fault, but it's done. DONE!" she screamed. "Nothing can change that, but sitting on the floor crying isn't going to help it either."

Wynona felt her tears dry a little as her sister spoke. The words were far from kind, but at the moment, they were sort of what she needed.

"The real question is…what do we do now?" Celia asked, pointedly looking at every individual around the room. "Somehow I don't think we can simply take down my dad because we're pretty sure he hired an assassin. If he hasn't been caught by now, there's a good reason for it."

Lusgu snorted.

Celia smirked. "So?" She looked at Wynona. "Are you going to take him out, or what?"

All eyes went to Wynona and she wanted to cower. She wanted nothing to do with any of this. Power and prestige were so far from her ideal lifestyle that it was laughable.

"At this point in time, I'm not prepared to do that," Wynona said carefully.

Celia tsked her tongue and shook her head. "Better get prepared, sis. Because I have a feeling that the war is coming whether you want it to or not." Spinning on her heel, she stomped out the door.

After a moment, Chief Ligurio cleared his throat. "I'm going to make sure she doesn't run anyone over." Then he too was gone.

"Will you walk me home?" Rayn asked softly, her eyes on Lusgu.

Lusgu almost smiled and it melted Wynona's heart just a bit, all while adding to her guilt. "It would be my pleasure."

The sight of the tall woman and the small brownie walking hand in hand was one Wynona wasn't sure she'd ever forget. She stood at the kitchen sink, watching through the window as they strolled, in no hurry to separate again.

"Wynona…"

Wynona turned to see Daemon standing a few feet behind her, his fully black eyes fixated on the window as well. "What?" She looked around for whatever he was worried about.

"Use your vision." Daemon nodded to the window.

Frowning, Wynona turned and looked out the window again. Rascal stepped up to her side and put a hand on her waist. "What is it?"

"I don't know." Wynona blinked and brought her magic into her eyes. She blinked again. "Oh my word…"

"Wy! What?"

Wynona turned to Rascal. "I can see the curse on Rayn," she croaked. "It's like a brown scarf around her neck. There's one on

Lusgu as well." Wynona turned to Daemon, who nodded his agreement.

"Okay…" Rascal said. "We already determined they'd been cursed and unable to talk about the murder."

Wynona shook her head. "But that's not the problem."

"Then what is it?"

Wynona took one last look out the window. "Lusgu has another curse," she whispered hoarsely. "It goes around his entire body and looks like barbed wire." She swallowed, trying to bring moisture back to her suddenly dry throat. "It's like he's been trapped inside his own body."

"He's not really a brownie," Daemon stated, his voice dark.

Wynona slumped and Rascal caught her. "He's not really a brownie…" Skittering caught her attention and Wynona looked at Violet, who was on her hind legs on the table. "He's not really a brownie," she said again.

Violet hesitated only momentarily before nodding. *He's not really a brownie.*

COMING NEXT

Thank you so much for joining me on Wynona's journey!

If you haven't already joined me newsletter,
you should!
You'll love being part of my reader family
and our weekly chats. Not to mention
you'll receive a FREE scene from Rascal's
point of view.

And if you're ready to figure out a few more answers
about Lusgu, don't worry! You can grab that
HERE!

Don't miss "No Matcha For Murder"
Grab Your Copy Today!

Made in the USA
Monee, IL
05 February 2023